編者的話

　　教育部推行「**全民英語能力檢定測驗**」後，預計在未來，所有大學生，包括四年制軍事院校學生、以及一般社會人士，如公務人員、工程師、外事警政人員、空服員、海關人員、新聞從業人員、資訊管理人員等，均必須通過「**中高級英語能力檢定測驗**」，以作為畢業、就業、升遷時之英語能力證明，此項測驗的重要性，可見一斑。

　　在任何英語測驗中，字彙都是最基本的一環，掌握字彙考題，即是掌握先機。因此，繼「中高級英語聽力檢定①、②」之後，我們再推出這本「**中高級英語字彙 420 題**」，完全仿照「中高級英語能力檢定測驗」中的詞彙題題型，為讀者精心設計了 **42** 回測驗題，所有題目均有詳細的中文翻譯，及單字註解，提供讀者充分的練習機會，增加你應試時的實力及信心。同時，熟背書中所列出的字彙，在你準備**轉學考試**、研究所、托福或 TOEIC 考試時，也是一大助益。

　　感謝這麼多讀者，給我們鼓勵。編輯好書，是「學習」一貫的宗旨，讀者若需要任何學習英文的書，都可以提供意見給我們，我們的目標是，**學英文的書**，「**學習**」都有；「學習」出版、天天進步。也盼望讀者們不吝給我們批評指教。

劉 毅

製作過程

　　這本書的完成，要歸功於許多「學習」的
工作夥伴，本書由蔡琇瑩老師擔任總指揮，經
過美籍老師 Laura Stewart 和 Andy Swarzman
的審慎校閱，張家慈小姐，非常詳盡地核對單
字及音標，黃淑貞小姐及蘇淑玲小姐，負責打
字、排版，還有白雪嬌小姐，為本書設計了美
麗的封面，感謝他們辛苦的付出。

HIGH-INTERMEDIATE LEVEL ENGLISH VOCABULARY TEST

中高級字彙420題

TEST 1

Directions: *The following questions are incomplete sentences. You are to choose the one word that best completes the sentence.*

1. Labor unions are _____ for shorter hours, higher pay and better medical benefits.
   (A) searching
   (B) qualifying
   (C) confronting
   (D) battling （　）

2. Too little calcium can _____ a child's growth.
   (A) retard
   (B) inherit
   (C) accumulate
   (D) monitor （　）

3. Much of the waste produced by modern people can be reduced by _____.
   (A) frugality
   (B) dump
   (C) recycling
   (D) circulation （　）

4. It is a mere _____ that the president is to meet with the Secretary of Defense.
   (A) description
   (B) subscription
   (C) consumption
   (D) assumption （　）

5. Children whose parents cannot afford to feed them properly often suffer from _____.
   (A) malnutrition
   (B) obesity
   (C) diabetes
   (D) insomnia （　）

6. Three decades ago, mainland China was _____ shut off from the world.
   - (A) vividly
   - (B) familiarly
   - (C) virtually
   - (D) mutually   (   )

7. Most of the people living in the mountainous slum areas are _____ laborers.
   - (A) literary
   - (B) worth
   - (C) illiterate
   - (D) spacious   (   )

8. Steven went through about four years of being _____ to video games. He finally overcame the bad habit.
   - (A) addicted
   - (B) irrational
   - (C) workaholic
   - (D) convicted   (   )

9. A further _____ of the New Taiwan dollar may prove to be beneficial to our international trade.
   - (A) depreciation
   - (B) deception
   - (C) desperation
   - (D) detection   (   )

10. A doctor's first step in treating a sick person is making a(n) _____ to find out why the patient is sick.
    - (A) prescription
    - (B) experiment
    - (C) therapy
    - (D) diagnosis   (   )

TEST 1 詳解

1. (**D**) Labor unions are <u>battling</u> for shorter hours, higher pay and better medical benefits.

工會正在<u>努力爭取</u>較短的工時、較高的薪資，以及較佳的醫療福利。

    (A) search〔sɝtʃ〕*v.* 尋找＜*for*＞

    (B) qualify〔'kwɑlə,faɪ〕*v.* 有～資格＜*for*＞

    (C) confront〔kən'frʌnt〕*v.* 面對

    (D) *battle*〔'bætḷ〕*v.* 戰鬥；努力

    ＊ *labor union* 工會   benefit〔'bɛnəfɪt〕*n.* 福利

2. (**A**) Too little calcium can <u>retard</u> a child's growth.

鈣質太少可能會<u>阻礙</u>小孩的生長。

    (A) *retard*〔rɪ'tɑrd〕*v.* 阻礙

    (B) inherit〔ɪn'hɛrɪt〕*v.* 遺傳

    (C) accumulate〔ə'kjumjə,let〕*v.* 累積

    (D) monitor〔'mɑnətɚ〕*v.* 監視

    ＊ calcium〔'kælsɪəm〕*n.* 鈣質

3. (**C**) Much of the waste produced by modern people can be reduced by <u>recycling</u>.

現代人所製造的許多廢物可以經由<u>資源回收</u>減少。

    (A) frugality〔fru'gælətɪ〕*n.* 節儉

    (B) dump〔dʌmp〕*n.* 垃圾場

    (C) *recycling*〔ri'saɪklɪŋ〕*n.* 資源回收

    (D) circulation〔,sɝkjə'leʃən〕*n.* 循環

4. (**D**) It is a mere <u>assumption</u> that the president is to meet with the Secretary of Defense.

總統將與國防部長會面一事，純屬臆測。

(A) description〔dɪˋskrɪpʃən〕*n.* 描述

(B) subscription〔səbˋskrɪpʃən〕*n.* 訂閱＜ *to* ＞

(C) consumption〔kənˋsʌmpʃən〕*n.* 消耗

(D) *assumption*〔əˋsʌmpʃən〕*n.* 假說；臆測

* mere〔mɪr〕*adj.* 僅僅　　*meet with* 與～會面

defense〔dɪˋfɛns〕*n.* 防衛；國防

the Secretary of Defense 國防部長

5. (**A**) Children whose parents cannot afford to feed them properly often suffer from <u>malnutrition</u>.

父母若無力提供孩子適當的食物，小孩通常會<u>營養不良</u>。

(A) *malnutrition*〔͵mælnjuˋtrɪʃən〕*n.* 營養不良

(B) obesity〔oˋbisətɪ〕*n.* 肥胖

(C) diabetes〔͵daɪəˋbitɪs〕*n.* 糖尿病

(D) insomnia〔ɪnˋsɑmnɪə〕*n.* 失眠

6. (**C**) Three decades ago, mainland China was <u>virtually</u> shut off from the world.

三十年前，中國大陸<u>幾乎</u>是與世隔絕。

(A) vividly〔ˋvɪvɪdlɪ〕*adv.* 生動地

(B) familiarly〔fəˋmɪljəlɪ〕*adv.* 熟悉地

(C) *virtually*〔ˋvɝtʃuəlɪ〕*adv.* 實質上；幾乎

(D) mutually〔ˋmjutʃuəlɪ〕*adv.* 彼此；互相地

* *shut off* 隔絕

7. (**C**) Most of the people living in the mountainous slum areas are <u>illiterate</u> laborers.

大部份住在山地貧窮地區的都是<u>不識字的</u>工人。

(A) literary (ˈlɪtəˌrɛrɪ) adj. 文學的

(B) worth (wɝθ) adj. 值得的 (不置於名詞之前)

(C) ***illiterate*** (ɪˈlɪtərɪt) adj. 不識字的；文盲的
(↔ literate adj. 識字的)

(D) spacious (ˈspeʃəs) adj. 寬敞的

* mountainous (ˈmauntṇəs) adj. 山地的
slum (slʌm) n. 貧民區
laborer (ˈlebərə) n. 勞工；工人

8. (**A**) Steven went through about four years of being <u>addicted</u> to video games. He finally overcame the bad habit.

史蒂芬經歷了四年<u>沈溺於</u>電動玩具的日子。他終於改掉了這個壞習慣。

(A) ***addicted*** (əˈdɪktɪd) adj. 沈溺於；上癮的 < *to* >

(B) irrational (ɪˈræʃənḷ) adj. 不理性的
(↔ rational adj. 理性的)

(C) workaholic (ˌwɝkəˈhɑlɪk) n. 工作狂

(D) convict (kənˈvɪkt) v. 判決

* ***go through*** 經歷
overcome (ˌovəˈkʌm) v. 克服

9. (**A**) A further <u>depreciation</u> of the New Taiwan dollar may prove to be beneficial to our international trade.

新台幣進一步<u>貶值</u>，對於我們的國際貿易也許有益。

   (A) ***depreciation*** (dɪˌpriʃɪ'eʃən) *n.* 貶值

   (B) deception (dɪ'sɛpʃən) *n.* 欺騙

   (C) desperation (ˌdɛspə'reʃən) *n.* 絕望

   (D) detection (dɪ'tɛkʃən) *n.* 探知；發現

   ＊ beneficial (ˌbɛnə'fɪʃəl) *adj.* 有益的

de	+ preci +	ation		dia	+ gnos +	is
down	+ *price* +	*n.*		*through*	+ *know* +	*n.*

10. (**D**) A doctor's first step in treating a sick person is making a <u>diagnosis</u> to find out why the patient is sick. 醫生治療病人的第一步是，<u>診斷</u>出病人為何生病。

   (A) prescription (prɪ'skrɪpʃən) *n.* 藥方

   (B) experiment (ɪk'spɛrəmənt) *n.* 實驗

   (C) therapy ('θɛrəpɪ) *n.* 治療法

   (D) ***diagnosis*** (ˌdaɪəg'nosɪs) *n.* 診斷

TEST 2

Directions: *The following questions are incomplete sentences. You are to choose the one word that best completes the sentence.*

1. College students now still have to attend lectures, do _____ and take quizzes.
   - (A) assignments
   - (B) graduates
   - (C) scores
   - (D) degrees   (   )

2. After a _____ defeat in the election, the political party vowed to reform.
   - (A) dishearten
   - (B) humiliated
   - (C) devastating
   - (D) impressive   (   )

3. The company gave hard workers extra _____ as a reward.
   - (A) burdens
   - (B) penalties
   - (C) bonuses
   - (D) contexts   (   )

4. It was a(n) _____ that they both applied for the same job.
   - (A) occurrence
   - (B) similarity
   - (C) confidence
   - (D) coincidence   (   )

5. As citizens, we should never _____ our right to vote.
   - (A) renounce
   - (B) recommend
   - (C) record
   - (D) regret   (   )

6. Because of the wage cut, the workers voiced their
   _____ to the company's head.
   (A) grievance
   (B) oppose
   (C) agreement
   (D) complain   (   )

7. The _____ of the "Cry Wolf" story is that
   dishonesty will never pay.
   (A) moral
   (B) mortgage
   (C) morale
   (D) mortal   (   )

8. Like people in any country, Americans enjoy following
   the lives of _____: movie stars, sports heroes,
   famous artists, and so on.
   (A) celebrities
   (B) fugitives
   (C) majorities
   (D) minorities   (   )

9. The Duke was _____ by the fear that he might be
   assassinated at any moment.
   (A) perspired
   (B) fascinated
   (C) conspired
   (D) obsessed   (   )

10. For modern youngsters, making money seems to be the
    most important thing, and other things are _____
    unimportant. In other words, compared with making
    money, other things are less important.
    (A) intuitively
    (B) independently
    (C) relatively
    (D) radically   (   )

TEST 2 詳解

1. (**A**) College students now still have to attend lectures,
   do <u>assignments</u> and take quizzes.
   現在的大學生仍然必須上課、做<u>作業</u>、考試。

   (A) ***assignment*** 〔 ə'saɪnmənt 〕 *n.* 作業

   (B) graduate 〔'grædʒuɪt 〕 *n.* 畢業生

   〔'grædʒu,et 〕 *v.* 畢業

   (C) score 〔 skor 〕 *n.* 分數

   (D) degree 〔 dɪ'gri 〕 *n.* 程度 (= *extent*)；學位

   ＊ attend 〔 ə'tɛnd 〕 *v.* 上 (課)

   lecture 〔'lɛktʃə 〕 *n.* 演講；講課

   quiz 〔 kwɪz 〕 *n.* 小考

2. (**C**) After a <u>devastating</u> defeat in the election, the
   political party vowed to reform.
   選舉<u>嚴重</u>挫敗後，該政黨誓言改革。

   (A) dishearten 〔 dɪs'hɑrtn̩ 〕 *v.* 使沮喪；使氣餒

   (此處應用 *disheartening*)

   (B) humiliate 〔 hju'mɪlɪ,et 〕 *v.* 使丟臉

   (此處應用 *humiliating*)

   (C) ***devastating*** 〔'dɛvəs,tetɪŋ 〕 *adj.* 嚴重的

   (D) impressive 〔 ɪm'prɛsɪv 〕 *adj.* 令人印象深刻的

   ＊ defeat 〔 dɪ'fit 〕 *n.* 失敗　　***political party*** 政黨

   vow 〔 vau 〕 *v.* 發誓　　reform 〔 rɪ'fɔrm 〕 *v.* 改革

3. (**C**) The company gave hard workers extra <u>bonuses</u> as a reward.

該公司給予工作努力的員工額外的<u>獎金</u>，做為報酬。

(A) burden〔'bɝdn̩〕*n.* 負擔；重擔

(B) penalty〔'pɛnl̩tɪ〕*n.* 處罰

(C) **bonus**〔'bonəs〕*n.* 獎金；紅利

(D) context〔'kɑntɛkst〕*n.* 上下文

＊ reward〔rɪ'wɔrd〕*n.* 報酬

4. (**D**) It was a <u>coincidence</u> that they both applied for the same job. 他們二人去應徵同一份工作，純屬<u>巧合</u>。

(A) occurrence〔ə'kɝəns〕*n.* 事件

(= *incident* ; *happening*)

(B) similarity〔,sɪmə'lærətɪ〕*n.* 相似之處

(C) confidence〔'kɑnfədəns〕*n.* 信心

(D) **coincidence**〔ko'ɪnsədəns〕*n.* 巧合

＊ **apply for** 申請；應徵

5. (**A**) As citizens, we should never <u>renounce</u> our right to vote. 身為公民，我們絕不應該<u>放棄</u>投票的權利。

(A) **renounce**〔rɪ'naʊns〕*v.* 放棄 (= *give up*)

(B) recommend〔,rɛkə'mɛnd〕*v.* 推薦

(C) record〔rɪ'kɔrd〕*v.* 記錄；錄音（影）

(D) regret〔rɪ'grɛt〕*v.* 後悔

＊ citizen〔'sɪtəzn̩〕*n.* 公民；國民

vote〔vot〕*v.* 投票

6. (**A**) Because of the wage cut, the workers voiced their
   <u>grievance</u> to the company's head.

   由於減薪，員工們將他們的<u>不滿</u>反應給老板。

   (A) ***grievance*** ('grivəns) *n.* 不滿；抱怨
   (B) oppose (ə'poz) *v.* 反對
   (C) agreement (ə'grimənt) *n.* 同意
   (D) complain (kəm'plen) *v.* 抱怨 (此處應用 *complaint*)

   * wage (wedʒ) *n.* 薪資　　cut (kʌt) *n.* 減少
     voice (vɔɪs) *v.* 用言語表達

7. (**A**) The <u>moral</u> of the "Cry Wolf" story is that dishonesty
   will never pay.

   「狼來了」這個故事的<u>寓意</u>就是，不誠實會得不償失。

   (A) ***moral*** ('mɔrəl) *n.* 寓意
   (B) mortgage ('mɔrgɪdʒ) *n., v.* 抵押
   (C) morale (mə'ræl) *n.* 士氣
   (D) mortal ('mɔrtḷ) *adj.* 會死的

   * pay (pe) *v.* 划算；有利

8. (**A**) Like people in any country, Americans enjoy
   following the lives of <u>celebrities</u>: movie stars,
   sports heroes, famous artists, and so on.

   和任何國家的人都一樣，美國人也喜歡追逐<u>名人</u>的生活：
   電影明星、運動英雄、知名藝術家等等。

   (A) ***celebrity*** (sə'lɛbrətɪ) *n.* 名人
   (B) fugitive ('fjudʒətɪv) *n.* 逃亡者
   (C) majority (mə'dʒɔrətɪ) *n.* 大多數
   (D) minority (mə'nɔrətɪ , maɪ-) *n.* 少數

9. (**D**) The Duke was <u>obsessed</u> by the fear that he might be assassinated at any moment.

公爵被他可能隨時會被暗殺的恐懼所<u>纏擾</u>。

(A) perspire〔 pɚˈspaɪr 〕*v.* 流汗（ = *sweat* ）

(B) fascinate〔ˈfæsn̩ˌet 〕*v.* 使著迷

(C) conspire〔 kənˈspaɪr 〕*v.* 陰謀

(D) *obsess*〔 əbˈsɛs 〕*v.* 困擾；纏住

＊ duke〔 djuk 〕*n.* 公爵
assassinate〔 əˈsæsn̩ˌet 〕*v.* 暗殺
at any moment 隨時

10. (**C**) For modern youngsters, making money seems to be the most important thing, and other things are <u>relatively</u> unimportant. In other words, compared with making money, other things are less important.

對現代年輕人而言，賺錢似乎是最重要的事，而其他事<u>相對</u><u>地</u>變得不重要。換句話說，和賺錢比起來，其他事較不重要。

(A) intuitively〔 ɪnˈtjuɪtɪvlɪ 〕*adv.* 直覺地

(B) independently〔ˌɪndɪˈpɛndəntlɪ 〕*adv.* 獨立地

(C) *relatively*〔ˈrɛlətɪvlɪ 〕*adv.* 相對地

(D) radically〔ˈrædɪkl̩ɪ 〕*adv.* 激烈地

＊ *in other words* 換句話說
compared with 和～比起來

TEST 3

Directions: *The following questions are incomplete sentences. You are to choose the one word that best completes the sentence.*

1. If the government doesn't take action to protect rare animals, these animals will become _____ soon.
   (A) instinct
   (B) distinct
   (C) extinct
   (D) explosive ( )

2. The messages were _____ to England by e-mail.
   (A) advanced
   (B) subscribed
   (C) transplanted
   (D) transmitted ( )

3. Well-educated young people form the _____ of our country's future development.
   (A) backbone
   (B) reliance
   (C) wishbone
   (D) alliance ( )

4. In order for knowledge to advance, scientists sometimes need to question _____.
   (A) invalids
   (B) authorities
   (C) emblems
   (D) superiority ( )

5. The mayor finally admitted that the accident was the result of an _____.
   (A) misunderstanding
   (B) oversight
   (C) assembly
   (D) insight ( )

6. Today we gather here to _____ the 70th birthday of Grandpa.
   (A) dispose
   (B) celebrate
   (C) allow
   (D) reveal   (   )

7. The first direct presidential election in Taiwan was a(n) _____ event in Chinese history.
   (A) commonplace
   (B) inspirational
   (C) medieval
   (D) momentous   (   )

8. The freshman _____ of that university this year is higher than it used to be; that is, there are more freshmen attending that university this year than before.
   (A) graduation
   (B) enrollment
   (C) enthusiasm
   (D) participation   (   )

9. _____ by the election loss, the party made the reform proposal.
   (A) Socialized
   (B) Stimulated
   (C) Pleasing
   (D) Encouraged   (   )

10. A cup of whole milk provides _____ one hundred sixty-six calories of energy.
    (A) widely
    (B) approximately
    (C) cowardly
    (D) coarsely   (   )

TEST 3 詳解

1. (**C**) If the government doesn't take action to protect rare animals, these animals will become <u>extinct</u> soon.

如果政府不採取行動來保護稀有動物，這些動物很快就會<u>絕種</u>了。

- (A) instinct (ˈɪnstɪŋkt) *n.* 本能
- (B) distinct (dɪˈstɪŋkt) *adj.* 不同的 <*from*>
- (C) *extinct* (ɪkˈstɪŋkt) *adj.* 絕種的
- (D) explosive (ɪkˈsplosɪv) *adj.* 爆炸的

* *take action* 採取行動　　rare (rɛr) *adj.* 稀有的

2. (**D**) The messages were <u>transmitted</u> to England by e-mail.

這些訊息利用電子郵件<u>傳送</u>到英國。

- (A) advance (ədˈvæns) *v.* 進步；前進
- (B) subscribe (səbˈskraɪb) *v.* 訂閱 <*to*>
- (C) transplant (trænsˈplænt) *v.* 移植
- (D) *transmit* (trænsˈmɪt) *v.* 傳送

3. (**A**) Well-educated young people form the <u>backbone</u> of our country's future development.

受過良好教育的青年，是我們國家未來發展的<u>中堅</u>。

- (A) *backbone* (ˈbækˌbon) *n.* 脊骨 (= *spine*)；
  中堅 <*of*>
- (B) reliance (rɪˈlaɪəns) *n.* 依賴 <*on*>
- (C) wishbone (ˈwɪʃˌbon) *n.* 叉骨；許願骨
- (D) alliance (əˈlaɪəns) *n.* 聯盟

4. (**B**) In order for knowledge to advance, scientists sometimes need to question <u>authorities</u>.

爲了讓知識進步，科學家有時必須質疑<u>權威</u>。

(A) invalid〔'ɪnvəlɪd〕 *n.* 病人 (= *patient*)

(B) ***authority***〔ə'θɔrətɪ〕 *n.* 權威

(C) emblem〔'ɛmbləm〕 *n.* 象徵 (= *symbol*)

(D) superiority〔sə͵pɪrɪ'ɔrətɪ , -'ɑrətɪ〕 *n.* 優越

* advance〔əd'væns〕 *v.* 進步

question〔'kwɛstʃən〕 *v.* 詢問；質疑

5. (**B**) The mayor finally admitted that the accident was the result of an <u>oversight</u>.

市長終於承認，這次意外是<u>疏失</u>造成的。

(A) misunderstanding〔͵mɪsʌndə'stændɪŋ〕 *n.* 誤解

(冠詞應用 *a*)

(B) ***oversight***〔'ovə͵saɪt〕 *n.* 疏忽

(C) assembly〔ə'sɛmblɪ〕 *n.* 集會；裝配

(D) insight〔'ɪn͵saɪt〕 *n.* 洞察力

* admit〔əd'mɪt〕 *v.* 承認   result〔rɪ'zʌlt〕 *n.* 結果

6. (**B**) Today we gather here to <u>celebrate</u> the 70th birthday of Grandpa.

今天我們齊聚一堂，來<u>慶祝</u>爺爺七十大壽。

(A) dispose〔dɪ'spoz〕 *v.* 處置

(B) ***celebrate***〔'sɛlə͵bret〕 *v.* 慶祝

(C) allow〔ə'laʊ〕 *v.* 允許

(D) reveal〔rɪ'vil〕 *v.* 揭露

* gather〔'gæðə〕 *v.* 聚集

7. (**D**) The first direct presidential election in Taiwan was a <u>momentous</u> event in Chinese history.
台灣首次總統直選，是中國歷史上的一件<u>重大</u>事件。

    (A) commonplace〔'kɑmən,ples〕*adj.* 普通的
       (= *common* ; *ordinary*)

    (B) inspirational〔,ınspə'reʃənḷ〕*adj.* 啓發靈感的

    (C) medieval〔,midɪ'ivḷ, ,mɛ-〕*adj.* 中世紀的

    (D) ***momentous***〔mo'mɛntəs〕*adj.* 重大的
      (= *important* ; *significant*)

    * direct〔də'rɛkt〕*adj.* 直接的
    presidential〔,prɛzə'dɛnʃəl〕*adj.* 總統的
    election〔ı'lɛkʃən〕*n.* 選舉

8. (**B**) The freshman <u>enrollment</u> of that university this year is higher than it used to be; that is, there are more freshmen attending that university this year than before.
那所大學今年的新生<u>註冊人數</u>比以往多，也就是說，今年就讀該大學的新生比以前多。

    (A) graduation〔,grædʒʊ'eʃən〕*n.* 畢業

    (B) ***enrollment***〔ın'rolmənt〕*n.* 登記；註冊人數

    (C) enthusiasm〔ın'θjuzɪ,æzəm〕*n.* 熱誠

    (D) participation〔pə,tısə'peʃən, par-〕*n.* 參加 < *in* >

    * freshman〔'frɛʃmən〕*n.* 大一新生
    attend〔ə'tɛnd〕*v.* 上 (學)

9. (**B**) <u>Stimulated</u> by the election loss, the party made the reform proposal.

受到選舉失利的<u>刺激</u>，該政黨提出改革的提議。

(A) socialize〔'soʃə,laɪz〕*v.* 社會化

(B) *stimulate*〔'stɪmjə,let〕*v.* 刺激；激勵

(C) please〔pliz〕*v.* 取悅

(D) encourage〔ɪn'kɝɪdʒ〕*v.* 鼓勵

* reform〔rɪ'fɔrm〕*n.* 改革
  proposal〔prə'pozḷ〕*n.* 提議

10. (**B**) A cup of whole milk provides <u>approximately</u> one hundred sixty-six calories of energy.

一杯全脂牛奶提供<u>大約</u>一百六十六卡的熱量。

(A) widely〔'waɪdlɪ〕*adv.* 廣泛地

(B) *approximately*〔ə'prɑksəmɪtlɪ〕*adv.* 大約
    (= *roughly* ; *about*)

(C) cowardly〔'kaʊədlɪ〕*adj.* 膽小的

(D) coarsely〔'kɔrslɪ〕*adv.* 粗糙地

* *whole milk* 全脂牛奶
  calorie〔'kælərɪ〕*n.* 卡路里
  energy〔'ɛnədʒɪ〕*n.* 熱量

ap	+ proxim	+ ate	+ ly
|	|	|	|
to	+ *near*	+ *adj.*	+ *adv.*

TEST 4

Directions: *The following questions are incomplete sentences. You are to choose the one word that best completes the sentence.*

1. Those people who find food _____ are usually overweight.
   (A) merciless
   (B) reckless
   (C) irregular
   (D) irresistible   (   )

2. A _____ is someone who uses violence or the threat of violence, often for political purposes.
   (A) pilgrim
   (B) kidnapper
   (C) participant
   (D) terrorist   (   )

3. Nutritionists _____ food into seven basic groups.
   (A) overthrow
   (B) grind
   (C) categorize
   (D) channel   (   )

4. As the world's natural _____ dwindle, we must be concerned and try to make the best use of them.
   (A) wealths
   (B) materials
   (C) resources
   (D) sources   (   )

5. Today, we are not _____ from the effects of financial crisis abroad.
   (A) escape
   (B) immune
   (C) connected
   (D) involved   (   )

6. The shoes are not _____ in my size; I have to get them elsewhere.

    (A) available
    (B) fictional
    (C) fundamental
    (D) customary   (   )

7. Democracy in Taiwan has won _____ from the West.

    (A) eloquence
    (B) compliments
    (C) competition
    (D) selection   (   )

8. Cross-strait talks between Taiwan and China were _____ after a two-year break.

    (A) recovered
    (B) recreated
    (C) regenerated
    (D) resumed   (   )

9. All of the patients like Ruth because she is kind and treats them _____ every day.

    (A) affectedly
    (B) affectionately
    (C) considerably
    (D) impatiently   (   )

10. These three boxes are _____. They are of the same size, shape, color and weight.

    (A) unique
    (B) individual
    (C) initiative
    (D) identical   (   )

TEST 4 詳解

1. (**D**) Those people who find food <u>irresistible</u> are usually overweight. 無法抗拒食物的人通常都體重過重。

    (A) merciless (ˈmɝsɪlɪs) *adj.* 無情的 < *to* >

    (B) reckless (ˈrɛklɪs) *adj.* 魯莽的 < *of* >

    (C) irregular (ɪˈrɛgjələ) *adj.* 不規則的

    (D) *irresistible* (ˌɪrɪˈzɪstəbl̩) *adj.* 無法抗拒的

    * overweight (ˈovəˈwet) *adj.* 體重過重的

2. (**D**) A <u>terrorist</u> is someone who uses violence or the threat of violence, often for political purposes.
恐怖分子就是使用暴力，或威脅要使用暴力的人，通常是爲了政治目的。

    (A) pilgrim (ˈpɪlgrɪm) *n.* 朝聖者

    (B) kidnapper (ˈkɪdnæpə) *n.* 綁匪

    (C) participant (pəˈtɪsəpənt) *n.* 參加者

    (D) *terrorist* (ˈtɛrərɪst) *n.* 恐怖分子

3. (**C**) Nutritionists <u>categorize</u> food into seven basic groups.
營養學家將食物分成七大基本種類。

    (A) overthrow (ˌovəˈθro) *v.* 推翻

    (B) grind (graɪnd) *v.* 磨碎

    (C) *categorize* (ˈkætəgəˌraɪz) *v.* 分類

    (D) channel (ˈtʃænl̩) *v.* 挖溝渠

    * nutritionist (njuˈtrɪʃənɪst) *n.* 營養學家

4. (**C**) As the world's natural <u>resources</u> dwindle, we must be concerned and try to make the best use of them.

隨著全世界的自然<u>資源</u>逐漸減少，我們必須關心，並努力善用。

    (A) wealth〔wɛlθ〕*n.* 財富（不用複數）

    (B) material〔mə'tɪrɪəl〕*n.* 材料

    (C) *resource*〔rɪ'sors〕*n.* 資源（通常用複數）

    (D) source〔sors〕*n.* 來源

    * dwindle〔'dwɪndḷ〕*v.* 逐漸減少
     concerned〔kən'sɜnd〕*adj.* 關心的
     make the best use of 善用

5. (**B**) Today, we are not <u>immune</u> from the effects of financial crisis abroad.

今日國外的金融危機，我們無法<u>不受影響</u>。

    (A) escape〔ə'skep〕*v.* 逃脫 <*from*>

      （應用 *We cannot escape from...*）

    (B) ***immune***〔ɪ'mjun〕*adj.* 免疫的；不受影響的
     <*from , to*>

    (C) connected〔kə'nɛktɪd〕*adj.* 有關的

    (D) involved〔ɪn'vɑlvd〕*adj.* 有牽連的 <*with*>

    * effect〔ɪ'fɛkt〕*n.* 影響
     financial〔fə'nænʃəl〕*adj.* 金融的；財務的
     crisis〔'kraɪsɪs〕*n.* 危機
     abroad〔ə'brɔd〕*adv.* 在國外

6. (**A**) The shoes are not <u>available</u> in my size; I have to get them elsewhere.

這些鞋子<u>沒有</u>我的尺寸；我得到別處去買。

(A) ***available*** 〔ə'veləbḷ 〕 *adj.* 可獲得的；買得到的

(B) fictional 〔'fɪkʃənḷ 〕 *adj.* 小說的；虛構的

(C) fundamental 〔ˌfʌndə'mɛntḷ 〕 *adj.* 基礎的 (= *basic*)

(D) customary 〔'kʌstəmˌɛrɪ 〕 *adj.* 習慣性的

7. (**B**) Democracy in Taiwan has won <u>compliments</u> from the West. 台灣的民主已贏得西方國家的<u>稱讚</u>。

(A) eloquence 〔'ɛləkwəns 〕 *n.* 雄辯

(B) ***compliment*** 〔'kɑmpləmənt 〕 *n.* 稱讚 (= *praise*)

(C) competition 〔ˌkɑmpə'tɪʃən 〕 *n.* 競爭；比賽

(D) selection 〔sə'lɛkʃən 〕 *n.* 選擇

* democracy 〔dɪ'mɑkrəsɪ 〕 *n.* 民主

8. (**D**) Cross-strait talks between Taiwan and China were <u>resumed</u> after a two-year break.

台灣和中國之間的兩岸對談，在中斷二年後<u>重新開始</u>。

(A) recover 〔rɪ'kʌvɚ 〕 *v.* 恢復 (健康等)

(B) recreate 〔'rɛkrɪˌet 〕 *v.* 消遣；娛樂

　　　　〔ˌrikrɪ'et 〕 *v.* 重新創造

(C) regenerate 〔rɪ'dʒɛnəˌret 〕 *v.* 再生；使復活

(D) ***resume*** 〔rɪ'zum 〕 *v.* (中斷後) 重新開始；繼續

* cross-strait 〔'krɔs'stret 〕 *adj.* 海峽兩岸的

break 〔brek 〕 *n.* 中斷

9. (**B**) All of the patients like Ruth because she is kind and
treats them <u>affectionately</u> every day.

所有的病人都喜歡露絲，因為她心地善良，而且每天都
<u>充滿愛心地</u>對待他們。

    (A) affectedly〔əˋfɛktɪdlɪ〕*adv.* 做作地

    (B) *affectionately*〔əˋfɛkʃənɪtlɪ〕*adv.* 充滿深情地

    (C) considerably〔kənˋsɪdərəblɪ〕*adv.* 相當地

      （此處應用 *considerately adv.* 體貼地）

    (D) impatiently〔ɪmˋpeʃəntlɪ〕*adv.* 不耐煩地

```
affection + ate  + ly
    |         |      |
  感情      + adj. + adv.
```

10. (**D**) These three boxes are <u>identical</u>. They are of the
same size, shape, color and weight.

這三個盒子<u>一模一樣</u>，大小、形狀、顏色、重量都相同。

    (A) unique〔juˋnik〕*adj.* 獨特的

    (B) individual〔͵ɪndəˋvɪdʒʊəl〕*adj.* 個別的

    (C) initiative〔ɪˋnɪʃɪ͵etɪv〕*n.* 主動權

    (D) *identical*〔aɪˋdɛntɪkḷ〕*adj.* 完全相同的

TEST 5

Directions: *The following questions are incomplete sentences. You are to choose the one word that best completes the sentence.*

1. A _____ mind will never find life uneventful.
   (A) futile
   (B) sterile
   (C) imaginative
   (D) fertile   (   )

2. The criminal has _____ all his wrongdoing.
   (A) vowed
   (B) disallowed
   (C) confessed
   (D) pronounced   (   )

3. It is essential to develop good _____ between teachers and students.
   (A) inscriptions
   (B) interactions
   (C) perfections
   (D) predictions   (   )

4. As my brother is color-blind, he cannot _____ between green and blue.
   (A) switch
   (B) distinguish
   (C) erase
   (D) attempt   (   )

5. While some bacteria are beneficial, others are _____ in that they cause disease.
   (A) harmful
   (B) profitable
   (C) invisible
   (D) corrupt   (   )

6. Last week, an armed robber shot two men when he robbed the City Bank. Afterwards, an ambulance rushed the two _____ to the hospital.

   (A) criminals
   (B) victims
   (C) witnesses
   (D) suspects   (   )

7. Although pencils are _____ made of graphite and not of lead, the term "lead pencil" has come to be widely used.

   (A) reportedly
   (B) actually
   (C) privately
   (D) originally   (   )

8. Being a _____ policeman, he knew how to deal with such criminals.

   (A) experienced
   (B) seasoned
   (C) fashionable
   (D) vital   (   )

9. A heavy rain _____ the city, and the citizens suffered from lack of dry clothing.

   (A) trenched
   (B) drenched
   (C) quenched
   (D) dripped   (   )

10. The whole society abhors the _____ treatment of animals.

   (A) benign
   (B) benevolent
   (C) inhumane
   (D) merciful   (   )

TEST 5 詳解

1. (**D**) A <u>fertile</u> mind will never find life uneventful.

有豐富創造力的人，永遠不會覺得生活單調。

  (A) futile〔ˈfjutḷ〕*adj.* 徒勞的；無用的（= *useless*）

  (B) sterile〔ˈstɛrəl〕*adj.* 貧瘠的

  (C) imaginative〔ɪˈmædʒəˌnetɪv〕*adj.* 想像的；
   富想像力的（冠詞應用 *an*）

  (D) *fertile*〔ˈfɝtḷ〕*adj.* 肥沃的；富創造力的

  * uneventful〔ˌʌnɪˈvɛntfəl〕*adj.* 平靜無事的；單調的

2. (**C**) The criminal has <u>confessed</u> all his wrongdoing.

犯人已<u>招認</u>所有罪行。

  (A) vow〔vaʊ〕*v.* 發誓

  (B) disallow〔ˌdɪsəˈlaʊ〕*v.* 不允許；駁回

  (C) *confess*〔kənˈfɛs〕*v.* 招認；自白

  (D) pronounce〔prəˈnaʊns〕*v.* 發音；宣告

  * criminal〔ˈkrɪmənḷ〕*n.* 犯人
   wrongdoing〔ˈrɔŋˈduɪŋ〕*n.* 爲非做歹；罪行

3. (**B**) It is essential to develop good <u>interactions</u> between teachers and students.

老師和學生之間發展良好的<u>互動關係</u>是必要的。

  (A) inscription〔ɪnˈskrɪpʃən〕*n.* 銘刻

  (B) *interaction*〔ˌɪntɚˈækʃən〕*n.* 互動

  (C) perfection〔pɚˈfɛkʃən〕*n.* 完美

  (D) prediction〔prɪˈdɪkʃən〕*n.* 預測

  * essential〔əˈsɛnʃəl〕*adj.* 必要的

4. (**B**) As my brother is color-blind, he cannot <u>distinguish</u> between green and blue.

由於我弟弟是色盲，他無法<u>辨別</u>綠色和藍色。

(A) switch〔swɪtʃ〕v. 轉變

(B) ***distinguish***〔dɪ'stɪŋgwɪʃ〕v. 辨別

(C) erase〔ɪ'res〕v. 擦掉；消除

(D) attempt〔ə'tɛmpt〕v., n. 嘗試

* color-blind〔'kʌlə‚blaɪnd〕adj. 色盲的
distinguish between A and B 辨別 A 和 B
(= *distinguish A from B*)

5. (**A**) While some bacteria are beneficial, others are <u>harmful</u> in that they cause disease.

雖然有些細菌是有益的，但有些是<u>有害的</u>，因為它們會導致疾病。

(A) ***harmful***〔'hɑrmfəl〕adj. 有害的

(B) profitable〔'prɑfɪtəbḷ〕adj. 有利可圖的

(C) invisible〔ɪn'vɪzəbḷ〕adj. 看不見的

(D) corrupt〔kə'rʌpt〕adj. 腐敗的

* while〔hwaɪl〕conj. 雖然 (= *although*)
bacteria〔bæk'tɪrɪə〕n. pl. 細菌
beneficial〔‚bɛnə'fɪʃəl〕adj. 有益的
in that 因為 (= *because*)

6. (**B**) Last week, an armed robber shot two men when he robbed the City Bank. Afterwards, an ambulance rushed the two <u>victims</u> to the hospital.

上週一名持槍搶匪，搶劫市銀行時，射殺了二個人。隨後，救護車將二名<u>傷者</u>緊急送醫。

(A) criminal〔'krɪmənḷ〕 *n.* 罪犯

(B) ***victim***〔'vɪktɪm〕 *n.* 受害者

(C) witness〔'wɪtnɪs〕 *n.* 目擊者

(D) suspect〔'sʌspɛkt〕 *n.* 嫌疑犯

* armed〔ɑrmd〕 *adj.* 武裝的   shoot〔ʃut〕 *v.* 射殺
afterwards〔'æftɚwɚdz〕 *adv.* 後來
ambulance〔'æmbjələns〕 *n.* 救護車
rush〔rʌʃ〕 *v.* 趕緊；火速

7. (**B**) Although pencils are <u>actually</u> made of graphite and not of lead, the term "lead pencil" has come to be widely used.

雖然鉛筆<u>實際</u>上是由石墨製成的，而不是鉛，但「鉛筆」這個名詞已經被廣泛使用。

(A) reportedly〔rɪ'portɪdlɪ〕 *adv.* 根據報導；據說

(B) ***actually***〔'æktʃʊəlɪ〕 *adv.* 實際上

(C) privately〔'praɪvɪtlɪ〕 *adv.* 個人地；私下地

(D) originally〔ə'rɪdʒənḷɪ〕 *adv.* 最初地

* graphite〔'græfaɪt〕 *n.* 石墨
lead〔lɛd〕 *n.* 鉛   term〔tɝm〕 *n.* 名詞

8. (**B**) Being a <u>seasoned</u> policeman, he knew how to deal with such criminals.

身為<u>經驗豐富的</u>警察，他知道如何應付這樣的罪犯。

    (A) experienced〔ɪkˈspɪrɪənst〕 *adj.* 有經驗的

    （冠詞應用 *an*）

    (B) ***seasoned***〔ˈsiznd〕 *adj.* 有經驗的；經過歷練的

    (C) fashionable〔ˈfæʃənəbl〕 *adj.* 流行的

    (D) vital〔ˈvaɪtl〕 *adj.* 非常重要的

    * ***deal with*** 應付

9. (**B**) A heavy rain <u>drenched</u> the city, and the citizens suffered from lack of dry clothing.

豪雨<u>使</u>整個城市<u>濕答答的</u>，市民們都快沒有乾衣服穿了。

    (A) trench〔trɛntʃ〕 *v.* 挖壕溝

    (B) ***drench***〔drɛntʃ〕 *v.* 使濕透

    (C) quench〔kwɛntʃ〕 *v.* 解（渴）；熄滅

    (D) drip〔drɪp〕 *v.* 滴落

    * citizen〔ˈsɪtəzn〕 *n.* 市民   ***suffer from*** 苦於

10. (**C**) The whole society abhors the <u>inhumane</u> treatment of animals. 全社會上的人都痛恨動物遭到<u>不人道的</u>對待。

    (A) benign〔bɪˈnaɪn〕 *adj.* 良性的

    (B) benevolent〔bəˈnɛvələnt〕 *adj.* 仁慈的

    (C) ***inhumane***〔ˌɪnhjuˈmen〕 *adj.* 不人道的

    (D) merciful〔ˈmɝsɪfəl〕 *adj.* 慈悲的

    * abhor〔əbˈhɔr〕 *v.* 痛恨；厭煩

    treatment〔ˈtritmənt〕 *n.* 對待

TEST 6

Directions: *The following questions are incomplete sentences. You are to choose the one word that best completes the sentence.*

1. Their divorce was _____; therefore, they remain friends despite their failed marriage.
   (A) amicable
   (B) progressive
   (C) solitary
   (D) soluble   (   )

2. The company will have to _____ a few persons because it is not as productive as it was.
   (A) reform
   (B) return
   (C) employ
   (D) dismiss   (   )

3. A chronic disease is a health _____.
   (A) hazard
   (B) benefit
   (C) component
   (D) ingredient   (   )

4. I could not correct your test paper because your handwriting was _____.
   (A) illegitimate
   (B) illegible
   (C) precise
   (D) tidy   (   )

5. Unemployment has reached _____ levels. The government has to do something about it.
   (A) unvarnished
   (B) unprecedented
   (C) unsuspecting
   (D) unscrupulous   (   )

6. The judge _____ the young woman to seven years'
   imprisonment for armed robbery.
   (A) accused
   (B) arrested
   (C) charged
   (D) sentenced   (   )

7. There are people who still cannot accept the fact that
   humans _____ from apes.
   (A) revolved
   (B) generated
   (C) derived
   (D) evolved   (   )

8. After flying an airplane all day, Norris liked to be a
   _____ and take a casual walk in the evening.
   (A) pediatrician
   (B) pedestrian
   (C) pedagogue
   (D) peddler   (   )

9. An _____ disease is usually caused by bacteria and
   can be spread from person to person.
   (A) inattentive
   (B) infectious
   (C) incidental
   (D) infinite   (   )

10. You must _____ in at the airport an hour before
    your plane leaves.
    (A) hug
    (B) check
    (C) pin
    (D) lash   (   )

TEST 6 詳解

1. (**A**) Their divorce was <u>amicable</u>; therefore, they remain friends despite their failed marriage.

他們的離婚很<u>平和</u>；因此，儘管婚姻失敗，他們仍是朋友。

(A) ***amicable*** (ˈæmɪkəbl̩) *adj.* 友好的；和平的

(B) progressive (prəˈgrɛsɪv) *adj.* 進步的

(C) solitary (ˈsɑlə͵tɛrɪ) *adj.* 單獨的；孤獨的

(D) soluble (ˈsɑljəbl̩) *adj.* 可解決的

* divorce (dəˈvors) *n.* 離婚

  despite (dɪˈspaɪt) *prep.* 儘管 (= *in spite of*)

2. (**D**) The company will have to <u>dismiss</u> a few persons because it is not as productive as it was.

該公司必須<u>解雇</u>一些人，因為生產力已不如從前。

(A) reform (rɪˈfɔrm) *v.* 改革

(B) return (rɪˈtɝn) *v.* 返回；歸還

(C) employ (ɪmˈplɔɪ) *v.* 雇用 (= *hire*)

(D) ***dismiss*** (dɪsˈmɪs) *v.* 解雇 (= *fire*)

* productive (prəˈdʌktɪv) *adj.* 有生產力的

3. (**A**) A chronic disease is a health <u>hazard</u>.

慢性疾病會<u>危及</u>健康。

(A) ***hazard*** (ˈhæzəd) *n.* 危險 (= *danger* ; *risk*)

(B) benefit (ˈbɛnəfɪt) *n.* 利益

(C) component (kəmˈponənt) *n.* 成分

(D) ingredient (ɪnˈgridɪənt) *n.* 原料

* chronic (ˈkrɑnɪk) *adj.* 慢性的

4. (**B**) I could not correct your test paper because your handwriting was <u>illegible</u>.

我無法批改你的考卷，因為你的字跡難以辨認。

(A) illegitimate〔͵ɪlɪˈdʒɪtəmɪt〕*adj.* 違法的

(B) ***illegible***〔ɪˈlɛdʒəbḷ〕*adj.* 難認的

(C) precise〔prɪˈsaɪs〕*adj.* 精確的

(D) tidy〔ˈtaɪdɪ〕*adj.* 整齊的

* correct〔kəˈrɛkt〕*v.* 批改；更正
handwriting〔ˈhænd͵raɪtɪŋ〕*n.* 字跡

5. (**B**) Unemployment has reached <u>unprecedented</u> levels. The government has to do something about it.

失業率已達到空前新高。政府必須採取行動了。

(A) unvarnished〔ʌnˈvɑrnɪʃt〕*adj.* 未修飾的

(B) ***unprecedented***〔ʌnˈprɛsə͵dɛntɪd〕*adj.* 空前的；
史無前例的

(C) unsuspecting〔͵ʌnsəˈspɛktɪŋ〕*adj.* 不懷疑的

(D) unscrupulous〔ʌnˈskrupjələs〕*adj.* 肆無忌憚的

* unemployment〔͵ʌnɪmˈplɔɪmənt〕*n.* 失業（率）
level〔ˈlɛvḷ〕*n.* 水準；高度
do something about it 採取行動（ *= take action* ）

un	+	pre	+ ced	+ ent	+ ed
not	+	*before*	+ *go*	+ *n.*	+ *adj.*	（沒有人走在前面）

6. (**D**) The judge <u>sentenced</u> the young woman to seven years' imprisonment for armed robbery.

法官<u>判決</u>這名年輕女子七年徒刑，罪名是持械搶劫。

　　(A) accuse〔ə'kjuz〕*v.* 控告 < *of* >

　　(B) arrest〔ə'rɛst〕*v.* 逮捕 < *for* >

　　(C) charge〔tʃɑrdʒ〕*v.* 控告 < *with* >

　　(D) *sentence*〔'sɛntəns〕*v.* 判刑 < *to* >

　　＊ imprisonment〔ɪm'prɪznmənt〕*n.* 監禁

　　　armed〔ɑrmd〕*adj.* 武裝的

7. (**D**) There are people who still cannot accept the fact that humans <u>evolved</u> from apes.

有些人仍然無法接受，人類是由猿猴<u>演化</u>而來的事實。

　　(A) revolve〔rɪ'vɑlv〕*v.* 旋轉

　　(B) generate〔'dʒɛnə,ret〕*v.* 產生

　　(C) derive〔də'raɪv〕*v.* 源於 < *from* >

　　(D) *evolve*〔ɪ'vɑlv〕*v.* 演化

　　＊ ape〔ep〕*n.* 猿

8. (**B**) After flying an airplane all day, Norris liked to be a <u>pedestrian</u> and take a casual walk in the evening.

搭了一整天的飛機之後，諾瑞斯只想當個<u>行人</u>，晚上去隨意地散個步。

　　(A) pediatrician〔,pidɪə'trɪʃən〕*n.* 小兒科醫師

　　(B) *pedestrian*〔pə'dɛstrɪən〕*n.* 行人

　　(C) pedagogue〔'pɛdə,gɑg〕*n.* 教師 (= *teacher*)

　　(D) peddler〔'pɛdlə〕*n.* 小販

　　＊ casual〔'kæʒuəl〕*adj.* 隨意的

9. (**B**) An <u>infectious</u> disease is usually caused by bacteria and can be spread from person to person.

傳<u>染</u>病通常由細菌所引起，會在人群中散播開來。

(A) inattentive〔͵ɪnə'tɛntɪv〕*adj.* 不注意的

(B) ***infectious***〔ɪn'fɛkʃəs〕*adj.* 會傳染的

(C) incidental〔͵ɪnsə'dɛntl̩〕*adj.* 偶發的

(D) infinite〔'ɪnfənɪt〕*adj.* 無限的

　＊ bacteria〔bæk'tɪrɪə〕*n. pl.* 細菌

　　spread〔sprɛd〕*v.* 散播

in + fect + ious
｜　　　　｜
in + make + adj.

10. (**B**) You must <u>check</u> in at the airport an hour before your plane leaves.

你必須在班機起飛前一小時先<u>辦理登機手續</u>。

(A) hug〔hʌg〕*v.,n.* 擁抱

(B) ***check in*** 　（機場）辦理登機手續；（飯店）登記住宿

　　（↔ check out（飯店）結帳退房）

(C) pin〔pɪn〕*v.* 別住

(D) lash〔læʃ〕*v.* 鞭打

TEST 7

Directions: *The following questions are incomplete sentences. You are to choose the one word that best completes the sentence.*

1. When I first moved to France, I felt very _____;
   I missed Taiwan very much.
   (A) tense
   (B) airsick
   (C) homesick
   (D) weary   (   )

2. Most people have become so _____ on TV that they
   cannot do without it in their lives.
   (A) dependent
   (B) dependable
   (C) concentrated
   (D) forgetful   (   )

3. A good salesman must be _____ if he wants to
   succeed.
   (A) cynical
   (B) conservative
   (C) aggressive
   (D) rude   (   )

4. It is _____ of you to be polite to that crude man.
   (A) gracious
   (B) courtesy
   (C) general
   (D) grace   (   )

5. Although fish have no vocal organs, they still are able
   to make _____.
   (A) movements
   (B) bubbles
   (C) sounds
   (D) ripples   (   )

6. The professor's latest study _____ mainly with the migration of birds.
   (A) collided
   (B) focused
   (C) dealt
   (D) absorbed   (   )

7. The effects of the financial _____ have been felt in stock markets around the world. Many companies have gone bankrupt.
   (A) blackout
   (B) disadvantage
   (C) urgency
   (D) crisis   (   )

8. In a democratic country, people are allowed to _____ against their government to express their political opinions.
   (A) determine
   (B) depict
   (C) discipline
   (D) demonstrate   (   )

9. The " _____ family," which consists of only one father, one mother and children, is becoming the main family structure everywhere.
   (A) typical
   (B) nuclear
   (C) formal
   (D) similar   (   )

10. Many Asian men think that American women are too _____ to make good wives.
   (A) reasonable
   (B) positive
   (C) persuasive
   (D) liberated   (   )

TEST 7 詳解

1. (**C**) When I first moved to France, I felt very <u>homesick</u>;
I missed Taiwan very much.
當我剛搬到法國時，我很<u>想家</u>；我十分想念台灣。

    (A) tense〔tɛns〕 *adj.* 緊張的

    (B) airsick〔'ɛr,sɪk〕 *adj.* 暈機的

    (C) ***homesick***〔'hom,sɪk〕 *adj.* 想家的

    (D) weary〔'wɪrɪ〕 *adj.* 疲倦的（= *tired* ）

2. (**A**) Most people have become so <u>dependent</u> on TV that
they cannot do without it in their lives.
大部分人已變得如此<u>依賴</u>電視，以至於生活中不能沒有電視。

    (A) ***dependent***〔dɪ'pɛndənt〕 *adj.* 依賴的 < *on* >

    (B) dependable〔dɪ'pɛndəbḷ〕 *adj.* 可靠的（= *reliable* ）

    (C) concentrated〔'kɑnsṇ,tretɪd〕 *adj.* 集中的；濃縮的

    (D) forgetful〔fə'gɛtfəl〕 *adj.* 健忘的

    * ***cannot do without*** 不能沒有

3. (**C**) A good salesman must be <u>aggressive</u> if he wants to
succeed. 要做個好的推銷員，一定要<u>有衝勁</u>才能成功。

    (A) cynical〔'sɪnɪkḷ〕 *adj.* 憤世嫉俗的

    (B) conservative〔kən'sɝvətɪv〕 *adj.* 保守的

    (C) ***aggressive***〔ə'grɛsɪv〕 *adj.* 積極的；有衝勁的

    (D) rude〔rud〕 *adj.* 粗魯的

4. (**A**) It is <u>gracious</u> of you to be polite to that crude man.

你真是<u>和善</u>，對那個粗野的人還那麼客氣。

(A) ***gracious*** 〔'greʃəs 〕 *adj.* 和善的

(B) courtesy 〔'kɜtəsɪ 〕 *n.* 禮貌

（此處應用形容詞 *courteous* 〔'kɜtɪəs 〕）

(C) general 〔'dʒɛnərəl 〕 *adj.* 一般的

(D) grace 〔 gres 〕 *n.* 優雅（此處應用形容詞 *graceful*）

＊ crude 〔 krud 〕 *adj.* 粗野的（＝ *unrefined*；*vulgar*）

5. (**C**) Although fish have no vocal organs, they still are able to make <u>sounds</u>.

雖然魚沒有發聲器官，它們仍然可以發出<u>聲音</u>。

(A) movement 〔'muvmənt 〕 *n.* 動作

(B) bubble 〔'bʌbḷ 〕 *n.* 泡泡

(C) ***sound*** 〔 saʊnd 〕 *n.* 聲音

(D) ripple 〔'rɪpḷ 〕 *n.* 漣漪

＊ vocal 〔'vokḷ 〕 *adj.* 聲音的　　organ 〔'ɔrgən 〕 *n.* 器官

6. (**C**) The professor's latest study <u>dealt</u> mainly with the migration of birds.

這位教授最新的研究主要<u>討論</u>鳥類的遷移。

(A) collide 〔 kə'laɪd 〕 *v.* 相撞＜*with*＞

(B) focus 〔'fokəs 〕 *v.* 集中＜*on*＞

(C) ***deal with*** 討論（主題）

(D) absorb 〔 əb'sɔrb 〕 *v.* 吸收

＊ migration 〔 maɪ'greʃən 〕 *n.* 遷移

7. (**D**) The effects of the financial <u>crisis</u> have been felt in stock markets around the world. Many companies have gone bankrupt.

金融危機的影響在全世界的股票市場都可感受到。很多公司已經破產了。

   (A) blackout ('blæk,aut) *n.* 停電
   (B) disadvantage (,dɪsəd'væntɪdʒ) *n.* 缺點
   (C) urgency ('ɜdʒənsɪ) *n.* 緊急
   (D) *crisis* ('kraɪsɪs) *n.* 危機

   * financial (fə'nænʃəl) *adj.* 金融的
     stock market 股票市場   *go bankrupt* 破產

8. (**D**) In a democratic country, people are allowed to <u>demonstrate</u> against their government to express their political opinions.

在民主國家中，人民可以向政府示威抗議，表達自己的政治理念。

   (A) determine (dɪ'tɜmɪn) *v.* 決定
   (B) depict (dɪ'pɪkt) *v.* 描繪
   (C) discipline ('dɪsəplɪn) *v.* 訓練
   (D) *demonstrate* ('dɛmən,stret) *v.* 示威

   * democratic (,dɛmə'krætɪk) *adj.* 民主的
     allow (ə'lau) *v.* 允許
     against (ə'gɛnst) *prep.* 反對；抗議
     political (pə'lɪtɪkḷ) *adj.* 政治的

9. (**B**) The "nuclear family," which consists of only one
father, one mother and children, is becoming the
main family structure everywhere.

只由父母和子女組成的「核心家庭」，現在正成為各地
主要的家庭型態。

(A) typical〔'tɪpɪkḷ〕*adj.* 典型的

(B) ***nuclear***〔'njuklɪə〕*adj.* 核心的；核子的
nuclear family 核心家庭；小家庭

(C) formal〔'fɔrmḷ〕*adj.* 正式的

(D) similar〔'sɪmələ〕*adj.* 相似的

* ***consist of*** 由～組成 (= *be made up of*)
structure〔'strʌktʃə〕*n.* 結構；型態

10. (**D**) Many Asian men think that American women are
too liberated to make good wives.

許多亞洲男性認為，美國女性太不受傳統束縛了，而不能
成為好太太。

(A) reasonable〔'riznəbḷ〕*adj.* 理性的 (= *rational*)

(B) positive〔'pɑzətɪv〕*adj.* 積極的

(C) persuasive〔pə'swesɪv〕*adj.* 有說服力的

(D) ***liberated***〔'lɪbəˌretɪd〕*adj.* 解放的；不受傳統束縛的

* ***too～to*** + ***V*** 太～而不能…
make〔mek〕*v.* 成為 (= *become*)

```
liber + ate
  |      |
free  + v.（解放）
```

TEST 8

Directions: *The following questions are incomplete sentences. You are to choose the one word that best completes the sentence.*

1. It is _____ that these buildings remain empty while thousands of people have no homes.
   - (A) outrageous
   - (B) coherent
   - (C) effective
   - (D) reverent   (　)

2. Many people are afraid to speak in public; psychologists call such a fear or anxiety _____ fright.
   - (A) stage
   - (B) publicity
   - (C) platform
   - (D) panel   (　)

3. A burnt child _____ the fire.
   - (A) dreads
   - (B) draws
   - (C) drags
   - (D) drifts   (　)

4. This travel agency _____ in arranging tours to European countries.
   - (A) concentrate
   - (B) specialties
   - (C) concerns
   - (D) specializes   (　)

5. Taiwan has become a hi-tech country by _____ heavily in the electronics industry.
   - (A) indicating
   - (B) investing
   - (C) injuring
   - (D) incorporating   (　)

6. AIDS is a(n) _____ illness for every patient who contracts it.

   (A) mild
   (B) itchy
   (C) decent
   (D) fatal   (   )

7. Although genetic research is progressing quickly, the old question of _____ versus environment is still being debated.

   (A) costume
   (B) nurture
   (C) upbringing
   (D) heredity   (   )

8. The _____ impact of these small changes was considerable.

   (A) cumulative
   (B) optimistic
   (C) conscientious
   (D) excessive   (   )

9. _____ your money in a savings account and you'll earn 5% interest.

   (A) Withdraw
   (B) Deposit
   (C) Balance
   (D) Remain   (   )

10. As the couple had no children, they decided to _____ a child.

   (A) acquire
   (B) adept
   (C) adapt
   (D) adopt   (   )

TEST 8 詳解

1. (**A**) It is <u>outrageous</u> that these buildings remain empty while thousands of people have no homes.

這些大樓空著沒人住，而卻有數千人無家可歸，這太<u>荒唐</u>了。

   (A) *outrageous* 〔 aut'redʒəs 〕 *adj.* 荒唐的
   (B) coherent 〔 ko'hɪrənt 〕 *adj.* 有條理的
   (C) effective 〔 ɪ'fɛktɪv 〕 *adj.* 有效的
   (D) reverent 〔'rɛvrənt 〕 *adj.* 恭敬的

2. (**A**) Many people are afraid to speak in public; psychologists call such a fear or anxiety <u>stage</u> fright.

許多人害怕公開發言；心理學家稱這種恐懼或焦慮為<u>怯場</u>。

   (A) *stage* 〔 stedʒ 〕 *n.* 舞台　　*stage fright* 怯場
   (B) publicity 〔 pʌb'lɪsətɪ 〕 *n.* 宣傳
   (C) platform 〔'plæt‚fɔrm 〕 *n.* 月台；講台
   (D) panel 〔'pænḷ 〕 *n.* 鑲板；小組

   ＊ psychologist 〔 saɪ'kɑlədʒɪst 〕 *n.* 心理學家
      anxiety 〔 æŋ'zaɪətɪ 〕 *n.* 焦慮
      fright 〔 fraɪt 〕 *n.* 害怕

3. (**A**) A burnt child <u>dreads</u> the fire.

【諺】燙傷的孩子<u>懼怕</u>火；一朝被蛇咬，十年怕草繩。

   (A) *dread* 〔 drɛd 〕 *v.* 害怕 (= *fear*)
   (B) draw 〔 drɔ 〕 *v.* 畫；拉；吸引
   (C) drag 〔 dræg 〕 *v.* 拖曳
   (D) drift 〔 drɪft 〕 *v.* 漂流

4. (**D**) This travel agency <u>specializes</u> in arranging tours to European countries. 這家旅行社<u>專門</u>安排歐洲的行程。

    (A) concentrate〔'kɑnsn̩,tret〕v. 專心 <*on*>

    (B) specialty〔'spɛʃəltɪ〕n. 特色

    (C) concern〔kən'sɜn〕v. 有關（爲及物動詞，不加介系詞）

    (D) *specialize*〔'spɛʃəl,aɪz〕v. 專門做 <*in*>

      * *travel agency* 旅行社

      arrange〔ə'rendʒ〕v. 安排

5. (**B**) Taiwan has become a hi-tech country by <u>investing</u> heavily in the electronics industry.

台灣能成爲高科技國家，乃是藉由大量<u>投資</u>電子業。

    (A) indicate〔'ɪndə,ket〕v. 顯示（= *show*）

    (B) *invest*〔ɪn'vɛst〕v. 投資

    (C) injure〔'ɪndʒɚ〕v. 傷害

    (D) incorporate〔ɪn'kɔrpə,ret〕v. 結合

      * electronics〔ɪ,lɛk'trɑnɪks〕n. 電子學

      industry〔'ɪndəstrɪ〕n. 工業

6. (**D**) AIDS is a <u>fatal</u> illness for every patient who contracts it. 對感染愛滋病的病人而言，這是<u>致命的</u>疾病。

    (A) mild〔maɪld〕adj. 溫和的

    (B) itchy〔'ɪtʃɪ〕adj. 發癢的；渴望的

    (C) decent〔'disn̩t〕adj. 合宜的

    (D) *fatal*〔'fetl̩〕adj. 致命的

      * contract〔kən'trækt〕v. 感染

7. (**D**) Although genetic research is progressing quickly, the old question of <u>heredity</u> versus environment is still being debated.

雖然基因研究進步神速，但<u>遺傳</u>相對於環境的老問題，仍有待討論。

    (A) costume〔'kɑstjum〕 *n.* 服裝

    (B) nurture〔'nɝtʃɚ〕 *n., v.* 養育

    (C) upbringing〔'ʌp‚brɪŋɪŋ〕 *n.* 養育

    (D) *heredity*〔hə'rɛdətɪ〕 *n.* 遺傳

    * genetic〔dʒə'nɛtɪk〕 *adj.* 遺傳的
       progress〔prə'grɛs〕 *v.* 進步
       versus〔'vɝsəs〕 *prep.* 相對；對抗 (略為 vs.)
       debate〔dɪ'bet〕 *v.* 辯論；討論

8. (**A**) The <u>cumulative</u> impact of these small changes was considerable. 這個小改變<u>累積起來的</u>影響是相當可觀的。

    (A) *cumulative*〔'kjumjə‚letɪv〕 *adj.* 累積的
       比較：accumulate〔ə'kjumjə‚ket〕 *v.* 累積

    (B) optimistic〔‚ɑptə'mɪstɪk〕 *adj.* 樂觀的

    (C) conscientious〔‚kɑnʃɪ'ɛnʃəs〕 *adj.* 有良心的

    (D) excessive〔ɪk'sɛsɪv〕 *adj.* 過度的

    * impact〔'ɪmpækt〕 *n.* 影響
       considerable〔kən'sɪdərəbl̩〕 *adj.* 相當大的；可觀的

ac + cumulate	cumulat + ive
| |	| |
to + *heap up* (累積)	*heap up* + *adj.*

9. (**B**) Deposit your money in a savings account and you'll earn 5% interest.

將錢存在儲蓄存款帳戶中，你可得到百分之五的利息。

(A) withdraw〔wɪð'drɔ〕v. 提（款）

(B) *deposit*〔dɪ'pɑzɪt〕v. 存（款）

(C) balance〔'bæləns〕v. 結算

(D) remain〔rɪ'men〕v. 剩餘

＊account〔ə'kaʊnt〕n. 帳戶

savings account 儲蓄存款帳戶

interest〔'ɪntrɪst〕n. 利息

```
de   + pos + it
 |       |      |
down + put  + 物（被置於下方的東西）
```

10. (**D**) As the couple had no children, they decided to adopt a child.

由於這對夫妻膝下無子，他們決定領養一個小孩。

(A) acquire〔ə'kwaɪr〕v. 獲得

(B) adept〔ə'dɛpt〕adj. 熟練的＜in＞

(C) adapt〔ə'dæpt〕v. 適應＜to＞

(D) *adopt*〔ə'dɑpt〕v. 領養；採取

TEST 9

Directions: The following questions are incomplete sentences. You are to choose the one word that best completes the sentence.

1. Nowadays many factories use machines like computers or computerized _____.
   (A) projects
   (B) robots
   (C) techniques
   (D) analysts (　)

2. Many scientists remain _____ about the value of his research program.
   (A) distract
   (B) skeptical
   (C) handicapped
   (D) influential (　)

3. I feel _____ — I wish I didn't have to work tonight.
   (A) complimentary
   (B) bold
   (C) involuntary
   (D) exhausted (　)

4. In an effort to _____ the nation's worst economic crisis, the President announced an emergency plan.
   (A) overcome
   (B) occupy
   (C) install
   (D) preserve (　)

5. Clinton has voiced _____ for inflicting pain on his marriage because of his behavior.
   (A) delight
   (B) remorse
   (C) fulfillment
   (D) bliss (　)

6. Neighborhood watch has greatly helped prevent _____ in this area.
   - (A) breakthroughs
   - (B) guilt
   - (C) garages
   - (D) burglaries   (   )

7. Due to a sharp _____ of the U.S. dollar, James lost much money.
   - (A) appreciation
   - (B) duration
   - (C) estimation
   - (D) eruption   (   )

8. Report the dormitory theft immediately to the campus police to ensure the _____ of students.
   - (A) procedure
   - (B) conscience
   - (C) security
   - (D) self-defense   (   )

9. We could not learn very much from him, for he _____ nearly every question we asked.
   - (A) evaded
   - (B) emitted
   - (C) eloped
   - (D) eclipsed   (   )

10. Almost everyone in the community has _____ either money or help to the building of this recreation center.
   - (A) attributed
   - (B) distributed
   - (C) contributed
   - (D) tributed   (   )

TEST 9 詳解

1. (**B**) Nowadays many factories use machines like computers or computerized <u>robots</u>.
   現在許多工廠使用機器，如電腦，或用電腦操作的<u>機器人</u>。

   (A) project〔'pradʒɛkt〕*n.* 計劃 (= *plan*)
   (B) ***robot***〔'robət〕*n.* 機器人
   (C) technique〔tɛk'nik〕*n.* 技術
   (D) analyst〔'ænḷɪst〕*n.* 分析師

   * factory〔'fæktrɪ〕*n.* 工廠
     computerize〔kəm'pjutə,raɪz〕*v.* 電腦化

2. (**B**) Many scientists remain <u>skeptical</u> about the value of his research program.
   許多科學家對於他的研究計劃的價值，保持<u>懷疑的</u>態度。

   (A) distract〔dɪ'strækt〕*v.* 使分心
   (B) ***skeptical***〔'skɛptɪkḷ〕*adj.* 懷疑的
   (C) handicapped〔'hændɪ,kæpt〕*adj.* 殘障的
   (D) influential〔,ɪnflʊ'ɛnʃəl〕*adj.* 有影響力的

3. (**D**) I feel <u>exhausted</u> — I wish I didn't have to work tonight. 我覺得好累 —— 真希望我今晚不必上班。

   (A) complimentary〔,kamplə'mɛntərɪ〕*adj.* 稱讚的
   (B) bold〔bold〕*adj.* 大膽的
   (C) involuntary〔ɪn'valən,tɛrɪ〕*adj.* 非自願的
   (D) ***exhausted***〔ɪg'zɔstɪd〕*adj.* 筋疲力盡的
     (= *tired out*)

4. (**A**) In an effort to <u>overcome</u> the nation's worst economic crisis, the President announced an emergency plan.

為努力克服該國最嚴重的經濟危機，總統宣布了一項緊急計劃。

    (A) ***overcome*** (͵ovɚˋkʌm) *v.* 克服

    (B) occupy (ˋɑkjə͵paɪ) *v.* 占據

    (C) install (ɪnˋstɔl) *v.* 安裝

    (D) preserve (prɪˋzɝv) *v.* 保存

     * effort (ˋɛfɚt) *n.* 努力

      in an effort to + *V*. 努力做～

      crisis (ˋkraɪsɪs) *n.* 危機

      announce (əˋnauns) *v.* 宣布

      emergency (ɪˋmɝdʒənsɪ) *n.* 緊急情況

5. (**B**) Clinton has voiced <u>remorse</u> for inflicting pain on his marriage because of his behavior.

柯林頓對於自己的行為所加諸於他的婚姻上的痛苦，表達<u>懺悔</u>之意。

    (A) delight (dɪˋlaɪt) *n.* 喜悅

    (B) ***remorse*** (rɪˋmɔrs) *n.* 懊悔 (= *regret*)

    (C) fulfillment (fulˋfɪlmənt) *n.* 履行

    (D) bliss (blɪs) *n.* 極大的幸福

     * voice (vɔɪs) *v.* 用言語表達

      inflict (ɪnˋflɪkt) *v.* 加諸 <*on*>

6. (**D**) Neighborhood watch has greatly helped prevent burglaries in this area.

守望相助對於預防此地區的<u>竊盜事件</u>大有幫助。

(A) breakthrough〔'brek͵θru〕*n.* 突破

(B) guilt〔gɪlt〕*n.* 罪

(C) garage〔gə'raʒ〕*n.* 車庫

(D) ***burglary***〔'bɝglərɪ〕*n.* 竊盜行為

* neighborhood〔'nebə͵hud〕*n.* 社區
watch〔watʃ〕*n.* 看守;警戒

7. (**A**) Due to a sharp <u>appreciation</u> of the U.S. dollar, James lost much money.

由於美金急速<u>升值</u>,詹姆斯損失了很多錢。

(A) ***appreciation***〔ə͵priʃɪ'eʃən〕*n.* 漲價;升值

(B) duration〔dju'reʃən〕*n.* 持續

(C) estimation〔͵ɛstə'meʃən〕*n.* 估計

(D) eruption〔ɪ'rʌpʃən〕*n.* 爆發

* sharp〔ʃarp〕*adj.* 急速的

8. (**C**) Report the dormitory theft immediately to the campus police to ensure the <u>security</u> of students.

立刻向校警報告這起宿舍竊案,以確保學生的<u>安全</u>。

(A) procedure〔prə'sidʒə〕*n.* 程序

(B) conscience〔'kanʃəns〕*n.* 良心

(C) ***security***〔sɪ'kjurətɪ〕*n.* 安全

(D) self-defense〔͵sɛlfdɪ'fɛns〕*n.* 自衛

* theft〔θɛft〕*n.* 竊盜事件　　ensure〔ɪn'ʃur〕*v.* 確保

9. (**A**) We could not learn very much from him, for he
evaded nearly every question we asked.

我們無法從他身上得知太多事，因為他幾乎迴避我們所問
的每個問題。

    (A) ***evade*** 〔 ɪ'ved 〕 *v.* 迴避

    (B) emit 〔 ɪ'mɪt 〕 *v.* 發出；排出

    (C) elope 〔 ɪ'lop 〕 *v.* 私奔

    (D) eclipse 〔 ɪ'klɪps 〕 *v.* 遮蔽（其他天體的光）

                 n. （日、月）蝕

10. (**C**) Almost everyone in the community has contributed
either money or help to the building of this
recreation center.

幾乎社區中的每個人都貢獻了金錢或協助，建造了這座娛
樂中心。

    (A) attribute 〔 ə'trɪbjut 〕 *v.* 歸因於 < *to* >

    (B) distribute 〔 dɪ'strɪbjut 〕 *v.* 分發

    (C) ***contribute*** 〔 kən'trɪbjut 〕 *v.* 貢獻 < *to* >

    (D) tribute 〔'trɪbjut 〕 *n.* 貢物

    * community 〔 kə'mjunətɪ 〕 *n.* 社區

       recreation 〔,rɛkrɪ'eʃən 〕 *n.* 娛樂

con + tribute	dis + tribute
| |	| |
together + *give*	*apart* + *give*

TEST 10

Directions: *The following questions are incomplete sentences. You are to choose the one word that best completes the sentence.*

1. I enjoyed the movie but the ending was too _____.
   (A) sentimental
   (B) hypothetical
   (C) courageous
   (D) courteous   (   )

2. The stories about King Arthur and his Knights of the Round Table are _____.
   (A) levels
   (B) legends
   (C) essays
   (D) flavors   (   )

3. The reporter's story about the fire was not only interesting, but also _____.
   (A) misleading
   (B) accurate
   (C) conductive
   (D) initial   (   )

4. Some people _____ illness in order to be admitted to hospital.
   (A) fabricate
   (B) eradicate
   (C) alternate
   (D) illuminate   (   )

5. A _____ disease is caused by not eating enough of particular kinds of food that are necessary for good health.
   (A) dental
   (B) digestion
   (C) deficiency
   (D) dismay   (   )

6. After nine days of warm weather the seeds began to
   _____.
   - (A) halt
   - (B) blight
   - (C) wither
   - (D) sprout   (   )

7. If we are _____ to cultural differences when dealing
   with people from other countries, miscommunication
   and conflict will easily occur.
   - (A) conscious
   - (B) ignorant
   - (C) indifferent
   - (D) attentive   (   )

8. Not all mathematical skills are learned in school;
   measuring and _____ the dimensions of objects
   is a part of the everyday life of students.
   - (A) disapproving
   - (B) disputing
   - (C) considering
   - (D) computing   (   )

9. To increase the number of female representatives, the
   committee decided to _____ in favor of women for
   three years.
   - (A) discriminate
   - (B) intimidate
   - (C) subtract
   - (D) elaborate   (   )

10. Modern transportation is more _____ than traditional
    modes of transport.
    - (A) numerous
    - (B) outdated
    - (C) efficient
    - (D) productive   (   )

TEST 10 詳解

1. (**A**) I enjoyed the movie but the ending was too
   <u>sentimental</u>. 我很喜歡這部電影，但結局太感傷了。

   (A) ***sentimental*** 〔͵sɛntə'mɛntḷ 〕 *adj.* 多愁善感的；
      感傷的

   (B) hypothetical 〔͵haɪpə'θɛtɪkḷ 〕 *adj.* 假設的

   (C) courageous 〔 kə'redʒəs 〕 *adj.* 勇敢的 (= *brave*)

   (D) courteous 〔'kɝtɪəs 〕 *adj.* 有禮貌的 (= *polite*)

   * ending 〔'ɛndɪŋ 〕 *n.* 結局

2. (**B**) The stories about King Arthur and his Knights of
   the Round Table are <u>legends</u>.
   有關亞瑟王和他的圓桌武士的故事都是傳說。

   (A) level 〔'lɛvḷ 〕 *n.* 水準；程度

   (B) ***legend*** 〔'lɛdʒənd 〕 *n.* 傳說；傳奇

   (C) essay 〔'ɛse 〕 *n.* 論文；文章

   (D) flavor 〔'flevɚ 〕 *n.* 味道；風味

   * knight 〔 naɪt 〕 *n.* 武士；騎士

3. (**B**) The reporter's story about the fire was not only
   interesting, but also <u>accurate</u>.
   這名記者所做的，關於這場火災的報導，不但有趣而且正確。

   (A) misleading 〔 mɪs'lidɪŋ 〕 *adj.* 誤導的

   (B) ***accurate*** 〔'ækjərɪt 〕 *adj.* 正確的

   (C) conductive 〔 kən'dʌktɪv 〕 *adj.* 傳導的

   (D) initial 〔 ɪ'nɪʃəl 〕 *adj.* 初期的

4. (**A**) Some people <u>fabricate</u> illness in order to be admitted to hospital. 有些人裝病是爲了住院。

    (A) *fabricate*〔'fæbrɪ͵ket〕 *v.* 假裝 (= *pretend*)

    (B) eradicate〔ɪ'rædɪ͵ket〕 *v.* 根除

    (C) alternate〔'ɔltə͵net〕 *v.* 交替；輪流

    (D) illuminate〔ɪ'lumə͵net〕 *v.* 照亮；啓發

    * admit〔əd'mɪt〕 *v.* 准許進入 < *to* >

5. (**C**) A <u>deficiency</u> disease is caused by not eating enough of particular kinds of food that are necessary for good health.

<u>營養失調</u>是由於沒有攝取足夠的，某些良好健康所需的食物，所導致的。

    (A) dental〔'dɛntḷ〕 *adj.* 牙齒的

    (B) digestion〔daɪ'dʒɛstʃən〕 *n.* 消化

    (C) *deficiency*〔dɪ'fɪʃənsɪ〕 *n.* 不足

        deficiency disease 營養失調

    (D) dismay〔dɪs'me〕 *n.* 驚慌；沮喪

6. (**D**) After nine days of warm weather the seeds began to <u>sprout</u>. 溫暖的天氣持續九天之後，種子開始<u>發芽</u>了。

    (A) halt〔hɔlt〕 *v.* 停止

    (B) blight〔blaɪt〕 *v.* 枯萎；病蟲害

    (C) wither〔'wɪðə〕 *v.* 枯萎

    (D) *sprout*〔spraut〕 *v.* 發芽

    * seed〔sid〕 *n.* 種子

7. (**C**) If we are <u>indifferent</u> to cultural differences when dealing with people from other countries, miscommunication and conflict will easily occur.

與其他國家的人相處時，如果我們對文化差異<u>漠不關心</u>，誤會和衝突很容易發生。

    (A) conscious〔'kɑnʃəs〕*adj.* 察覺的＜*of*＞

    (B) ignorant〔'ɪgnərənt〕*adj.* 無知的＜*of*＞

    (C) ***indifferent***〔ɪn'dɪfərənt〕*adj.* 漠不關心的＜*to*＞

    (D) attentive〔ə'tɛntɪv〕*adj.* 專注的＜*to*＞

    * ***deal with sb.*** 與某人相處（＝*get along with sb.*）
      conflict〔'kɑnflɪkt〕*n.* 衝突

8. (**D**) Not all mathematical skills are learned in school; measuring and <u>computing</u> the dimensions of objects is a part of the everyday life of students.

並非所有數學技巧都是在學校學的；測量、<u>計算</u>物體的三度空間，是學生日常生活的一部分。

    (A) disapprove〔‚dɪsə'pruv〕*v.* 不贊成

    (B) dispute〔dɪ'spjut〕*v.,n.* 爭論

    (C) consider〔kən'sɪdɚ〕*v.* 認為；考慮

    (D) ***compute***〔kəm'pjut〕*v.* 計算

    * measure〔'mɛʒɚ〕*v.* 測量
      dimension〔də'mɛnʃən〕*n.* 空間；次元
      object〔'ɑbdʒɪkt〕*n.* 物體

9. (**A**) To increase the number of female representatives, the committee decided to <u>discriminate</u> in favor of women for three years.

為了增加女性代表的人數，委員會決定連續三年優待女性。

(A) ***discriminate*** 〔 dɪˋskrɪməˌnet 〕 *v.* 差別待遇
discriminate in favor of 偏袒

(B) intimidate 〔 ɪnˋtɪməˌdet 〕 *v.* 威脅

(C) subtract 〔 səbˋtrækt 〕 *v.* 扣除

(D) elaborate 〔 ɪˋlæbəˌret 〕 *v.* 更詳細說明

* representative 〔ˌrɛprɪˋzɛntətɪv 〕 *n.* 代表
committee 〔 kəˋmɪtɪ 〕 *n.* 委員會
in favor of 有利；偏袒

10. (**C**) Modern transportation is more <u>efficient</u> than traditional modes of transport.

現代交通工具比傳統的運輸方式更<u>有效率</u>。

(A) numerous 〔ˋnjumərəs 〕 *adj.* 很多的（= *many* ）

(B) outdated 〔 aʊtˋdetɪd 〕 *adj.* 過時的（= *out of date* ）

(C) ***efficient*** 〔 əˋfɪʃənt 〕 *adj.* 有效率的

(D) productive 〔 prəˋdʌktɪv 〕 *adj.* 有生產力的

* transportation 〔ˌtrænspəˋteʃən 〕 *n.* 交通工具
mode 〔 mod 〕 *n.* 方式
transport 〔ˋtrænsport 〕 *n.* 運輸

TEST 11

Directions: *The following questions are incomplete sentences. You are to choose the one word that best completes the sentence.*

1. Taipower is warning that power _____ may not be far off if the mercury continues to climb.
   (A) banquet
   (B) rationing
   (C) antidote
   (D) corridor   (   )

2. The emperor sought only the _____ of his own power, not the well-being of his people.
   (A) amazement
   (B) aggrandizement
   (C) appearance
   (D) accusation   (   )

3. "Don't worry," he said _____. "Everything will be all right."
   (A) keenly
   (B) indefinitely
   (C) unconsciously
   (D) reassuringly   (   )

4. They are planning to _____ this open space into an amusement park.
   (A) measure
   (B) modify
   (C) circulate
   (D) convert   (   )

5. The chairman asked him to _____ just what he meant.
   (A) clarify
   (B) declare
   (C) classify
   (D) confirm   (   )

6. The river is half a mile wide at the point where the bridge
   _____ it.
   (A) scans
   (B) splits
   (C) spans
   (D) snaps   (   )

7. The new generation of goods is smarter and better
   designed than its _____.
   (A) descendants
   (B) enthusiasts
   (C) predecessors
   (D) ancestors   (   )

8. Some rice fields in southeast Asia require _____ to
   grow crops.
   (A) irritation
   (B) reservation
   (C) concentration
   (D) irrigation   (   )

9. Whether Taiwan should build more nuclear power
   _____ has triggered intense debates.
   (A) factories
   (B) armies
   (C) bases
   (D) plants   (   )

10. Since it was founded in 1971, Doctors Without Borders
    has sent many _____ doctors and nurses to Africa.
    (A) volunteer
    (B) compulsory
    (C) spontaneous
    (D) automatic   (   )

TEST 11 詳解

1. (**B**) Taipower is warning that power <u>rationing</u> may not be far off if the mercury continues to climb.

台電提出警告，如果溫度再持續上升，可能不久就會實施限電。

(A) banquet (ˈbæŋkwɪt) *n.* 宴會

(B) ***rationing*** (ˈræʃənɪŋ) *n.* 限量；配給

(C) antidote (ˈæntɪ͵dot) *n.* 解毒劑

(D) corridor (ˈkɔrədə) *n.* 走廊

* power (ˈpauə) *n.* 電力
mercury (ˈmɜkjərɪ) *n.* 水銀；(溫度計的) 水銀柱
(引申為「溫度」之意)

2. (**B**) The emperor sought only the <u>aggrandizement</u> of his own power, not the well-being of his people.

皇帝只尋求自己權力的<u>擴張</u>，而不顧人民的福祉。

(A) amazement (əˈmezmənt) *n.* 驚訝

(B) ***aggrandizement*** (əˈɡrændɪzmənt) *n.* 擴張

(C) appearance (əˈpɪrəns) *n.* 外表；出現

(D) accusation (͵ækjəˈzeʃən) *n.* 控訴

* emperor (ˈɛmpərə) *n.* 皇帝
well-being (ˈwɛlˈbiɪŋ) *n.* 幸福；福祉

ag	+ grand	+ ize	+ ment
to	+ large	+ v.	+ n.

3. (**D**) "Don't worry," he said <u>reassuringly</u>. "Everything will be all right."

「別擔心，」他<u>安慰地</u>說。「一切都會沒事的。」

    (A) keenly〔'kinlɪ〕*adv.* 敏銳地

    (B) indefinitely〔ɪn'dɛfənɪtlɪ〕*adv.* 不確定地

    (C) unconsciously〔ʌn'kɑnʃəslɪ〕*adv.* 無意識地

    (D) *reassuringly*〔ˏriə'ʃurɪŋlɪ〕*adv.* 令人安心地

4. (**D**) They are planning to <u>convert</u> this open space into an amusement park.

他們正在計劃，將這塊空地<u>改成</u>遊樂園。

    (A) measure〔'mɛʒɚ〕*v.* 測量

    (B) modify〔'mɑdəˏfaɪ〕*v.* 修正

    (C) circulate〔'sɝkjəˏlet〕*v.* 循環

    (D) *convert*〔kən'vɝt〕*v.* 改變 <*into*>

     * *amusement park* 遊樂園

5. (**A**) The chairman asked him to <u>clarify</u> just what he meant. 主席要求他<u>說清楚</u>他的原意。

    (A) *clarify*〔'klærəˏfaɪ〕*v.* 說清楚；澄清

      (= *make clear*)

    (B) declare〔dɪ'klɛr〕*v.* 宣布

    (C) classify〔'klæsəˏfaɪ〕*v.* 分類

    (D) confirm〔kən'fɝm〕*v.* 證實；確認

     * chairman〔'tʃɛrmən〕*n.* 主席

6. (**C**) The river is half a mile wide at the point where the bridge spans it. 這條河在橋跨過的那一段有半哩寬。

    (A) scan〔skæn〕*v.* 掃描

    (B) split〔splɪt〕*v.* 分裂

    (C) ***span***〔spæn〕*v.* (橋)跨過(河流)

    (D) snap〔snæp〕*v.* 劈啪作響；啪地一聲折斷

7. (**C**) The new generation of goods is smarter and better designed than its predecessors.

這項新一代的產品比它的前一代，更加聰明，設計得更好。

    (A) descendant〔dɪ'sɛndənt〕*n.* 子孫

    (B) enthusiast〔ɪn'θjuzɪˌæst〕*n.* 狂熱者

    (C) ***predecessor***〔'prɛdɪˌsɛsɚ,ˌprɛdɪ'sɛsɚ〕*n.* 前任；以前的東西

    (D) ancestor〔'ænsɛstɚ〕*n.* 祖先

    ＊ generation〔ˌdʒɛnə'reʃən〕*n.* 世代

8. (**D**) Some rice fields in southeast Asia require irrigation to grow crops. 東南亞有些稻田需要靠灌溉來種植農作。

    (A) irritation〔ˌɪrə'teʃən〕*n.* 激怒

    (B) reservation〔ˌrɛzɚ'veʃən〕*n.* 預約

    (C) concentration〔ˌkɑnsṇ'treʃən〕*n.* 專心

    (D) ***irrigation***〔ˌɪrə'geʃən〕*n.* 灌溉

    ＊ ***rice field*** 稻田　　require〔rɪ'kwaɪr〕*v.* 需要
    crop〔krɑp〕*n.* 農作物

9. (**D**) Whether Taiwan should build more nuclear power
plants has triggered intense debates.

台灣是否該建更多核能發電廠，已引發激烈的辯論。

(A) factory (ˈfækt(ə)rɪ) *n.* 工廠 (不用於發電廠)

(B) army (ˈɑrmɪ) *n.* 軍隊

(C) base (bes) *n.* 基地

(D) *plant* (plænt) *n.* 工廠

power plant 發電廠 (= *power station*)

* nuclear (ˈnjuklɪə) *adj.* 核能的

trigger (ˈtrɪgə) *v.* 引發

intense (ɪnˈtɛns) *adj.* 激烈的

debate (dɪˈbet) *n.* 辯論

10. (**A**) Since it was founded in 1971, Doctors Without
Borders has sent many volunteer doctors and nurses
to Africa.

自從一九七一年創立以來，「無國界醫生」組織已派遣許多
自願的醫生和護士到非洲去。

(A) *volunteer* (ˌvɑlənˈtɪr) *adj.* 自願的

(B) compulsory (kəmˈpʌlsərɪ) *adj.* 強迫的

(C) spontaneous (spɑnˈtenɪəs) *adj.* 自發性的

(D) automatic (ˌɔtəˈmætɪk) *adj.* 自動的

* found (faʊnd) *v.* 創立

border (ˈbɔrdə) *n.* 國界

TEST 12

Directions: The following questions are incomplete sentences. You are to choose the one word that best completes the sentence.

1. Owing to a serious hereditary disease, he was _____ from military service.
   - (A) resolved
   - (B) dissolved
   - (C) mentioned
   - (D) exempted   (   )

2. The wingbeats of hummingbirds are so _____ that their wings cannot be seen distinctly.
   - (A) sluggish
   - (B) rapid
   - (C) active
   - (D) obvious   (   )

3. Painkillers may only temporarily _____ your discomfort.
   - (A) relax
   - (B) relieve
   - (C) release
   - (D) relate   (   )

4. We laughed and laughed because the film was so _____.
   - (A) tragic
   - (B) touching
   - (C) hilarious
   - (D) pathetic   (   )

5. Many people in Taiwan think that the fist fights in the Legislative Yuan should be _____.
   - (A) ignored
   - (B) condemned
   - (C) acclaimed
   - (D) imitated   (   )

6. The objective of this study was to _____ some construction problems.
   (A) mobilize
   (B) launch
   (C) revive
   (D) investigate   (   )

7. Jackie and Kathy like to eat in all kinds of _____ restaurants. They enjoy tasting foods of different cultures.
   (A) extensive
   (B) ethnic
   (C) ethical
   (D) essential   (   )

8. Much to the investors' delight, the stocks eventually climbed 5 percent after a month-long _____.
   (A) slope
   (B) surge
   (C) soar
   (D) slump   (   )

9. It is important that readers are capable of _____ between facts and opinions while reading academic materials.
   (A) differentiating
   (B) originating
   (C) extending
   (D) emancipating   (   )

10. There seems to be a _____ between one's sex and one's status in society. On the whole, men enjoy higher status than women.
    (A) correlation
    (B) nomination
    (C) boundary
    (D) variation   (   )

TEST 12 詳解

1. (**D**) Owing to a serious hereditary disease, he was
   <u>exempted</u> from military service.
   由於罹患嚴重的遺傳性疾病，他<u>免</u>服兵役。

   (A) resolve〔rɪˋzɑlv〕v. 決心
   (B) dissolve〔dɪˋzɑlv〕v. 溶解
   (C) mention〔ˋmɛnʃən〕v. 提及
   (D) *exempt*〔ɪgˋzɛmpt〕v. 免除 <*from*>

   * *owing to* 由於 (= *because of*)
     hereditary〔həˋrɛdə͵tɛrɪ〕adj. 遺傳性的
     military〔ˋmɪlə͵tɛrɪ〕adj. 軍事的
     military service 兵役

2. (**B**) The wingbeats of hummingbirds are so <u>rapid</u> that
   their wings cannot be seen distinctly.
   蜂鳥的翅膀振動太<u>快速</u>了，以至於無法清楚地看到牠們的
   翅膀。

   (A) sluggish〔ˋslʌgɪʃ〕adj. 遲緩的
   (B) *rapid*〔ˋræpɪd〕adj. 快速的
   (C) active〔ˋæktɪv〕adj. 活躍的
   (D) obvious〔ˋɑbvɪəs〕adj. 明顯的

   * wingbeat〔ˋwɪŋ͵bit〕n. (鳥) 翅膀的振動
     hummingbird〔ˋhʌmɪŋ͵bɝd〕n. 蜂鳥
     wing〔wɪŋ〕n. 翅膀
     distinctly〔dɪˋstɪŋktlɪ〕adv. 清楚地 (= *clearly*)

3. (**B**) Painkillers may only temporarily <u>relieve</u> your discomfort. 止痛藥或許只能暫時<u>減輕</u>你的不適。

    (A) relax〔rɪ'læks〕*v.* 放鬆

    (B) *relieve*〔rɪ'liv〕*v.* 減輕 (= *ease*)

    (C) release〔rɪ'lis〕*v.* 釋放

    (D) relate〔rɪ'let〕*v.* 使有關 < *to* >

     * painkiller〔'pen,kɪlə〕*n.* 止痛藥
       temporarily〔'tɛmpə,rɛrəlɪ〕*adv.* 暫時地
       discomfort〔dɪs'kʌmfət〕*n.* 不舒服；不適

4. (**C**) We laughed and laughed because the film was so <u>hilarious</u>. 我們一直笑、一直笑，因爲這部電影太<u>滑稽</u>了。

    (A) tragic〔'trædʒɪk〕*adj.* 悲慘的

    (B) touching〔'tʌtʃɪŋ〕*adj.* 感人的

    (C) *hilarious*〔hɪ'lɛrɪəs〕*adj.* 滑稽的

    (D) pathetic〔pə'θɛtɪk〕*adj.* 可悲的

5. (**B**) Many people in Taiwan think that the fist fights in the Legislative Yuan should be <u>condemned</u>.
在台灣，有許多人認爲，立法院裏的打架行爲應該受到<u>譴責</u>。

    (A) ignore〔ɪg'nor〕*v.* 忽視；不理會

    (B) *condemn*〔kən'dɛm〕*v.* 譴責

    (C) acclaim〔ə'klem〕*v.* 歡呼

    (D) imitate〔'ɪmə,tet〕*v.* 模仿

     * *fist fight* 打架；互毆
       legislative〔'lɛdʒɪs,letɪv〕*adj.* 立法的
       the Legislative Yuan 立法院

6. (**D**) The objective of this study was to <u>investigate</u> some
   construction problems.
   這次研究的目標，是要<u>調查</u>某些結構上的問題。

   (A) mobilize 〔'mobḷ,aɪz 〕 v. 動員
   (B) launch 〔 lɔntʃ 〕 v. 發射；著手開始
   (C) revive 〔 rɪ'vaɪv 〕 v. 使復活
   (D) ***investigate*** 〔 ɪn'vɛstə,get 〕 v. 調查 (= *look into*)

   * objective 〔 əb'dʒɛktɪv 〕 n. 目標
   construction 〔 kən'strʌkʃən 〕 n. 結構

7. (**B**) Jackie and Kathy like to eat in all kinds of <u>ethnic</u>
   restaurants. They enjoy tasting foods of different
   cultures. 傑奇和凱西喜歡到各種<u>民族</u>風味的餐廳用餐。
   他們喜歡品嘗不同文化的食物。

   (A) extensive 〔 ɪk'stɛnsɪv 〕 adj. 廣泛的
   (B) ***ethnic*** 〔'ɛθnɪk 〕 adj. 民族的
   (C) ethical 〔'ɛθɪkḷ 〕 adj. 倫理道德的
   (D) essential 〔 ə'sɛnʃəl 〕 adj. 必要的

8. (**D**) Much to the investors' delight, the stocks eventually
   climbed 5 percent after a month-long <u>slump</u>.
   令投資人感到非常高興的是，股票在長達一個月<u>暴跌</u>後，
   終於攀升了百分之五。

   (A) slope 〔 slop 〕 n. 斜坡
   (B) surge 〔 sɝdʒ 〕 n. 巨浪；高漲
   (C) soar 〔 sor 〕 v., n. 翱翔；高漲
   (D) ***slump*** 〔 slʌmp 〕 n., v. 掉落；暴跌

   * investor 〔 ɪn'vɛstə 〕 n. 投資人
   delight 〔 dɪ'laɪt 〕 n. 高興   stock 〔 stɑk 〕 n. 股票

9. (**A**) It is important that readers are capable of
<u>differentiating</u> between facts and opinions while
reading academic materials.

讀者在閱讀學術性資料時，要能夠<u>區分</u>事實和意見，這是
非常重要的。

(A) ***differentiate*** ﹝͵dɪfəˈrɛnʃɪ͵et﹞ *v.* 區分
(= *distinguish*)

differentiate between A and B 區分 A 和 B

(B) originate ﹝əˈrɪdʒə͵net﹞ *v.* 起源於

(C) extend ﹝ɪkˈstɛnd﹞ *v.* 延伸

(D) emancipate ﹝ɪˈmænsə͵pet﹞ *v.* 解放 < *from* >

* ***be capable of*** + *N/V-ing* 能夠
academic ﹝͵ækəˈdɛmɪk﹞ *adj.* 學術性的

10. (**A**) There seems to be a <u>correlation</u> between one's sex
and one's status in society. On the whole, men
enjoy higher status than women.

一個人的性別與其在社會上的地位似乎有<u>關連</u>。就整體而
言，男性享有比女性高的社會地位。

(A) ***correlation*** ﹝͵kɔrəˈleʃən﹞ *n.* 相互關係；關連

(B) nomination ﹝͵nɑməˈneʃən﹞ *n.* 提名

(C) boundary ﹝ˈbaʊndərɪ﹞ *n.* 邊界

(D) variation ﹝͵vɛrɪˈeʃən﹞ *n.* 變化

* status ﹝ˈstetəs﹞ *n.* 地位
on the whole 就整體而言

TEST 13

Directions: *The following questions are incomplete sentences. You are to choose the one word that best completes the sentence.*

1. Each _____ should contain the exact amount of medicine the doctor wants.
   (A) hypothesis
   (B) overdose
   (C) concept
   (D) capsule
   (　　)

2. Better _____ can cut indoor air pollution to a safe level.
   (A) violation
   (B) adventure
   (C) ventilation
   (D) sprayer
   (　　)

3. Historical records show that Confucius _____ his ideas about education.
   (A) reiterated
   (B) exchanged
   (C) denounced
   (D) retracted
   (　　)

4. The drug is extremely _____, but causes unpleasant side effects.
   (A) potent
   (B) omnipresent
   (C) potential
   (D) visible
   (　　)

5. When Daniel was six, he had a heart transplant. The _____ of the organ was a five-year-old boy.
   (A) receiver
   (B) donor
   (C) recipient
   (D) researcher
   (　　)

6. _____ complaints could harm one's marriage or life in general.
   (A) Stiff
   (B) External
   (C) Depressed
   (D) Chronic   (   )

7. Foreign investors are _____ on the Taiwan stock market. They think there is still room for it to soar.
   (A) pessimistic
   (B) bullish
   (C) bearish
   (D) primary   (   )

8. Princess Diana died after suffering massive _____ injuries in a high-speed car crash.
   (A) inferior
   (B) innocent
   (C) internal
   (D) inclusive   (   )

9. He was usually very kind, so his sudden _____ greatly surprised us.
   (A) uprightness
   (B) harshness
   (C) mishap
   (D) heartiness   (   )

10. Both experienced and _____ subjects were used in the research.
   (A) novice
   (B) residual
   (C) infuriated
   (D) miscellaneous   (   )

TEST 13 詳解

1. (**D**) Each <u>capsule</u> should contain the exact amount of medicine the doctor wants.

每顆<u>膠囊</u>都應該包含醫生要求的正確的藥量。

    (A) hypothesis〔haɪˋpɑθəsɪs〕 *n.* 假說

    (B) overdose〔͵ovɚˋdos〕 *n.* 用藥過量

    (C) concept〔ˋkɑnsɛpt〕 *n.* 概念 (= *idea*)

    (D) *capsule*〔ˋkæpsḷ〕 *n.* 膠囊

    * contain〔kənˋten〕 *v.* 包含

2. (**C**) Better <u>ventilation</u> can cut indoor air pollution to a safe level. 較良好的<u>通風</u>可以將室內的空氣污染減至安全的標準。

    (A) violation〔͵vaɪəˋleʃən〕 *n.* 違反

    (B) adventure〔ədˋvɛntʃɚ〕 *n.* 冒險

    (C) *ventilation*〔͵vɛntḷˋeʃən〕 *n.* 通風

    (D) sprayer〔ˋspreɚ〕 *n.* 噴霧器

    * level〔ˋlɛvḷ〕 *n.* 標準

3. (**A**) Historical records show that Confucius <u>reiterated</u> his ideas about education.

史料顯示，孔子<u>一再重述</u>他對教育的想法。

    (A) *reiterate*〔riˋɪtə͵ret〕 *v.* 反覆地說 (= *repeat*)

    (B) exchange〔ɪksˋtʃendʒ〕 *v.,n.* 交換

    (C) *denounce*〔dɪˋnaʊns〕 *v.* 譴責

    (D) retract〔rɪˋtrækt〕 *v.* 取消；撤回

    * Confucius〔kənˋfjuʃəs〕 *n.* 孔子

4. (**A**) The drug is extremely <u>potent</u>, but causes unpleasant side effects. 這個藥非常<u>有效</u>，但會導致令人不適的副作用。

    (A) ***potent***〔'potn̩t〕 *adj.* 有效的

    (B) omnipresent〔ˌɑmnɪ'prɛzn̩t〕 *adj.* 無所不在的

    (C) potential〔pə'tɛnʃəl〕 *adj.* 有潛力的；可能的

    (D) visible〔'vɪzəbl̩〕 *adj.* 看得見的

    * unpleasant〔ʌn'plɛzn̩t〕 *adj.* 不愉快的
     side effect 副作用

5. (**B**) When Daniel was six, he had a heart transplant. The <u>donor</u> of the organ was a five-year-old boy.
丹尼爾六歲時動過心臟移殖手術。器官<u>捐贈者</u>是一個五歲的男孩。

    (A) receiver〔rɪ'sivɚ〕 *n.* 接受者；電話聽筒

    (B) ***donor***〔'donɚ〕 *n.* 捐贈者

    (C) recipient〔rɪ'sɪpɪənt〕 *n.* 接受者

    (D) researcher〔rɪ'sɝtʃɚ〕 *n.* 研究人員

    * transplant〔'træns,plænt〕 *n.* 移殖
     organ〔'ɔrgən〕 *n.* 器官

6. (**D**) <u>Chronic</u> complaints could harm one's marriage or life in general.
長期<u>不斷</u>的抱怨，有損一個人的婚姻或日常生活。

    (A) stiff〔stɪf〕 *adj.* 僵硬的

    (B) external〔ɪk'stɝnl̩〕 *adj.* 外在的

    (C) depressed〔dɪ'prɛst〕 *adj.* 沮喪的

    (D) ***chronic***〔'krɑnɪk〕 *adj.* 長期不斷的

    * ***in general*** 一般的

7. (**B**) Foreign investors are <u>bullish</u> on the Taiwan stock
market. They think there is still room for it to soar.
外國投資人對台灣股市很<u>樂觀</u>。他們認為仍有上漲的空間。

 (A) pessimistic〔͵pɛsə'mɪstɪk〕*adj.* 悲觀的
  (↔ optimistic *adj.* 樂觀的)
 (B) ***bullish***〔'bʊlɪʃ〕*adj.* 看漲的；樂觀的
  a bull/bullish market　市場看漲
 (C) bearish〔'bɛrɪʃ〕*adj.* 股票下跌的
  a bear/bearish market　下跌的市場
 (D) primary〔'praɪ͵mɛrɪ〕*adj.* 主要的

 * investor〔ɪn'vɛstɚ〕*n.* 投資人
  stock market 股票市場
  soar〔sor〕*v.* 上漲

8. (**C**) Princess Diana died after suffering massive <u>internal</u>
injuries in a high-speed car crash.
戴安娜王妃在高速車禍中，受到嚴重的<u>內傷</u>而香消玉殞。

 (A) inferior〔ɪn'fɪrɪɚ〕*adj.* 較差的 < *to* >
 (B) innocent〔'ɪnəsn̩t〕*adj.* 無辜的
 (C) ***internal***〔ɪn'tɝnl̩〕*adj.* 內部的
  (↔ external *adj.* 外在的)
 (D) inclusive〔ɪn'klusɪv〕*adj.* 包括在內的 < *of* >

 * massive〔'mæsɪv〕*adj.* 大量的
  injury〔'ɪndʒərɪ〕*n.* 傷害
  crash〔kræʃ〕*n.* 撞毀

9. (**B**) He was usually very kind, so his sudden <u>harshness</u>
  greatly surprised us.

  他通常很親切，所以他突然變很<u>無情</u>，使我們大吃一驚。

  (A) uprightness〔'ʌp,raɪtnɪs〕*n.* 正直

  (B) ***harshness***〔'harʃnɪs〕*n.* 嚴厲；無情
    (= *severity* ; *cruelty*)

  (C) mishap〔'mɪs,hæp , mɪs'hæp〕*n.* 不幸

  (D) heartiness〔'hartɪnɪs〕*n.* 誠摯

10. (**A**) Both experienced and <u>novice</u> subjects were used
  in the research.

  此次研究中被研究的對象，有經驗者及<u>新手</u>皆有。

  (A) ***novice***〔'navɪs〕*n.* 初學者；新手　*adj.* 新的
    比較：novel〔'navḷ〕*n.* 小說　*adj.* 新奇的

  (B) residual〔rɪ'zɪdʒʊəl〕*adj.* 剩餘的

  (C) infuriated〔ɪn'fjʊrɪ,etɪd〕*adj.* 生氣的

  (D) miscellaneous〔,mɪsḷ'enɪəs〕*adj.* 各種的
    (= *various*)

  * subject〔'sʌbdʒɪkt〕*n.* 被研究的對象

nov + ice	nov + el
|　　|	|　　|
new + 行為者	new + adj.

TEST 14

Directions: *The following questions are incomplete sentences. You are to choose the one word that best completes the sentence.*

1. Having been abandoned by her boyfriend, Janet was so sad that she experienced a nervous _____.
   - (A) influenza
   - (B) amnesia
   - (C) breakdown
   - (D) allergy   (   )

2. The orator's _____ speech left the audience weeping and applauding.
   - (A) impassioned
   - (B) impassive
   - (C) impartial
   - (D) passion   (   )

3. Test results have _____ worries that the reactor could overheat.
   - (A) entertained
   - (B) enlightened
   - (C) provoked
   - (D) departed   (   )

4. It is so _____ in the classroom that everyone hopes the school will buy an air conditioner.
   - (A) humid
   - (B) plain
   - (C) urban
   - (D) scarce   (   )

5. A bicycle is a two-wheeled _____ propelled by pedals.
   - (A) vessel
   - (B) structure
   - (C) vehicle
   - (D) furniture   (   )

6. Human cloning is most _____, for it arouses many disputes and arguments.
   (A) contrast
   (B) comparative
   (C) compassionate
   (D) controversial   (   )

7. He has been _____ from New York to Boston.
   (A) initiated
   (B) defended
   (C) enhanced
   (D) transferred   (   )

8. She managed to stay _____, even when an emergency came up.
   (A) distracted
   (B) endangered
   (C) composed
   (D) indebted   (   )

9. America is a country of _____ who moved to America at different periods of time and thus is called a "melting pot" of different races.
   (A) tourists
   (B) immigrants
   (C) emigrants
   (D) entrepreneurs   (   )

10. Juvenile _____ is becoming serious in Taiwan, for we can see many robbers and gangsters are teenagers.
   (A) definition
   (B) delinquency
   (C) destination
   (D) designation   (   )

TEST 14 詳解

1. (**C**) Having been abandoned by her boyfriend, Janet was so sad that she experienced a nervous <u>breakdown</u>.

被男友拋棄後，珍娜非常傷心，以至於神經衰弱。

(A) influenza〔,ɪnflʊˈɛnzə〕 *n.* 流行性感冒 (= *flu*)

(B) amnesia〔 æmˈniʒə〕 *n.* 失憶症

(C) ***breakdown*** 〔ˈbrek,daʊn〕 *n.* 衰弱；崩潰

(D) allergy〔ˈælədʒɪ〕 *n.* 過敏症 < *to* >

* abandon〔 əˈbændən〕 *v.* 拋棄

nervous〔ˈnɝvəs〕 *adj.* 神經的

2. (**A**) The orator's <u>impassioned</u> speech left the audience weeping and applauding.

演說者慷慨激昂的演說，使得聽眾熱淚盈眶、掌聲不斷。

(A) ***impassioned*** 〔 ɪmˈpæʃənd〕 *adj.* 慷慨激昂的；熱情洋溢的

(B) impassive〔 ɪmˈpæsɪv〕 *adj.* 無表情的；無動於衷的

(C) impartial〔 ɪmˈparʃəl〕 *adj.* 公平的；不偏袒的

(D) passion〔ˈpæʃən〕 *n.* 熱情

（此處應用形容詞 *passionate* ）

* orator〔ˈɔrətɚ, ˈɑrətɚ〕 *n.* 演說者

audience〔ˈɔdɪəns〕 *n.* 聽眾

weep〔 wip〕 *v.* 哭泣

applaud〔 əˈplɔd〕 *v.* 鼓掌

im + passion + ed
| | |
in + 熱情 + *adj.*

3. (**C**) Test results have <u>provoked</u> worries that the reactor could overheat.

測試結果<u>引</u>發原子反應爐可能會過熱的憂慮。

    (A) entertain〔ˌɛntəˈten〕*v.* 款待；娛樂

    (B) enlighten〔ɪnˈlaɪtn̩〕*v.* 啓蒙；使明白

    (C) ***provoke***〔prəˈvok〕*v.* 激怒；引發

    (D) depart〔dɪˈpɑrt〕*v.* 出發；離開 (= *leave*)

      * reactor〔rɪˈæktɚ〕*n.* 原子反應爐
        overheat〔ˈovɚˈhit〕*v.* 過熱

4. (**A**) It is so <u>humid</u> in the classroom that everyone hopes the school will buy an air conditioner.

教室裏太<u>潮濕</u>了，所以大家希望學校能購買冷氣機。

    (A) ***humid***〔ˈhjumɪd〕*adj.* 潮濕的

    (B) plain〔plen〕*adj.* 明白的；平的

    (C) urban〔ˈɝbən〕*adj.* 都市的

    (D) scarce〔skɛrs〕*adj.* 稀少的；不足的

      * ***air conditioner*** 空調機；冷氣機

5. (**C**) A bicycle is a two-wheeled <u>vehicle</u> propelled by pedals.　腳踏車是兩輪的<u>交通工具</u>，由踩踏板使之前進。

    (A) vessel〔ˈvɛsl̩〕*n.* 容器；船

    (B) structure〔ˈstrʌktʃɚ〕*n.* 構造

    (C) ***vehicle***〔ˈviɪkl̩〕*n.* 陸上交通工具；車輛

    (D) furniture〔ˈfɝnɪtʃɚ〕*n.* 家具

      * wheel〔hwil〕*n.* 輪子
        propel〔prəˈpɛl〕*v.* 推進；使前進
        pedal〔ˈpɛdl̩〕*n.* 踏板

6. (**D**) Human cloning is most <u>controversial</u>, for it arouses many disputes and arguments.

複製人非常<u>具爭議性</u>，引起許多爭執及辯論。

    (A) contrast〔'kɑntræst〕*n.* 對比

    (B) comparative〔kəm'pærətɪv〕*adj.* 比較的

    (C) compassionate〔kəm'pæʃənɪt〕*adj.* 同情的

    (D) ***controversial***〔͵kɑntrə'vɝʃəl〕*adj.* 引起爭議的

      ＊ cloning〔'klonɪŋ〕*n.* 複製
        arouse〔ə'rauz〕*v.* 引起
        dispute〔dɪ'spjut〕*n.* 爭論 (= *argument*)

7. (**D**) He has been <u>transferred</u> from New York to Boston.

他從紐約被<u>調</u>到波士頓。

    (A) initiate〔ɪ'nɪʃɪ͵et〕*v.* 創始

    (B) defend〔dɪ'fɛnd〕*v.* 保衛

    (C) enhance〔ɪn'hæns〕*v.* 提高

    (D) ***transfer***〔træns'fɝ〕*v.* 調職

8. (**C**) She managed to stay <u>composed</u>, even when an emergency came up.

即使是緊急事件發生，她也設法保持<u>鎮定</u>。

    (A) distracted〔dɪ'stræktɪd〕*adj.* 分心的；心煩的

    (B) endangered〔ɪn'dendʒəd〕*adj.* 瀕臨絕種的

    (C) ***composed***〔kəm'pozd〕*adj.* 冷靜的；鎮定的
        (= *calm*)

    (D) indebted〔ɪn'dɛtɪd〕*adj.* 感激的 < *to* >

      ＊ ***manage to*** + ***V.*** 設法
        emergency〔ɪ'mɝdʒənsɪ〕*n.* 緊急事件
        come up 發生 (= *occur* ; *arise*)

9. (**B**) America is a country of <u>immigrants</u> who moved to America at different periods of time and thus is called a "melting pot" of different races.

美國是由不同時期移入的<u>移民</u>所組成的國家，因此被稱為民族的「融爐」。

(A) tourist〔'turɪst〕*n.* 遊客

(B) ***immigrant***〔'ɪməgrənt〕*n.*（移入的）移民

(C) emigrant〔'ɛməgrənt〕*n.*（移出的）移民

(D) entrepreneur〔ˌɑntrəprə'nɝ〕*n.* 企業家

* melt〔mɛlt〕*v.* 融化
pot〔pɑt〕*n.* 鍋；盆
race〔res〕*n.* 民族；種族

im + migr + ant
in + move + 人

10. (**B**) Juvenile <u>delinquency</u> is becoming serious in Taiwan, for we can see many robbers and gangsters are teenagers.

少年<u>犯罪</u>在台灣日漸嚴重，因為我們可以看到很多搶匪、歹徒都是青少年。

(A) definition〔ˌdɛfə'nɪʃən〕*n.* 定義

(B) ***delinquency***〔dɪ'lɪŋkwənsɪ〕*n.* 犯罪

(C) destination〔ˌdɛstə'neʃən〕*n.* 目的地

(D) designation〔ˌdɛzɪg'neʃən〕*n.* 指示

* juvenile〔'dʒuvənḷ〕*adj.* 少年的
gangster〔'gæŋstɚ〕*n.* 歹徒

TEST 15

Directions: *The following questions are incomplete sentences. You are to choose the one word that best completes the sentence.*

1. Our research is _____ and there are problems with the other statistics.
   (A) serviceable
   (B) torrent
   (C) tangible
   (D) exploratory   (　　)

2. A miser is very _____ with his money.
   (A) stingy
   (B) generous
   (C) selfish
   (D) charitable   (　　)

3. Medical researchers are _____ every possible treatment of cancer.
   (A) exploring
   (B) auditioning
   (C) avoiding
   (D) escorting   (　　)

4. The experience of the older workers in these specific jobs may have _____ for their reduced stamina.
   (A) compensated
   (B) contemplated
   (C) conveyed
   (D) commenced   (　　)

5. In this criminal case the body had been badly burned, so _____ is difficult.
   (A) identification
   (B) sanitation
   (C) identity
   (D) impulsion   (　　)

6. The motorist is _____ to the policeman not to write him a ticket.
   (A) appealing
   (B) appalling
   (C) assisting
   (D) appointing   (   )

7. Because of the heroic efforts of the firemen, the people on the roof of the building were _____.
   (A) trapped
   (B) proved
   (C) rescued
   (D) doomed   (   )

8. Sometimes politicians give jobs to their friends who really don't know the work. It is easy for politicians to _____ their power.
   (A) promote
   (B) neglect
   (C) fasten
   (D) abuse   (   )

9. The government has decided to enforce the laws to fight against the _____ of the civil servants, for it is destroying the nation's economy.
   (A) contempt
   (B) compassion
   (C) corruption
   (D) corporation   (   )

10. One major principle of Marxist _____ claims that the conflicts between the laborers and the capitalists are inevitable.
   (A) protest
   (B) patriotism
   (C) indulgence
   (D) ideology   (   )

TEST 15 詳解

1. (**D**) Our research is <u>exploratory</u> and there are problems with the other statistics.

我們的研究是經過實地調查的，而其他的統計數字則有問題。

(A) serviceable〔'sɜvɪsəbḷ〕*adj.* 有用的（＝*useful*）

(B) torrent〔'tɔrənt〕*n.* 湍流

(C) tangible〔'tændʒəbḷ〕*adj.* 明白的

(D) *exploratory*〔ɪk'splɔrə,torɪ〕*adj.* 實地調查的

＊statistics〔stə'tɪstɪks〕*n. pl.* 統計數字

2. (**A**) A miser is very <u>stingy</u> with his money.

守財奴對於錢十分吝嗇。

(A) *stingy*〔'stɪndʒɪ〕*adj.* 吝嗇的；小氣的

(B) generous〔'dʒɛnərəs〕*adj.* 慷慨的

(C) selfish〔'sɛlfɪʃ〕*adj.* 自私的

(D) charitable〔'tʃærətəbḷ〕*adj.* 慈善的

＊miser〔'maɪzə〕*n.* 守財奴

3. (**A**) Medical researchers are <u>exploring</u> every possible treatment of cancer.

醫學研究人員正在探索各種可能治療癌症的方法。

(A) *explore*〔ɪk'splor〕*v.* 探索

(B) audition〔ɔ'dɪʃən〕*v.* 試演；試唱

(C) avoid〔ə'vɔɪd〕*v.* 避免

(D) escort〔ɪ'skɔrt〕*v.* 護送

＊treatment〔'tritmənt〕*n.* 治療方法

4. (**A**) The experience of the older workers in these specific jobs may have <u>compensated</u> for their reduced stamina.

在這些特定工作中，老員工的經驗可<u>彌補</u>他們體力的不足。

　　(A) ***compensate***〔'kɑmpən,set〕 *v.* 彌補 < *for* >
　　　　(= *make up for*)

　　(B) contemplate〔'kɑntəm,plet〕 *v.* 沈思；考慮
　　　　(= *consider*)

　　(C) convey〔kən've〕 *v.* 傳送

　　(D) commence〔kə'mɛns〕 *v.* 開始 (= *begin* ; *start*)

　　* specific〔spɪ'sɪfɪk〕 *adj.* 特定的
　　　reduced〔rɪ'djust〕 *adj.* 減少的
　　　stamina〔'stæmənə〕 *n.* 精力；體力

5. (**A**) In this criminal case the body had been badly burned, so <u>identification</u> is difficult.

在這起刑案中，屍體被嚴重焚毀，所以<u>身分辨識</u>很困難。

　　(A) ***identification***〔aɪ,dɛntəfə'keʃən〕 *n.* 身分辨認

　　(B) sanitation〔,sænə'teʃən〕 *n.* 公共衛生

　　(C) identity〔aɪ'dɛntətɪ〕 *n.* 身分

　　(D) impulsion〔ɪm'pʌlʃən〕 *n.* 推進；刺激

　　* criminal〔'krɪmənḷ〕 *adj.* 刑事的
　　　criminal case 刑案

6. (**A**) The motorist is <u>appealing</u> to the policeman not to write him a ticket.

這名汽車駕駛人，正在<u>懇求</u>警察先生不要開罰單給他。

  (A) ***appeal*** 〔 ə'pil 〕 *v.* 懇求 < *to sb.* >

  (B) appall 〔 ə'pɔl 〕 *v.* 使驚嚇

  (C) assist 〔 ə'sɪst 〕 *v.* 幫助 (= *help*)

  (D) appoint 〔 ə'pɔɪnt 〕 *v.* 指派

  * motorist 〔'motərɪst 〕 *n.* 汽車駕駛人

7. (**C**) Because of the heroic efforts of the firemen, the people on the roof of the building were <u>rescued</u>.

由於消防隊員英勇努力救人，大樓屋頂的人都被<u>救出來</u>了。

  (A) trap 〔 træp 〕 *v.* 困住

  (B) prove 〔 pruv 〕 *v.* 證明

  (C) ***rescue*** 〔'rɛskju 〕 *v.* 解救 (= *save*)

  (D) doom 〔 dum 〕 *v.* 命中註定 (不好的結果)

  * heroic 〔 hɪ'roɪk 〕 *adj.* 英勇的

    effort 〔'ɛfət 〕 *n.* 努力

8. (**D**) Sometimes politicians give jobs to their friends who really don't know the work. It is easy for politicians to <u>abuse</u> their power.

有時，政客會提供工作給自己的朋友，而那些人根本不了解自己的工作要做什麼。政客很容易<u>濫用</u>自己的權力。

  (A) promote 〔 prə'mot 〕 *v.* 升職

  (B) neglect 〔 nɪ'glɛkt 〕 *v.* 忽略

  (C) fasten 〔'fæsn̩ 〕 *v.* 繫緊

  (D) ***abuse*** 〔 ə'bjuz 〕 *v.* 濫用

9. (**C**) The government has decided to enforce the laws to fight against the <u>corruption</u> of the civil servants, for it is destroying the nation's economy.

政府決定執法掃蕩公務人員貪污，因為這已危害國家經濟。

   (A) contempt〔kən'tɛmpt〕*n.* 輕視

   (B) compassion〔kəm'pæʃən〕*n.* 同情

   (C) ***corruption***〔kə'rʌpʃən〕*n.* 貪污

   (D) corporation〔ˌkɔrpə'reʃən〕*n.* 公司

   * enforce〔ɪn'fɔrs , -'fors〕*v.* 執行
     civil servant 公務員

10. (**D**) One major principle of Marxist <u>ideology</u> claims that the conflicts between the laborers and the capitalists are inevitable.

馬克思意識的主要原則之一聲稱，勞工和資本家之間的衝突是無法避免的。

   (A) protest〔'protɛst〕*n.* 抗議 < *against* >

   (B) patriotism〔'petrɪətɪzəm〕*n.* 愛國心

   (C) indulgence〔ɪn'dʌldʒəns〕*n.* 沈溺；縱容

   (D) ***ideology***〔ˌaɪdɪ'ɑlədʒɪ , ˌɪdɪ-〕*n.* 意識型態

   * principle〔'prɪnsəpḷ〕*n.* 原則
     Marxist〔'mɑrksɪst〕*adj.* 馬克思主義的
     claim〔klem〕*v.* 聲稱
     conflict〔'kɑnflɪkt〕*n.* 衝突
     laborer〔'lebərɚ〕*n.* 勞工
     capitalist〔'kæpətḷɪst〕*n.* 資本家
     inevitable〔ɪn'ɛvətəbḷ〕*adj.* 無法避免的

TEST 16

Directions: *The following questions are incomplete sentences. You are to choose the one word that best completes the sentence.*

1. Political _____ spoils the booming economy of Taiwan.
   - (A) debate
   - (B) turmoil
   - (C) involvement
   - (D) compromise   (   )

2. The _____ of gasoline caused the price to rise.
   - (A) shortage
   - (B) abundance
   - (C) enrich
   - (D) lessen   (   )

3. If the crops are not irrigated soon, the _____ will be poor.
   - (A) planters
   - (B) rice
   - (C) grains
   - (D) harvest   (   )

4. Aunt Martha left a _____ of only one acre of land, but that is now in the middle of Times Square.
   - (A) suspense
   - (B) legacy
   - (C) maintenance
   - (D) quantity   (   )

5. Young people are taught to _____ elderly citizens for their wisdom and experience.
   - (A) rebel
   - (B) revere
   - (C) revenge
   - (D) repent   (   )

6. The Chinese Lantern Festival falls on the 15th day of the first _____ month.
   (A) lunatic
   (B) loony
   (C) liberal
   (D) lunar   (   )

7. The present study assessed the _____ of performance standards on the social behavior of Type A and Type B children.
   (A) shutters
   (B) impact
   (C) chore
   (D) league   (   )

8. Because a high degree of variability was found in the data, it would be _____ to replicate this study on larger and different populations.
   (A) immortal
   (B) hygienic
   (C) beneficial
   (D) magnitude   (   )

9. Christopher Columbus's _____ to the New World was sponsored by the Queen of Spain.
   (A) navigation
   (B) pilgrimage
   (C) voyage
   (D) sailing   (   )

10. The world is turning into a " _____ village"; that is, people can travel fast to a foreign country or communicate easily with friends far away.
    (A) local
    (B) earthly
    (C) global
    (D) terrific   (   )

TEST 16 詳解

1. (**B**) Political <u>turmoil</u> spoils the booming economy of Taiwan. 政治的<u>混亂</u>會破壞台灣日漸繁榮的經濟。

    (A) debate〔dɪ'bet〕*n.* 辯論

    (B) **turmoil**〔'tɝmɔɪl〕*n.* 混亂

    (C) involvement〔ɪn'vɑlvmənt〕*n.* 牽涉 < *in* >

    (D) compromise〔'kɑmprə,maɪz〕*n.,v.* 妥協

    * political〔pə'lɪtɪkl̩〕*adj.* 政治的
        spoil〔spɔɪl〕*v.* 破壞
        booming〔'bumɪŋ〕*adj.* 日漸繁榮的

2. (**A**) The <u>shortage</u> of gasoline caused the price to rise. 汽油的<u>不足</u>導致價格上漲。

    (A) **shortage**〔'ʃɔrtɪdʒ〕*n.* 不足

    (B) abundance〔ə'bʌndəns〕*n.* 豐富

    (C) enrich〔ɪn'rɪtʃ〕*v.* 使豐富

    (D) lessen〔'lɛsn̩〕*v.* 減少

3. (**D**) If the crops are not irrigated soon, the <u>harvest</u> will be poor. 如果農作物沒有趕快灌溉，<u>收成</u>就會不好。

    (A) planter〔'plæntɚ〕*n.* 種植者；農場主人

    (B) rice〔raɪs〕*n.* 稻米

    (C) grain〔gren〕*n.* 穀類

    (D) **harvest**〔'hɑrvɪst〕*n.,v.* 收成；收穫

    * crop〔krɑp〕*n.* 農作物
        irrigate〔'ɪrə,get〕*v.* 灌溉

4. (**B**) Aunt Martha left a <u>legacy</u> of only one acre of land, but that is now in the middle of Times Square.

瑪莎姨媽留下了僅僅一英畝土地的<u>遺產</u>，但卻是在時代廣場的中央。

    (A) suspense〔səˈspɛns〕*n.* 懸疑

    (B) *legacy*〔ˈlɛgəsɪ〕*n.* 遺產

    (C) maintenance〔ˈmentənəns〕*n.* 維持

    (D) quantity〔ˈkwɑntətɪ〕*n.* 量

    ＊ acre〔ˈekɚ〕*n.* 英畝

5. (**B**) Young people are taught to <u>revere</u> elderly citizens for their wisdom and experience.

年輕人被教導要<u>尊敬</u>長者，因為他們有智慧、有經驗。

    (A) rebel〔rɪˈbɛl〕*v.* 反叛

    (B) *revere*〔rɪˈvɪr〕*v.* 尊敬 (= *respect*)

    (C) revenge〔rɪˈvɛndʒ〕*v.* 報復

    (D) repent〔rɪˈpɛnt〕*v.* 後悔

    ＊ citizen〔ˈsɪtəzn̩〕*n.* 市民；公民

6. (**D**) The Chinese Lantern Festival falls on the 15th day of the first <u>lunar</u> month.

中國的元宵節在<u>陰曆</u>正月十五。

    (A) lunatic〔ˈlunəˌtɪk〕*adj.* 瘋狂的 (= *insane*)

    (B) loony〔ˈlunɪ〕*adj.* 發瘋的 (= *crazy*)

    (C) liberal〔ˈlɪbərəl〕*adj.* 自由的

    (D) *lunar*〔ˈlunɚ〕*adj.* 月亮的　　*lunar month* 陰曆月

    ＊ lantern〔ˈlæntən〕*n.* 燈籠　　*fall on* 適逢；落在

7. (**B**) The present study assessed the <u>impact</u> of performance standards on the social behavior of Type A and Type B children.

目前這項研究評估，A 型和 B 型的小孩在表現標準上，對他們的社會行為上產生的<u>影響</u>。

(A) shutter〔ˈʃʌtɚ〕 n. 快門；(pl.) 百葉窗
(B) ***impact***〔ˈɪmpækt〕 n. 影響 < on >
(C) chore〔tʃɔr〕 n. 雜事
(D) league〔lig〕 n. 聯盟

* present〔ˈprɛznt〕 adj. 現在的
assess〔əˈsɛs〕 v. 評估
performance〔pɚˈfɔrməns〕 n. 表現
standard〔ˈstændɚd〕 n. 標準

8. (**C**) Because a high degree of variability was found in the data, it would be <u>beneficial</u> to replicate this study on larger and different populations.

由於在資料中發現很大的變數，所以將這份研究重新用在數量較多且不同的人口中，可能是<u>有益的</u>。

(A) immortal〔ɪˈmɔrtl̩〕 adj. 不朽的
(B) hygienic〔ˌhaɪdʒɪˈɛnɪk〕 adj. 衛生的
(C) ***beneficial***〔ˌbɛnəˈfɪʃəl〕 adj. 有益的
(D) magnitude〔ˈmægnəˌtjud〕 n. 大小；規模

* degree〔dɪˈgri〕 n. 程度
variability〔ˌvɛrɪəˈbɪlətɪ〕 n. 可變性
data〔ˈdetə〕 n. pl. 資料
replicate〔ˈrɛplɪˌket〕 v. 複製

9. (**C**) Christopher Columbus's <u>voyage</u> to the New World
was sponsored by the Queen of Spain.

哥倫布的新大陸之<u>旅</u>是由西班牙王后贊助的。

(A) navigation〔͵nævə'geʃən〕n. 航海（術）

(B) pilgrimage〔'pɪlgrəmɪdʒ〕n. 朝聖之旅

(C) *voyage*〔'vɔɪ‧ɪdʒ〕n. 航海（之旅）

(D) sailing〔'selɪŋ〕n. 駕帆船、遊艇出遊

* sponsor〔'spɑnsɚ〕v. 贊助

Spain〔spen〕n. 西班牙

```
voy  +  age
 |       |
way  +  n.（走過的路）
```

10. (**C**) The world is turning into a "<u>global</u> village"; that
is, people can travel fast to a foreign country or
communicate easily with friends far away.

全世界正逐漸成爲一個「<u>地球</u>村」；也就是，人們可以快
速出國旅行，或輕鬆地與遠方的朋友交談。

(A) local〔'lokḷ〕adj. 當地的

(B) earthly〔'ɝθlɪ〕adj. 世俗的（= *worldly*）

(C) *global*〔'globḷ〕adj. 全球的

(D) terrific〔tə'rɪfɪk〕adj. 很棒的

```
glob(e)  +  al
  |          |
地球    +   adj.
```

```
earth  +  ly
 |        |
地球   +  adj.
```

TEST 17

Directions: *The following questions are incomplete sentences. You are to choose the one word that best completes the sentence.*

1. John was _____ in his attempt to climb to the top of the mountain.
   (A) redundant
   (B) reconcilable
   (C) resistant
   (D) resolute   (   )

2. Peter did hurt his arm, but it was only a _____, not a break.
   (A) sponge
   (B) spray
   (C) sprain
   (D) splash   (   )

3. Management is weak, morale is low and punishment is _____.
   (A) conceit
   (B) subsequent
   (C) arbitrary
   (D) mischievous   (   )

4. Steve's _____ about school disappeared when his teacher greeted him warmly.
   (A) satisfaction
   (B) fiction
   (C) apprehension
   (D) comprehension   (   )

5. Prince Charles is the _____ to the throne.
   (A) heir
   (B) hammer
   (C) hirer
   (D) hinder   (   )

6. Throughout the world, the language with the largest number of native speakers is _____ Chinese.
   (A) Dialect
   (B) Linguistic
   (C) Mandarin
   (D) Oral   ( )

7. Action must be taken to reduce the _____ between medium education levels and the readability of instruction booklets.
   (A) disorder
   (B) disposal
   (C) disparity
   (D) disgust   ( )

8. The best-selling novel has been _____ into more than twenty languages.
   (A) transformed
   (B) transported
   (C) transited
   (D) translated   (·)

9. Does what we propose about the affairs meet with your _____?
   (A) appointment
   (B) approval
   (C) aggression
   (D) adjournment   ( )

10. The number of robberies in the area has _____ recently because residents have learned to protect their property.
   (A) declined
   (B) intensified
   (C) increased
   (D) resided   ( )

TEST 17 詳解

1. (**D**) John was <u>resolute</u> in his attempt to climb to the top of the mountain.

約翰很<u>堅決</u>，試著要爬上山頂。

   (A) redundant〔rɪ'dʌndənt〕*adj.* 多餘的

   (B) reconcilable〔'rɛkən,saɪləbḷ〕*adj.* 可和解的

   (C) resistant〔rɪ'zɪstənt〕*adj.* 抵抗的 < *to* >

   (D) ***resolute***〔'rɛzə,lut〕*adj.* 堅決的

   * attempt〔ə'tɛmpt〕*n.* 嘗試

2. (**C**) Peter did hurt his arm, but it was only a <u>sprain</u>, not a break. 彼德眞的傷了手臂，但只是<u>扭傷</u>，不是骨折。

   (A) sponge〔spʌndʒ〕*n.* 海綿

   (B) spray〔spre〕*n.* 噴霧（器）

   (C) ***sprain***〔spren〕*n.* 扭傷

   (D) splash〔splæʃ〕*n.* 濺起

3. (**C**) Management is weak, morale is low and punishment is <u>arbitrary</u>. 管理薄弱，士氣低落，而處罰又很<u>專制</u>。

   (A) conceit〔kən'sit〕*n.* 自大

   (B) subsequent〔'sʌbsɪ,kwɛnt〕*adj.* 接著發生的

   (C) ***arbitrary***〔'ɑrbə,trɛrɪ〕*adj.* 專制的

   (D) mischievous〔'mɪstʃɪvəs〕*adj.* 頑皮的

   * management〔'mænɪdʒmənt〕*n.* 管理
     morale〔mə'ræl〕*n.* 士氣

4. (**C**) Steve's <u>apprehension</u> about school disappeared when his teacher greeted him warmly.

當老師很親切地和他打招呼時，史蒂夫對學校的<u>恐懼</u>消失了。

    (A) satisfaction〔͵sætɪs'fækʃən〕*n.* 滿意

    (B) fiction〔'fɪkʃən〕*n.* 小說

    (C) ***apprehension***〔͵æprɪ'hɛnʃən〕*n.* 恐懼；憂慮
        (= *fear* ; *anxiety*)

    (D) comprehension〔͵kɑmprɪ'hɛnʃən〕*n.* 理解

   * greet〔grit〕*v.* 打招呼

5. (**A**) Prince Charles is the <u>heir</u> to the throne.

查爾斯王子是王位<u>繼承人</u>。

    (A) ***heir***〔ɛr〕*n.* 繼承人 < *to* >

    (B) hammer〔'hæmɚ〕*n.* 鐵鎚

    (C) hirer〔'haɪrɚ〕*n.* 雇主 (= *employer*)

    (D) hinder〔'haɪndɚ〕*adj.* 後方的　〔'hɪndɚ〕*v.* 妨礙

   * throne〔θron〕*n.* 王位

6. (**C**) Throughout the world, the language with the largest number of native speakers is <u>Mandarin</u> Chinese.

全世界最多人使用做為母語的語言是<u>國語</u>。

    (A) dialect〔'daɪəlɛkt〕*n.* 方言

    (B) linguistic〔lɪŋ'gwɪstɪk〕*adj.* 語言 (學) 的

    (C) ***Mandarin***〔'mændərɪn〕*n.* 國語

    (D) oral〔'ɔrəl〕*adj.* 口頭的

7. (**C**) Action must be taken to reduce the <u>disparity</u> between medium education levels and the readability of instruction booklets.

必須採取行動，減少中等教育程度和指導手冊的易讀性之間的<u>差異</u>。

(A) disorder〔dɪsˈɔrdɚ〕*n.* 混亂

(B) disposal〔dɪˈspozḷ〕*n.* 處置

(C) *disparity*〔dɪsˈpærətɪ〕*n.* 差異

(D) disgust〔dɪsˈgʌst〕*n.,v.* 厭惡

＊ medium〔ˈmidɪəm〕*adj.* 中等的
readability〔ˌridəˈbɪlətɪ〕*n.* 易讀性
instruction〔ɪnˈstrʌkʃən〕*n.* 指導
booklet〔ˈbʊklɪt〕*n.* 小冊子

dis + par + ity	trans + late
apart + equal + n.	across + carry

8. (**D**) The best-selling novel has been <u>translated</u> into more than twenty languages.

這本暢銷小說已被<u>翻譯</u>成二十多種語言。

(A) transform〔trænsˈfɔrm〕*v.* 改變

(B) transport〔trænsˈport〕*v.* 運輸

(C) transit〔ˈtrænsɪt〕*n.* 運輸

(D) *translate*〔trænsˈlet〕*v.* 翻譯

＊ best-selling〔ˈbɛstˈsɛlɪŋ〕*adj.* 暢銷的

9. (**B**) Does what we propose about the affairs meet with your <u>approval</u>?

關於這些事項，我們的提議你<u>同意</u>嗎？

    (A) appointment〔ə'pɔɪntmənt〕*n.* 約會

    (B) ***approval***〔ə'pruvḷ〕*n.* 同意；贊成

    (C) aggression〔ə'grɛʃən〕*n.* 侵略；攻擊＜ *on* ＞

    (D) adjournment〔ə'dʒɝnmənt〕*n.* 休會；延期

    ＊ propose〔prə'poz〕*v.* 提議

```
ap  +   prov  + al
|        |       |
to  + test , try +  n.
```

10. (**A**) The number of robberies in the area has <u>declined</u> recently because residents have learned to protect their property.

此地的搶案最近<u>減少</u>了，因爲居民已經學會保護自己的財產。

    (A) ***decline***〔dɪ'klaɪn〕*v.* 下降；減少
        (= *decrease* ; *reduce*)

    (B) intensify〔ɪn'tɛnsə,faɪ〕*v.* 增強

    (C) increase〔ɪn'kris〕*v.* 增加

    (D) reside〔rɪ'zaɪd〕*v.* 居住 (= *live*)

    ＊ resident〔'rɛzədənt〕*n.* 居民
       property〔'prɑpətɪ〕*n.* 財產

```
de   + cline
|        |
down + bend
```

TEST 18

Directions: *The following questions are incomplete sentences. You are to choose the one word that best completes the sentence.*

1. Discrimination on the grounds of race, religion or sex is _____.
   - (A) valid
   - (B) vacant
   - (C) illegal
   - (D) integral   (   )

2. The advertising campaign is intended to _____ sales.
   - (A) impart
   - (B) observe
   - (C) conform
   - (D) boost   (   )

3. People like to talk to Mike because he knows so many funny _____ and stories.
   - (A) triplets
   - (B) frolics
   - (C) pamphlets
   - (D) anecdotes   (   )

4. Her remarkable success as a rock star is partly due to her ability to _____ the media.
   - (A) heighten
   - (B) manipulate
   - (C) prescribe
   - (D) mourn   (   )

5. The theory of economics states that effectiveness of production can be enhanced via _____ production.
   - (A) scorn
   - (B) scope
   - (C) mass
   - (D) scale   (   )

6. One of Taiwan's most _____ problems is garbage disposal.
   - (A) miraculous
   - (B) acute
   - (C) unexpected
   - (D) groundless   (   )

7. During the past twenty years, Taiwan has _____ from a manufacturing economy to a service economy.
   - (A) bargained
   - (B) shifted
   - (C) hesitated
   - (D) reproved   (   )

8. The students working for McDonald's are only part-time or _____ employees.
   - (A) temporary
   - (B) registered
   - (C) professional
   - (D) well-trained   (   )

9. He paid $5000 as a down payment for the car and the rest will be paid in _____.
   - (A) installments
   - (B) installations
   - (C) instilments
   - (D) institutions   (   )

10. Our amusements must be really _____ because some people cannot stand ordinary pleasures.
    - (A) tropical
    - (B) recreational
    - (C) original
    - (D) mineral   (   )

TEST 18 詳解

1. (**C**) Discrimination on the grounds of race, religion or
   sex is <u>illegal</u>. 種族、宗教、性別上的歧視是<u>非法的</u>。
   - (A) valid〔'vælɪd〕*adj.* 有效的
   - (B) vacant〔'vekənt〕*adj.* 空的
   - (C) ***illegal***〔ɪ'ligl〕*adj.* 非法的
   - (D) integral〔'ɪntəgrəl〕*adj.* 必要的；不可或缺的
   - * discrimination〔dɪ,skrɪmə'neʃən〕*n.* 歧視
     on the grounds of 基於

2. (**D**) The advertising campaign is intended to <u>boost</u> sales.
   這個宣傳活動是爲了要<u>增加</u>銷售量。
   - (A) impart〔ɪm'part〕*v.* 傳授；賦與 *< to >*
   - (B) observe〔əb'zɜv〕*v.* 觀察
   - (C) conform〔kən'fɔrm〕*v.* 遵從；一致 *< to >*
   - (D) ***boost***〔bust〕*v.* 增加；提高
   - * campaign〔kæm'pen〕*n.* 活動
     intend〔ɪn'tɛnd〕*v.* 打算

3. (**D**) People like to talk to Mike because he knows so
   many funny <u>anecdotes</u> and stories.
   大家都喜歡和麥克聊天，因爲他知道好多有趣的<u>軼事</u>和故事。
   - (A) triplet〔'trɪplɪt〕*n.* 三胞胎；三個一組
   - (B) frolic〔'fralɪk〕*n.* 狂歡
   - (C) pamphlet〔'pæmflɪt〕*n.* 小册子 (= ***booklet***)
   - (D) ***anecdote***〔'ænɪk,dot〕*n.* 軼事

4. (**B**) Her remarkable success as a rock star is partly
due to her ability to <u>manipulate</u> the media.
她之所以能成為搖滾巨星，部分是由於她懂得<u>巧妙運用</u>
媒體。

    (A) heighten〔'haɪtn̩〕*v.* 升高

    (B) ***manipulate***〔mə'nɪpjə,let〕*v.* 巧妙運用；操縱

    (C) prescribe〔prɪ'skraɪb〕*v.* 開藥方

    (D) mourn〔morn〕*v.* 哀悼

    ＊ remarkable〔rɪ'mɑrkəbl̩〕*adj.* 卓越的
       media〔'midɪə〕*n.* 媒體

5. (**C**) The theory of economics states that effectiveness of
production can be enhanced via <u>mass</u> production.
經濟學的理論提到，產能可以經由<u>大量</u>生產提高。

    (A) scorn〔skɔrn〕*n.,v.* 輕視

    (B) scope〔skop〕*n.* 範圍；領域

    (C) ***mass***〔mæs〕*n.* 大量；大眾
       mass production 大量生產

    (D) scale〔skel〕*n.* 規模

    ＊ theory〔'θɪərɪ〕*n.* 理論
       economics〔,ikə'nɑmɪks〕*n.* 經濟學
       state〔stet〕*v.* 提到
       effectiveness〔ɪ'fɛktɪvnɪs〕*n.* 效能
       enhance〔ɪn'hæns〕*v.* 提升
       via〔'vaɪə〕*prep.* 藉由（= *by means of*）

6. (**B**) One of Taiwan's most <u>acute</u> problems is garbage
disposal. 台灣最<u>嚴重的</u>問題之一就是垃圾處理。

    (A) miraculous〔məˈrækjələs〕*adj.* 奇蹟似的

    (B) ***acute***〔əˈkjut〕*adj.* 嚴重的；激烈的

    (C) unexpected〔ˌʌnɪkˈspɛktɪd〕*adj.* 意想不到的

    (D) groundless〔ˈɡraʊndlɪs〕*adj.* 無根據的

    * disposal〔dɪˈspozl̩〕*n.* 處理

7. (**B**) During the past twenty years, Taiwan has <u>shifted</u>
from a manufacturing economy to a service economy.
過去二十年來，台灣經濟已經從製造業經濟<u>轉變</u>成為服務業。

    (A) bargain〔ˈbɑrgɪn〕*v.* 討價還價

    (B) ***shift***〔ʃɪft〕*v.* 轉移

    (C) hesitate〔ˈhɛzəˌtet〕*v.* 猶豫

    (D) reprove〔rɪˈpruv〕*v.* 責備（= *blame*；*scold*）

    * manufacturing〔ˌmænjəˈfæktʃərɪŋ〕*adj.* 製造業的

8. (**A**) The students working for McDonald's are only
part-time or <u>temporary</u> employees.
在麥當勞工作的學生們都只是兼職的，也就是<u>臨時的</u>雇員。

    (A) ***temporary***〔ˈtɛmpəˌrɛrɪ〕*adj.* 臨時的

    (B) registered〔ˈrɛdʒɪstəd〕*adj.* 掛號的

    (C) professional〔prəˈfɛʃənl̩〕*adj.* 專業的

    (D) well-trained〔ˈwɛlˈtrend〕*adj.* 受過良好訓練的

    * employee〔ˌɛmplɔɪˈi〕*n.* 員工

9. (**A**) He paid $5000 as a down payment for the car and the rest will be paid in <u>installments</u>.

這部車他付了五千元美金當頭期款，其餘的金額則用<u>分期付款</u>。

    (A) ***installment*** 〔 ɪn'stɔlmənt 〕 *n.* 分期付款

       in installments 以分期付款方式

    (B) installation 〔 ͵ɪnstə'leʃən 〕 *n.* 安裝；任命

    (C) instilment 〔 ɪn'stɪlmənt 〕 *n.* 灌輸

    (D) institution 〔 ͵ɪnstə'tjuʃən 〕 *n.* 制定

    * ***down payment*** （分期付款的）頭期款

in + stall + ment	in + stall + ation
in + stand + n.	in + stand + n.

10. (**C**) Our amusements must be really <u>original</u> because some people cannot stand ordinary pleasures.

我們的娛樂一定要很<u>有創意</u>，因為有些人無法忍受普通的娛樂。

    (A) tropical 〔'trɑpɪkḷ 〕 *adj.* 熱帶的

    (B) recreational 〔 ͵rɛkrɪ'eʃənḷ 〕 *adj.* 娛樂的

    (C) ***original*** 〔 ə'rɪdʒənḷ 〕 *adj.* 有創意的

    (D) mineral 〔'mɪnərəl 〕 *adj.* 礦物的

    * amusement 〔 ə'mjuzmənt 〕 *n.* 娛樂

TEST 19

Directions: *The following questions are incomplete sentences. You are to choose the one word that best completes the sentence.*

1. The previous _____ had left the house a terrible mess.
   (A) habitations
   (B) principals
   (C) artisans
   (D) occupants   (   )

2. We are the most intimate _____ when serving in the army.
   (A) comrades
   (B) foes
   (C) opponents
   (D) rivals   (   )

3. A _____ is a building where people can study stars.
   (A) gymnasium
   (B) planetarium
   (C) aquarium
   (D) auditorium   (   )

4. After he died, his whole family suddenly lost a _____.
   (A) pause
   (B) pillar
   (C) pill
   (D) pillage   (   )

5. His desire for _____ was obvious because he repeatedly attempted to say what he had done.
   (A) recognition
   (B) secrecy
   (C) integrity
   (D) despair   (   )

6. It is my _____ as president of the university to welcome you to Princeton.
   (A) significance
   (B) stimulus
   (C) privilege
   (D) institute   (   )

7. In order to discover who had a natural ability to learn languages, the students were given tests to determine their language _____.
   (A) appetite
   (B) aptitude
   (C) solitude
   (D) candidate   (   )

8. Chimpanzees in the wild use simple objects as tools, but in laboratory situations they can use more _____ items.
   (A) homemade
   (B) thorough
   (C) user-friendly
   (D) sophisticated   (   )

9. The U.S. President and his Canadian _____ signed a bilateral treaty.
   (A) counterpart
   (B) edition
   (C) version
   (D) publication   (   )

10. This car accident is all _____ to Adam's careless driving.
    (A) announced
    (B) affected
    (C) afforded
    (D) ascribed   (   )

TEST 19 詳解

1. (**D**) The previous <u>occupants</u> had left the house a terrible
mess. 前任<u>房客</u>離開後，房子凌亂不堪。

 (A) habitation〔,hæbə'teʃən〕 *n.* 住所
 (B) principal〔'prɪnsəpḷ〕 *n.* 校長
 (C) artisan〔'ɑrtəzn̩〕 *n.* 工匠 (= *craftsman*)
 (D) *occupant*〔'ɑkjəpənt〕 *n.* 居住者

 * previous〔'priviəs〕 *adj.* 先前的
  mess〔mɛs〕 *n.* 凌亂

2. (**A**) We are the most intimate <u>comrades</u> when serving in
the army. 在軍中服役時，我們是最親密的<u>夥伴</u>。

 (A) *comrade*〔'kɑmræd〕 *n.* 同志；夥伴
 (B) foe〔fo〕 *n.* 敵人
 (C) opponent〔ə'ponənt〕 *n.* 對手
 (D) rival〔'raɪvḷ〕 *n.* 對手

 * intimate〔'ɪntəmɪt〕 *adj.* 親密的 (= *close*)
  serve in the army 在軍中服役

3. (**B**) A <u>planetarium</u> is a building where people can study
stars. <u>天文館</u>是人們可以去研究星星的建築物。

 (A) gymnasium〔dʒɪm'neziəm〕 *n.* 健身房；體育館
 (B) *planetarium*〔,plænə'tɛrɪəm〕 *n.* 天文館
 (C) aquarium〔ə'kwɛrɪəm〕 *n.* 水族館
 (D) auditorium〔,ɔdə'torɪəm〕 *n.* 大禮堂；演講廳

4. (**B**) After he died, his whole family suddenly lost a
pillar. 他死後，他全家頓時失去了支柱。

(A) pause〔pɔz〕*n.,v.* 暫停

(B) *pillar*〔'pɪlɚ〕*n.* 柱子；支柱

(C) pill〔pɪl〕*n.* 藥丸

(D) pillage〔'pɪlɪdʒ〕*n.* 戰利品

5. (**A**) His desire for recognition was obvious because he
repeatedly attempted to say what he had done.
很明顯地，他渴望受到認可，因為他不斷地企圖說明自己
做過什麼事。

(A) *recognition*〔ˌrɛkəg'nɪʃən〕*n.* 認可

(B) secrecy〔'sikrəsɪ〕*n.* 祕密

(C) integrity〔ɪn'tɛgrətɪ〕*n.* 正直

(D) despair〔dɪ'spɛr〕*n.* 絕望

* desire〔dɪ'zaɪr〕*n.* 渴望
  obvious〔'ɑbvɪəs〕*adj.* 明顯的
  repeatedly〔rɪ'pitɪdlɪ〕*adv.* 不斷地
  attempt〔ə'tɛmpt〕*v.* 嘗試

6. (**C**) It is my privilege as president of the university to
welcome you to Princeton.
身為本校校長，我很榮幸歡迎各位來到普林斯頓大學。

(A) significance〔sɪg'nɪfəkəns〕*n.* 重要性

(B) stimulus〔'stɪmjələs〕*n.* 興奮劑

(C) *privilege*〔'prɪvlɪdʒ〕*n.* 特權；殊榮

(D) institute〔'ɪnstəˌtjut〕*n.* 學會

7. (**B**) In order to discover who had a natural ability to learn languages, the students were given tests to determine their language <u>aptitude</u>.

為了要發現誰具有學習語言的天分，學生們參加測驗來測出他們的語言<u>才能</u>。

(A) appetite〔ˈæpəˌtaɪt〕*n.* 食慾

(B) *aptitude*〔ˈæptəˌtjud〕*n.* 才能；性向

(C) solitude〔ˈsɑləˌtjud〕*n.* 孤獨

(D) candidate〔ˈkændəˌdet〕*n.* 候選人

```
apt + itude
 |      |
fit  +  n.
```

8. (**D**) Chimpanzees in the wild use simple objects as tools, but in laboratory situations they can use more <u>sophisticated</u> items.

野外的黑猩猩會使用簡單的物品做工具，但在實驗情況中，他們會使用更<u>複雜的</u>物品。

(A) homemade〔ˈhomˈmed〕*adj.* 自製的

(B) thorough〔ˈθɝo〕*adj.* 徹底的

(C) user-friendly〔ˈjuzɚˈfrɛndlɪ〕*adj.* 容易使用的

(D) *sophisticated*〔səˈfɪstɪˌketɪd〕*adj.* 複雜的

＊chimpanzee〔ˌtʃɪmpænˈzi〕*n.* 黑猩猩
laboratory〔ˈlæbrəˌtorɪ〕*n.* 實驗室
item〔ˈaɪtəm〕*n.* 物品

9. (**A**) The U.S. President and his Canadian <u>counterpart</u> signed a bilateral treaty.

美國總統和加拿大總理簽署了一份互惠條約。

    (A) ***counterpart*** ﹝'kaʊntə͵pɑrt﹞ *n.* 對應的人或物

    (B) edition ﹝ɪ'dɪʃən﹞ *n.* (發行物的) 版

    (C) version ﹝'vɝʒən﹞ *n.* 版本

    (D) publication ﹝͵pʌblə'keʃən﹞ *n.* 出版 (品)

    ＊ bilateral ﹝baɪ'lætərəl﹞ *adj.* 雙邊的；互惠的
       treaty ﹝'tritɪ﹞ *n.* 條約

```
counter    +  part
   |            |
matching , against + part
```

10. (**D**) This car accident is all <u>ascribed</u> to Adam's careless driving. 這次車禍全都<u>歸因於</u>亞當開車不小心。

    (A) announce ﹝ə'naʊns﹞ *v.* 宣布

    (B) affect ﹝ə'fɛkt﹞ *v.* 影響

    (C) afford ﹝ə'fɔrd﹞ *v.* 負擔得起

    (D) ***ascribe*** ﹝ə'skraɪb﹞ *v.* 歸因於

    ascribe A to B 把 A 歸因於 B

    (＝ *attribute A to B*)

```
a  +  scribe
|       |
to  +  write
```

TEST 20

Directions: *The following questions are incomplete sentences. You are to choose the one word that best completes the sentence.*

1. _____ is the emotional part of someone's character, especially how likely they are to be happy, angry etc.
   (A) Gloom
   (B) Excursion
   (C) Gravity
   (D) Temperament   (   )

2. Oil resources are not _____; luckily, now we can also use the sun's energy.
   (A) sparse
   (B) massive
   (C) finite
   (D) inexhaustible   (   )

3. Never keep valuables such as expensive _____ in your house; put them in the bank where they'll be safe.
   (A) checkbook
   (B) detergent
   (C) passport
   (D) jewelry   (   )

4. The weather seemed _____ for hiking.
   (A) advantage
   (B) hospitable
   (C) favorable
   (D) helping   (   )

5. Her strong sense of professional ambition _____ her to seek a promotion.
   (A) weakens
   (B) discourages
   (C) menaces
   (D) impels   (   )

6. Since 1972, the International Criminal Police Organization has been fighting against international _____ and drug trafficking.
   - (A) terrorism
   - (B) charity
   - (C) boycott
   - (D) tournament   (   )

7. Linda is regarded as a _____ woman because she shows much worldly experience and knowledge of fashionable life.
   - (A) juvenile
   - (B) self-centered
   - (C) cultured
   - (D) complacent   (   )

8. A _____ is a terrible event in which there is a lot of destruction or many people are injured or die.
   - (A) principle
   - (B) glimpse
   - (C) catastrophe
   - (D) hostility   (   )

9. My passport expired last month and I need to have it _____.
   - (A) purchased
   - (B) postponed
   - (C) prolonged
   - (D) renewed   (   )

10. The jury was _____ in the decision that the defendant was guilty.
    - (A) animated
    - (B) notorious
    - (C) anonymous
    - (D) unanimous   (   )

TEST 20 詳解

1. (**D**) <u>Temperament</u> is the emotional part of someone's character, especially how likely they are to be happy, angry etc.

性情即為一個人性格中感情的部分，尤其指他們易喜、易怒等的程度。

    (A) gloom〔glum〕*n.* 憂鬱

    (B) excursion〔ɪk'skɝʃən〕*n.* 遠足

    (C) gravity〔'grævətɪ〕*n.* 重力

    (D) *temperament*〔'tɛmprəmənt〕*n.* 性情

     * character〔'kærɪktɚ〕*n.* 性格

      likely〔'laɪklɪ〕*adj.* 可能的

2. (**D**) Oil resources are not <u>inexhaustible</u>; luckily, now we can also use the sun's energy.

石油資源並非<u>取之不盡、用之不竭</u>的；幸好，現在我們也可使用太陽能。

    (A) sparse〔spɑrs〕*adj.* 稀疏的

    (B) massive〔'mæsɪv〕*adj.* 大量的

    (C) finite〔'faɪnaɪt〕*adj.* 有限的

    (D) *inexhaustible*〔,ɪnɪg'zɔstəbḷ〕*adj.* 用之不竭的

     * resource〔rɪ'sors〕*n.* 資源

      energy〔'ɛnɚdʒɪ〕*n.* 能源

```
in  +  exhaust  +  ible
 |        |         |
not +    耗盡    +  可以
```

3. (**D**) Never keep valuables such as expensive <u>jewelry</u> in your house; put them in the bank where they'll be safe. 不要把貴重物品，如昂貴的<u>珠寶</u>擺在家裏；放在銀行比較安全。

    (A) checkbook〔'tʃɛk,bʊk〕*n.* 支票簿

    (B) detergent〔dɪ'tɝdʒənt〕*n.* 清潔劑

    (C) passport〔'pæs,port〕*n.* 護照

    (D) *jewelry*〔'dʒuəlrɪ〕*n.* 珠寶

    * valuables〔'væljuəblz〕*n. pl.* 貴重物品

4. (**C**) The weather seemed <u>favorable</u> for hiking.
天氣看起來很<u>適合</u>健行。

    (A) advantage〔əd'væntɪdʒ〕*n.* 優點

    (B) hospitable〔'hɑspɪtəbl〕*adj.* 好客的

    (C) *favorable*〔'fevərəbl〕*adj.* 有利的 < *for* >

    (D) helping〔'hɛlpɪŋ〕*n.* (食物的) 一份

5. (**D**) Her strong sense of professional ambition <u>impels</u> her to seek a promotion. 她強烈的事業心<u>驅使</u>她尋求升遷。

    (A) weaken〔'wikən〕*v.* 使虛弱

    (B) discourage〔dɪs'kɝɪdʒ〕*v.* 使氣餒

    (C) menace〔'mɛnɪs〕*v., n.* 威脅

    (D) *impel*〔ɪm'pɛl〕*v.* 驅使

    * ambition〔æm'bɪʃən〕*n.* 雄心
      promotion〔prə'moʃən〕*n.* 升遷

6. (**A**) Since 1972, the International Criminal Police
Organization has been fighting against international
<u>terrorism</u> and drug trafficking.

自從一九七二年以來，國際刑警組織一直在對抗國際<u>恐怖</u>
<u>行動</u>和毒品交易。

(A) ***terrorism*** 〔'tɛrə,rɪzəm 〕 *n.* 恐怖行動

(B) charity 〔'tʃærətɪ 〕 *n.* 慈善

(C) boycott 〔'bɔɪ,kɑt 〕 *n.* 抵制；杯葛

(D) tournament 〔't͡ɜnəmənt 〕 *n.* 錦標賽

* criminal 〔'krɪmənḷ 〕 *adj.* 刑事的

organization 〔,ɔrgənə'zeʃən 〕 *n.* 組織

fight against 對抗

traffic 〔'træfɪk 〕 *v.* (非法) 交易

7. (**C**) Linda is regarded as a <u>cultured</u> woman because she
shows much worldly experience and knowledge of
fashionable life.

琳達被認為是一位<u>有教養的</u>女性，因為她對世俗的閱歷頗深，
並對時尚生活相當有研究。

(A) juvenile 〔'dʒuvənḷ 〕 *adj.* 青少年的

(B) self-centered 〔'sɛlf'sɛntəd 〕 *adj.* 自我為中心的；
自私的 (= *selfish*)

(C) ***cultured*** 〔'kʌltʃəd 〕 *adj.* 有教養的

(D) complacent 〔 kəm'plesṇt 〕 *adj.* 自滿的

* worldly 〔'wɜldlɪ 〕 *adj.* 世俗的

fashionable 〔'fæʃənəbḷ 〕 *adj.* 流行的

8. (**C**) A <u>catastrophe</u> is a terrible event in which there is a lot of destruction or many people are injured or die.
所謂<u>大災難</u>即指有嚴重的破壞，或是很多人死傷的可怕事件。

    (A) principle〔'prɪnsəpl̩〕*n.* 原則

    (B) glimpse〔glɪmps〕*n.* 瞥一眼

    (C) *catastrophe*〔kə'tæstrəfɪ〕*n.* 大災難

    (D) hostility〔hɑs'tɪlətɪ〕*n.* 敵意

    ＊ destruction〔dɪ'strʌkʃən〕*n.* 破壞
       injure〔'ɪndʒɚ〕*v.* 受傷

9. (**D**) My passport expired last month and I need to have it <u>renewed</u>. 我的護照上個月到期了，我必須再拿去<u>更新</u>。

    (A) purchase〔'pɝtʃəs〕*v.,n.* 購買

    (B) postpone〔post'pon〕*v.* 拖延（＝*delay*）

    (C) prolong〔prə'lɔŋ〕*v.* 延長

    (D) *renew*〔rɪ'nju〕*v.* 更新

    ＊ expire〔ɪk'spaɪr〕*v.* 到期

10. (**D**) The jury was <u>unanimous</u> in the decision that the defendant was guilty. 陪審團<u>一致</u>決定被告有罪。

    (A) animated〔'ænə,metɪd〕*adj.* 有生氣的

    (B) notorious〔no'torɪəs〕*adj.* 惡名昭彰的

    (C) anonymous〔ə'nɑnəməs〕*adj.* 匿名的

    (D) *unanimous*〔ju'nænəməs〕*adj.* 全體一致的

    ＊ jury〔'dʒʊrɪ〕*n.* 陪審團
       decision〔dɪ'sɪʒən〕*n.* 決定
       defendant〔dɪ'fɛndənt〕*n.* 被告
       guilty〔'gɪltɪ〕*adj.* 有罪的

TEST 21

Directions: *The following questions are incomplete sentences. You are to choose the one word that best completes the sentence.*

1. We just came back from an _____ walk in the mountains.
   (A) adhesive
   (B) exhilarating
   (C) adolescent
   (D) erudite   (   )

2. The board of directors is _____ to vote on increasing the percentage of overseas investments on Wednesday.
   (A) scheduled
   (B) eliminated
   (C) intruded
   (D) extinguished   (   )

3. Most successful people say that effort was the most important _____ leading to their success.
   (A) suggestion
   (B) proposal
   (C) factor
   (D) consequence   (   )

4. The manager successfully made his branch into a _____ winner of performance awards.
   (A) frequent
   (B) commercial
   (C) populous
   (D) dominant   (   )

5. I'm going to _____ a model of a spacecraft.
   (A) soften
   (B) dial
   (C) assemble
   (D) probe   (   )

6. _____ punishment is not allowed in most schools, because it is illegal for teachers to hit students.
   (A) Capital
   (B) Corporate
   (C) Corporal
   (D) Decapitation   (   )

7. It is a _____ that in such a rich country there should be so many poor people.
   (A) paraphrase
   (B) paradox
   (C) proverb
   (D) prohibition   (   )

8. There are two _____ in the word "welfare": "wel-" and "-fare."
   (A) syllables
   (B) syllabuses
   (C) synonyms
   (D) symbols   (   )

9. To avoid contamination, surgeons wash their hands _____ before starting each operation.
   (A) hastily
   (B) reluctantly
   (C) scrupulously
   (D) extensively   (   )

10. To avoid an unnecessary abortion, couples should use effective _____ devices, for instance, condoms.
    (A) corresponding
    (B) confidential
    (C) corrosive
    (D) contraceptive   (   )

TEST 21 詳解

1. (**B**) We just came back from an <u>exhilarating</u> walk in the mountains.

我們在山上做完一趟<u>令人心情愉快</u>的步行，剛剛回來。

(A) adhesive〔əd'hisɪv〕*adj.* 有黏性的

(B) ***exhilarating***〔ɪg'zɪlə,retɪŋ〕*adj.* 令人心情愉快的；令人興奮的

(C) adolescent〔,ædḷ'ɛsṇt〕*adj.* 青春期的

(D) erudite〔'ɛru,daɪt〕*adj.* 博學的

```
ex  + hilar + at(e) + ing
 |      |       |       |
out + glad  +  v.   + adj.
```

2. (**A**) The board of directors is <u>scheduled</u> to vote on increasing the percentage of overseas investments on Wednesday.

董事會<u>預定</u>在星期三，投票表決是否要增加海外投資的比率。

(A) ***schedule***〔'skɛdʒʊl〕*v.* 排定時間；預定

(B) eliminate〔ɪ'lɪmə,net〕*v.* 消除（= *get rid of* ）

(C) intrude〔ɪn'trud〕*v.* 入侵

(D) extinguish〔ɪk'stɪŋgwɪʃ〕*v.* 熄滅（= *put out* ）

* ***board of directors*** 董事會

vote〔vot〕*v.* 投票

percentage〔pə'sɛntɪdʒ〕*n.* 百分比

overseas〔'ovə'siz〕*adj.* 海外的

investment〔ɪn'vɛstmənt〕*n.* 投資

3. (**C**) Most successful people say that effort was the most important <u>factor</u> leading to their success.

許多成功的人說，努力是導致他們成功最重要的<u>因素</u>。

(A) suggestion〔 səg'dʒɛstʃən 〕 *n.* 建議

(B) proposal〔 prə'pozḷ 〕 *n.* 提議；求婚

(C) *factor*〔'fæktɚ〕 *n.* 因素

(D) consequence〔'kɑnsə,kwɛns 〕 *n.* 結果

＊ effort〔'ɛfɚt 〕 *n.* 努力

4. (**A**) The manager successfully made his branch into a <u>frequent</u> winner of performance awards.

該名經理很成功地帶領整個分行，<u>經常</u>贏得業績獎。

(A) *frequent*〔'frikwənt 〕 *adj.* 經常的

(B) commercial〔 kə'mɝʃəl 〕 *adj.* 商業的

(C) populous〔'pɑpjələs 〕 *adj.* 人口稠密的

(D) dominant〔'dɑmənənt 〕 *adj.* 支配的

＊ branch〔 bræntʃ 〕 *n.* 分行

performance〔 pɚ'fɔrməns 〕 *n.* 性能；績效

award〔 ə'wɔrd 〕 *n.* 獎

5. (**C**) I'm going to <u>assemble</u> a model of a spacecraft.

我將要<u>組合</u>一台模型飛機。

(A) soften〔'sɔfən 〕 *v.* 軟化

(B) dial〔'daɪəl 〕 *v.* 撥號

(C) *assemble*〔 ə'sɛmbḷ 〕 *v.* 組合；裝配

(D) probe〔 prob 〕 *v.* 刺探；探索

＊ model〔'mɑdḷ 〕 *n.* 模型

spacecraft〔'spes,kræft 〕 *n.* 飛機；太空船

6. (**C**) <u>Corporal</u> punishment is not allowed in most schools, because it is illegal for teachers to hit students.

大部分學校不允許<u>體罰</u>，因為老師打學生是違法的。

    (A) capital〔'kæpətl〕*adj.* 首都的；致命的
        capital punishment 死刑
    (B) corporate〔'kɔrprɪt〕*adj.* 法人的
    (C) ***corporal***〔'kɔrprəl〕*adj.* 身體的
        corporal punishment 體罰
    (D) decapitation〔dɪ,kæpə'teʃən〕*n.* 斬首；砍頭

7. (**B**) It is a <u>paradox</u> that in such a rich country there should be so many poor people.

在如此富有的國家中，居然有這麼多窮人，真是<u>矛盾</u>。

    (A) paraphrase〔'pærə,frez〕*n.* 意譯
    (B) ***paradox***〔'pærə,daks〕*n.* 矛盾；似非而是的理論
    (C) proverb〔'pravɝb〕*n.* 諺語
    (D) prohibition〔,proə'bɪʃən〕*n.* 禁止

8. (**A**) There are two <u>syllables</u> in the word "welfare": "wel-" and "-fare."

"welfare"這個字有二個<u>音節</u>："wel-"和"-fare"。

    (A) ***syllable***〔'sɪləbl〕*n.* 音節
    (B) syllabus〔'sɪləbəs〕*n.* 課程綱要
    (C) synonym〔'sɪnə,nɪm〕*n.* 同義字
    (D) symbol〔'sɪmbl〕*n.* 象徵

    * welfare〔'wɛl,fɛr〕*n.* 福祉；福利

9. (**C**) To avoid contamination, surgeons wash their hands
<u>scrupulously</u> before starting each operation.
為了避免感染，外科醫生在開始動手術之前，會審慎地把手
洗乾淨。

    (A) hastily〔'hestɪlɪ〕*adv.* 匆忙地

    (B) reluctantly〔rɪ'lʌktəntlɪ〕*adv.* 不願意地
       (= *unwillingly*)

    (C) ***scrupulously***〔'skrupjələslɪ〕*adv.* 審慎地；
       小心翼翼地 (= *very carefully*)

    (D) extensively〔ɪk'stɛnsɪvlɪ〕*adv.* 廣泛地

    * avoid〔ə'vɔɪd〕*v.* 避免
      contamination〔kən,tæmə'neʃən〕*n.* 污染
      surgeon〔'sɝdʒən〕*n.* 外科醫生
      operation〔,ɑpə'reʃən〕*n.* 手術

10. (**D**) To avoid an unnecessary abortion, couples should
use effective <u>contraceptive</u> devices, for instance,
condoms. 為了避免不必要的墮胎，夫妻應該使用有效的
<u>避孕</u>用具，例如保險套。

    (A) corresponding〔,kɔrə'spɑndɪŋ〕*adj.* 對應的

    (B) confidential〔,kɑnfə'dɛnʃəl〕*adj.* 機密的

    (C) corrosive〔kə'rosɪv〕*adj.* 腐蝕的

    (D) ***contraceptive***〔,kɑntrə'sɛptɪv〕*adj.* 避孕的

    * abortion〔ə'bɔrʃən〕*n.* 墮胎
      effective〔ɪ'fɛktɪv〕*adj.* 有效的
      device〔dɪ'vaɪs〕*n.* 裝置；用具
      for instance 例如 (= *for example*)
      condom〔'kɑndəm〕*n.* 保險套

TEST 22

Directions: *The following questions are incomplete sentences. You are to choose the one word that best completes the sentence.*

1. His ingenuous remarks often embarrassed the audience because of their _____.
   (A) sarcasm
   (B) relevance
   (C) frankness
   (D) coherence   (   )

2. The level of indentation that seems to produce _____ results in comprehension is between 2 and 4 spaces.
   (A) optimal
   (B) inaccessible
   (C) pious
   (D) sociable   (   )

3. _____ is the receipt of the item with the letter of complaint.
   (A) Registered
   (B) Settled
   (C) Enclosed
   (D) Processed   (   )

4. The Islamic year is based on the moon and has 12 months, _____ 30 and 29 days long.
   (A) simultaneously
   (B) alternately
   (C) sluggishly
   (D) meditatively   (   )

5. Influenza is a viral disease that is extremely _____.
   (A) communicative
   (B) toxic
   (C) communicable
   (D) grateful   (   )

6. In June or July, the U.S. _____ is going to reassess trade relations with China.
   (A) Embassy
   (B) Congress
   (C) Capitol
   (D) Cabinet   (   )

7. Bill taught his dog to _____ sticks when he threw them.
   (A) retrieve
   (B) ponder
   (C) conceal
   (D) substitute   (   )

8. The doctor said that the rash was a definite _____ of the disease and that there was a cure for it.
   (A) sympathy
   (B) symphony
   (C) symmetry
   (D) symptom   (   )

9. When difficulties _____ concerning the negotiation, both parties refused to compromise.
   (A) raised
   (B) aroused
   (C) arose
   (D) rose   (   )

10. The old woman is too _____ to cross the street without her nephew's help.
    (A) mature
    (B) fluent
    (C) swift
    (D) feeble   (   )

TEST 22 詳解

1. (**C**) His ingenuous remarks often embarrassed the
audience because of their <u>frankness</u>.
他率直的言論常使觀衆很困窘，因爲他的話太<u>坦白</u>了。

    (A) sarcasm〔'sɑrkæzəm〕 *n.* 諷刺

    (B) relevance〔'rɛləvəns〕 *n.* 關連

    (C) *frankness*〔'fræŋknɪs〕 *n.* 坦白

    (D) coherence〔ko'hɪrəns〕 *n.* 有條理

    * ingenuous〔ɪn'dʒɛnjuəs〕 *adj.* 率直的
        remark〔rɪ'mɑrk〕 *n.* 評論；話
        embarrass〔ɪm'bærəs〕 *v.* 使困窘
        audience〔'ɔdɪəns〕 *n.* 觀衆

2. (**A**) The level of indentation that seems to produce
<u>optimal</u> results in comprehension is between 2 and
4 spaces. 段落縮排能達成<u>最佳</u>理解效果，大約是二至四格。

    (A) *optimal*〔'ɑptəməl〕 *adj.* 最理想的；最適合的

    (B) inaccessible〔,ɪnək'sɛsəbḷ〕 *adj.* 達不到的；
        無法接近的

    (C) pious〔'paɪəs〕 *adj.* 虔誠的

    (D) sociable〔'soʃəbḷ〕 *adj.* 善交際的

    * level〔'lɛvḷ〕 *n.* 程度
        indentation〔,ɪndɛn'teʃən〕 *n.* (段落開端的) 縮排
        comprehension〔,kɑmprɪ'hɛnʃən〕 *n.* 理解
        space〔spes〕 *n.* 空白

3. (**C**) <u>Enclosed</u> is the receipt of the item with the letter of complaint. 除了抱怨信外，順便<u>附寄</u>該項商品的收據。

   (A) register〔'rɛdʒɪstə〕 v. 登記；掛號

   (B) settle〔'sɛtḷ〕 v. 解決

   (C) **enclose**〔ɪn'kloz〕 v. 附寄

   (D) process〔'prɑsɛs〕 v. 加工

4. (**B**) The Islamic year is based on the moon and has 12 months, <u>alternately</u> 30 and 29 days long.

   回敎的年是根據月球來計算的，一年有十二個月，分爲三十天、二十九天二種，<u>互相交替</u>。

   (A) simultaneously〔ˌsaɪmḷ'tenɪəslɪ〕 adv. 同時地

   (B) **alternately**〔'ɔltəˌnɪtlɪ〕 adv. 輪流地；交替地

   (C) sluggishly〔'slʌgɪʃlɪ〕 adv. 遲鈍地

   (D) meditatively〔'mɛdəˌtetɪvlɪ〕 adv. 沉思地

   * Islamic〔ɪs'læmɪk〕 adj. 回敎的
     be based on 以～爲根據

5. (**C**) Influenza is a viral disease that is extremely <u>communicable</u>.

   流行性感冒是由濾過性病毒引起的疾病，具<u>有</u>高度<u>傳染性</u>。

   (A) communicative〔kə'mjunɪˌketɪv〕 adj. 健談的

   (B) toxic〔'tɑksɪk〕 adj. 有毒的

   (C) **communicable**〔kə'mjunɪkəbḷ〕 adj. 會傳染的

   (D) grateful〔'gretfəl〕 adj. 感激的

   * influenza〔ˌɪnfluˈɛnzə〕 n. 流行性感冒
     viral〔'vaɪrəl〕 adj. 濾過性病毒引起的

6. (**B**) In June or July, the U.S. <u>Congress</u> is going to reassess trade relations with China.

在六月或七月，美國<u>國會</u>將重新評估與中國的貿易關係。

   (A) embassy〔ˈɛmbəsɪ〕*n.* 大使館

   (B) ***Congress***〔ˈkɑŋgrəs〕*n.* 國會

   (C) Capitol〔ˈkæpətḷ〕*n.* 國會山莊

   (D) Cabinet〔ˈkæbənɪt〕*n.* 內閣

    * reassess〔ˌriəˈsɛs〕*v.* 重新評估

7. (**A**) Bill taught his dog to <u>retrieve</u> sticks when he threw them. 比爾教他的狗，當他把棍子丟出去，牠會去<u>撿回來</u>。

   (A) ***retrieve***〔rɪˈtriv〕*v.* 取回

   (B) ponder〔ˈpɑndɚ〕*v.* 沉思

   (C) conceal〔kənˈsil〕*v.* 隱藏

   (D) substitute〔ˈsʌbstəˌtjut〕*v.* 代替

    * stick〔stɪk〕*n.* 棍子

8. (**D**) The doctor said that the rash was a definite <u>symptom</u> of the disease and that there was a cure for it.

醫生說，出疹子是這種疾病很明確的<u>症狀</u>，也有治療方法。

   (A) sympathy〔ˈsɪmpəθɪ〕*n.* 同情

   (B) symphony〔ˈsɪmfənɪ〕*n.* 交響樂

   (C) symmetry〔ˈsɪmɪtrɪ〕*n.* 對稱

   (D) ***symptom***〔ˈsɪmptəm〕*n.* 症狀

    * rash〔ræʃ〕*n.* 疹子

     definite〔ˈdɛfənɪt〕*adj.* 明確的

9. (**C**) When difficulties <u>arose</u> concerning the negotiation, both parties refused to compromise.

當協商<u>產生</u>困難時，雙方都拒絕妥協。

(A) raise〔rez〕*v.* 舉起；提高（為及物動詞）

(B) arouse〔ə'rauz〕*v.* 喚醒（情緒）（為及物動詞）

(C) *arise*〔ə'raɪz〕*v.*（抽象事情）產生；發生

（為不及物動詞）

(D) rise〔raɪz〕*v.*（太陽）升起；（價格、溫度等）上升

（為不及物動詞）

* concerning〔kən'sɝnɪŋ〕*prep.* 有關（= *about*）

negotiation〔nɪ,goʃɪ'eʃən〕*n.* 協商；談判

party〔'partɪ〕*n.* 一方；關係人

compromise〔'kamprə,maɪz〕*v.* 妥協

< *with sb. on sth.* >

10. (**D**) The old woman is too <u>feeble</u> to cross the street without her nephew's help.

這位老婦人太<u>虛弱</u>了，沒有她姪子的幫助，無法過馬路。

(A) mature〔mə'tjʊr〕*adj.* 成熟的

(B) fluent〔'fluənt〕*adj.* 流利的

(C) swift〔swɪft〕*adj.* 迅速的

(D) *feeble*〔'fibl̩〕*adj.* 虛弱的（= *weak*）

* nephew〔'nɛfju〕*n.* 姪兒；外甥

TEST 23

Directions: *The following questions are incomplete sentences. You are to choose the one word that best completes the sentence.*

1. Clothing made of artificial _____ does not decompose the way natural things do.
   (A) organs
   (B) linings
   (C) genes
   (D) fibers   (　　)

2. Researchers said Taiwanese youths were becoming too fat because they had poor _____ habits.
   (A) dietitian
   (B) dietary
   (C) diary
   (D) dairy   (　　)

3. When the king _____ his throne, his brother succeeded him.
   (A) exploited
   (B) deprived
   (C) flattered
   (D) abdicated   (　　)

4. Since there are many ethnic groups in Taiwan, it is hard to reach a _____ on this political issue.
   (A) consensus
   (B) conservation
   (C) conference
   (D) conquest   (　　)

5. He is a _____; he does not eat any meat at all.
   (A) veteran
   (B) veterinarian
   (C) vegetarian
   (D) gourmet   (　　)

6. The doctor _____ her illness as pneumonia and she was hospitalized immediately.
   (A) diagnosed
   (B) sponsored
   (C) neutralized
   (D) fetched   (   )

7. A _____ examination is needed to conclude the cause of death.
   (A) postmodern
   (B) postmortem
   (C) posthumous
   (D) postscript   (   )

8. Rod got _____ in a serious crime while trying to help a friend in trouble.
   (A) entangled
   (B) ensured
   (C) accommodated
   (D) displayed   (   )

9. Today more and more people rarely consider the _____ of their actions, so the crime rate has been rising.
   (A) tradition
   (B) morality
   (C) evidence
   (D) patent   (   )

10. The management has decided to take a series of _____ measures.
    (A) furious
    (B) bankrupt
    (C) devout
    (D) expedient   (   )

TEST 23 詳解

1. (**D**) Clothing made of artificial <u>fibers</u> does not decompose the way natural things do.

人造纖維做成的衣物，不會像天然材質一般分解掉。

    (A) organ〔'ɔrgən〕*n.* 器官

    (B) lining〔'laɪnɪŋ〕*n.* 襯裏

    (C) gene〔dʒin〕*n.* 基因

    (D) *fiber*〔'faɪbɚ〕*n.* 纖維

    ＊ artificial〔,artə'fɪʃəl〕*adj.* 人造的

        decompose〔,dikəm'poz〕*v.* 分解

2. (**B**) Researchers said Taiwanese youths were becoming too fat because they had poor <u>dietary</u> habits.

研究人員說，台灣的年輕人變得太胖，是因爲<u>飲食</u>習慣不良。

    (A) dietitian〔,daɪə'tɪʃən〕*n.* 營養師

    (B) *dietary*〔'daɪə,tɛrɪ〕*adj.* 飲食的

    (C) diary〔'daɪərɪ〕*n.* 日記

    (D) dairy〔'dɛrɪ〕*n.* 酪農場

3. (**D**) When the king <u>abdicated</u> his throne, his brother succeeded him. 國王<u>退位</u>之後，他的弟弟繼承王位。

    (A) exploit〔ɪk'splɔɪt〕*v.* 開發；剝削

    (B) deprive〔dɪ'praɪv〕*v.* 剝奪

    (C) flatter〔'flætɚ〕*v.* 諂媚

    (D) *abdicate*〔'æbdə,ket〕*v.* 放棄；退（位）

    ＊ throne〔θron〕*n.* 王位   succeed〔sək'sid〕*v.* 繼承

4. (**A**) Since there are many ethnic groups in Taiwan, it is hard to reach a <u>consensus</u> on this political issue.

由於台灣有許多種族團體，關於這個政治議題，很難達成<u>共識</u>。

    (A) *consensus*〔kən'sɛnsəs〕 *n.* 共識

    (B) conservation〔͵kɑnsə'veʃən〕 *n.* 保育

    (C) conference〔'kɑnfərəns〕 *n.* 會議

    (D) conquest〔'kɑŋkwɛst〕 *n.* 征服

    * ethnic〔'ɛθnɪk〕 *adj.* 種族的
      political〔pə'lɪtɪkl̩〕 *adj.* 政治的
      issue〔'ɪʃjʊ〕 *n.* 議題

con +	sens	+ us
all +	*sense , feel* +	*n.*

5. (**C**) He is a <u>vegetarian</u>; he does not eat any meat at all.

他是個<u>素食者</u>；他不吃任何肉類。

    (A) veteran〔'vɛtərən〕 *n.* 退伍軍人；老兵

    (B) veterinarian〔͵vɛtərə'nɛrɪən〕 *n.* 獸醫 (= *vet*)

    (C) *vegetarian*〔͵vɛdʒə'tɛrɪən〕 *n.* 素食者

    (D) gourmet〔'gʊrme〕 *n.* 美食家

6. (**A**) The doctor <u>diagnosed</u> her illness as pneumonia and
she was hospitalized immediately.
醫生診斷她的病是肺炎，她立刻住進醫院。

   (A) ***diagnose***〔͵daɪəg'noz〕 v. 診斷
   (B) sponsor〔'spɑnsɚ〕 v. 贊助
   (C) neutralize〔'njutrəl͵aɪz〕 v. 使中和；中立
   (D) fetch〔fɛtʃ〕 v. 去取來

   ＊pneumonia〔nju'monjə〕 n. 肺炎
   hospitalize〔'hɑspɪtl͵aɪz〕 v. 使住院

7. (**B**) A <u>postmortem</u> examination is needed to conclude
the cause of death. 為確定死因為何，必須要驗屍。

   (A) postmodern〔post'mɑdɚn〕 adj. 後現代的
   (B) ***postmortem***〔post'mɔrtəm〕 adj. 死後的
   postmortem examination 驗屍
   (C) posthumous〔'pɑstʃuməs〕 adj. 死後出版、出生的
   (D) postscript〔'pos‧skrɪpt〕 n. 附註（略為 p.s.）

   ＊conclude〔kən'klud〕 v. 確定

8. (**A**) Rod got <u>entangled</u> in a serious crime while trying
to help a friend in trouble.
羅德試著想幫助一位有難的朋友，卻被捲入一宗重案。

   (A) ***entangle***〔ɪn'tæŋgl̩〕 v. 連累；捲入 <in>
   (B) ensure〔ɪn'ʃur〕 v. 保證
   (C) accommodate〔ə'kɑmə͵det〕 v. 容納
   (D) display〔dɪ'sple〕 v. 展示

9. (**B**) Today more and more people rarely consider the
<u>morality</u> of their actions, so the crime rate has
been rising.

今日，越來越多人很少考慮到自己的行爲是否合乎<u>道德</u>，
因此犯罪率一直在上升。

　　(A) tradition〔trəˋdɪʃən〕*n.* 傳統

　　(B) *morality*〔mɔˋrælətɪ〕*n.* 道德

　　(C) evidence〔ˋɛvədəns〕*n.* 證據

　　(D) patent〔ˋpætn̩t〕*n.* 專利

　　* rarely〔ˋrɛrlɪ〕*adv.* 很少（= *seldom*）
　　　crime rate 犯罪率

10. (**D**) The management has decided to take a series of
<u>expedient</u> measures. 資方決定採取一連串的<u>權宜</u>措施。

　　(A) furious〔ˋfjʊrɪəs〕*adj.* 憤怒的

　　(B) bankrupt〔ˋbæŋkrʌpt〕*adj.* 破產的

　　(C) devout〔dɪˋvaʊt〕*adj.* 虔誠的

　　(D) *expedient*〔ɪkˋspidɪənt〕*adj.* 權宜的

　　* *the management* 資方　　*a series of* 一系列的
　　　measure〔ˋmɛʒɚ〕*n.* 措施

```
ex   +  ped  +  ient
 |       |       |
out  +  foot  +  adj. ( 有助於前進的 )
```

TEST 24

Directions: *The following questions are incomplete sentences. You are to choose the one word that best completes the sentence.*

1. Don't put the glass at the _____ of the table; it may fall.
   (A) frontier
   (B) edge
   (C) angle
   (D) corner   (   )

2. People in that country _____ a lot of coffee and drink a large amount of alcohol.
   (A) admit
   (B) presume
   (C) submit
   (D) consume   (   )

3. Many big cities have _____ because of the global economic recession.
   (A) disconnected
   (B) decreased
   (C) deteriorated
   (D) dislocated   (   )

4. _____ qualities are important for achievement in coaching a basketball team.
   (A) Countenance
   (B) Fantasy
   (C) Leadership
   (D) Physics   (   )

5. The news of the businessman's kidnapping and murder _____ the country.
   (A) atoned
   (B) dumbfounded
   (C) alerted
   (D) incited   (   )

6. If you are ill, you should go and _____ a physician.
   - (A) consult
   - (B) result
   - (C) insult
   - (D) examine   (   )

7. Though women make valuable contributions, they have not been able to _____ the same social and economic status as men.
   - (A) retain
   - (B) pretend
   - (C) attain
   - (D) contain   (   )

8. In order to settle the strike, both management and labor have to make _____.
   - (A) medications
   - (B) interpretations
   - (C) concessions
   - (D) recessions   (   )

9. Some people are _____ and learn only those things for which they see immediate value.
   - (A) realistic
   - (B) remote
   - (C) industrious
   - (D) industrial   (   )

10. Union and management hope they can _____ a contract before the workers strike.
   - (A) negotiate
   - (B) reciprocate
   - (C) stipulate
   - (D) correlate   (   )

TEST 24 詳解

1. (**B**) Don't put the glass at the <u>edge</u> of the table; it may fall.

不要把杯子放在桌<u>邊</u>；可能會掉下去。

    (A) frontier〔frʌn'tɪr〕 *n.* 邊界；邊疆

    (B) *edge*〔ɛdʒ〕 *n.* 邊緣

    (C) angle〔'æŋgl̩〕 *n.* 角度

    (D) corner〔'kɔrnɚ〕 *n.* 角落

2. (**D**) People in that country <u>consume</u> a lot of coffee and drink a large amount of alcohol.

那個國家的人咖啡和酒都<u>喝</u>很多。

    (A) admit〔əd'mɪt〕 *v.* 承認；許入

    (B) presume〔prɪ'zum〕 *v.* 假定

    (C) submit〔səb'mɪt〕 *v.* 屈服

    (D) *consume*〔kən'sum , -'sjum〕 *v.* 消耗；吃（喝）

3. (**C**) Many big cities have <u>deteriorated</u> because of the global economic recession.

由於全球經濟衰退，許多大都市都已<u>墮落</u>。

    (A) disconnect〔ˌdɪskə'nɛkt〕 *v.* 分開

    (B) decrease〔dɪ'kris〕 *v.* 減少

    (C) *deteriorate*〔dɪ'tɪrɪəˌret〕 *v.* 墮落；惡化

    (D) dislocate〔'dɪsloˌket〕 *v.* 使脫離原位

    ＊ global〔'globl̩〕 *adj.* 全球的

      recession〔rɪ'sɛʃən〕 *n.*（經濟）衰退

4. (**C**) <u>Leadership</u> qualities are important for achievement in coaching a basketball team.

想要擔任教練來訓練籃球隊，<u>領導能力</u>的特質十分重要。

(A) countenance〔'kaʊntənəns〕 *n.* 面容

(B) fantasy〔'fæntəsɪ〕 *n.* 幻想

(C) ***leadership***〔'lidɚˏʃɪp〕 *n.* 領導能力

(D) physics〔'fɪzɪks〕 *n.* 物理學

＊ quality〔'kwɑlətɪ〕 *n.* 特質

achievement〔ə'tʃivmənt〕 *n.* 成就；達成

coach〔kotʃ〕 *v.* 擔任教練；訓練

5. (**B**) The news of the businessman's kidnapping and murder <u>dumbfounded</u> the country.

該名商人被綁架撕票的新聞<u>震驚</u>全國。

(A) atone〔ə'ton〕 *v.* 彌補 *< for >*

(B) ***dumbfound***〔dʌm'faʊnd〕 *v.* 使驚愕 (*= astonish*)

(C) alert〔ə'lɝt〕 *v.* 使警覺

(D) incite〔ɪn'saɪt〕 *v.* 激起；煽動

＊ kidnap〔'kɪdnæp〕 *v.* 綁架

6. (**A**) If you are ill, you should go and <u>consult</u> a physician.

如果你生病了，你應該去<u>看</u>醫生。

(A) ***consult***〔kən'sʌlt〕 *v.* 請教

(B) result〔rɪ'zʌlt〕 *v.* 導致 *< in >*；起因於 *< from >*

(C) insult〔ɪn'sʌlt〕 *v.* 侮辱

(D) examine〔ɪg'zæmɪn〕 *v.* 檢查；測驗

＊ physician〔fə'zɪʃən〕 *n.* (內科) 醫生

7. (**C**) Though women make valuable contributions, they have not been able to <u>attain</u> the same social and economic status as men.

雖然女性有寶貴的貢獻，但她們仍無法<u>達到</u>和男性一樣的社會、經濟地位。

    (A) retain〔rɪˋten〕*v.* 保留

    (B) pretend〔prɪˋtɛnd〕*v.* 假裝

    (C) *attain*〔əˋten〕*v.* 達到 (= *achieve*)

    (D) contain〔kənˋten〕*v.* 包含

    ＊ contribution〔͵kɑntrəˋbjuʃən〕*n.* 貢獻
        status〔ˋstetəs〕*n.* 地位

8. (**C**) In order to settle the strike, both management and labor have to make <u>concessions</u>.

為了要解決罷工，勞資雙方都必須<u>讓步</u>。

    (A) medication〔͵mɛdɪˋkeʃən〕*n.* 藥物

    (B) interpretation〔ɪn͵tɝprɪˋteʃən〕*n.* 解釋

    (C) *concession*〔kənˋsɛʃən〕*n.* 讓步

    (D) recession〔rɪˋsɛʃən〕*n.* 衰退

    ＊ settle〔ˋsɛtl̩〕*v.* 解決   strike〔straɪk〕*n.* 罷工
        management〔ˋmænɪdʒmənt〕*n.* 資方
        labor〔ˋlebɚ〕*n.* 勞方

con	+	cess	+	ion
|		|		|
together	+	*go*	+	*n.*

re	+	cess	+	ion
|		|		|
back	+	*go*	+	*n.*

9. (**A**) Some people are <u>realistic</u> and learn only those things for which they see immediate value.

有些人非常<u>現實</u>，只學那些他們認為立刻有用的東西。

(A) *realistic* 〔ˌriəˈlɪstɪk 〕 *adj.* 現實的

(B) remote 〔 rɪˈmot 〕 *adj.* 遙遠的

(C) industrious 〔 ɪnˈdʌstrɪəs 〕 *adj.* 勤奮的 (= *diligent*)

(D) industrial 〔 ɪnˈdʌstrɪəl 〕 *adj.* 工業的

cf. industry 〔ˈɪndʌstrɪ 〕 *n.* 勤奮；工業

industr + ious	industr + ial
勤奮 + *adj.*	工業 + *adj.*

10. (**A**) Union and management hope they can <u>negotiate</u> a contract before the workers strike.

勞資雙方希望能在員工罷工之前，<u>商訂</u>一個契約。

(A) *negotiate* 〔 nɪˈgoʃɪˌet 〕 *v.* 商訂

(B) reciprocate 〔 rɪˈsɪprəˌket 〕 *v.* 回報

(C) stipulate 〔ˈstɪpjəˌlet 〕 *v.* 規定；約定

(D) correlate 〔ˈkɔrəˌlet 〕 *v.* 有相互關係 < *with* >

* union 〔ˈjunjən 〕 *n.* 工會

contract 〔ˈkɑntrækt 〕 *n.* 契約

strike 〔 straɪk 〕 *v.* 罷工

TEST 25

Directions: *The following questions are incomplete sentences. You are to choose the one word that best completes the sentence.*

1. I am very _____ about whether I can pass the examination.
   (A) sorrowful
   (B) nervous
   (C) emphasis
   (D) content   (   )

2. I heard that Mr. Wang is Chris's _____ father, not his real father.
   (A) adoptive
   (B) biological
   (C) legal
   (D) adaptive   (   )

3. Although _____ efforts have been made, the work still needs to be improved.
   (A) selective
   (B) elective
   (C) considerable
   (D) considerate   (   )

4. His suggestion was so _____ that no one would even consider it.
   (A) significant
   (B) ridiculous
   (C) poisonous
   (D) contemporary   (   )

5. Your daily diet should _____ fruits and vegetables.
   (A) include
   (B) exclude
   (C) resist
   (D) proceed   (   )

6. Some people cannot borrow money from the bank because they do not own any real _____.

   (A) capacity
   (B) ownership
   (C) possession
   (D) estate   (   )

7. In today's society, there are lots of so-called single-parent families, where children live with just one of their parents, usually after a _____.

   (A) segregation
   (B) divorce
   (C) pursue
   (D) lawsuit   (   )

8. New discoveries enable scientists to explain why off-spring should _____ or differ from their parents.

   (A) mimic
   (B) accomplish
   (C) resemble
   (D) terrify   (   )

9. Despite his declination, we still _____ on his coming to the party.

   (A) contracted
   (B) contacted
   (C) insisted
   (D) persisted   (   )

10. In order to _____ Chinese, Sylvia stayed in main-land China for ten years.

   (A) multiply
   (B) memorize
   (C) maintain
   (D) master   (   )

TEST 25 詳解

1. (**B**) I am very <u>nervous</u> about whether I can pass the examination.　我很緊張不知是否能通過考試。

    (A) sorrowful〔'sɑrofəl〕*adj.* 悲傷的

    (B) ***nervous***〔'nɝvəs〕*adj.* 緊張的

    (C) emphasis〔'ɛmfəsɪs〕*n.* 強調

    (D) content〔kən'tɛnt〕*adj.* 滿足的 < *with* >

2. (**A**) I heard that Mr. Wang is Chris's <u>adoptive</u> father, not his real father.

    我聽說，王先生是克利斯的養父，而非他眞正的父親。

    (A) ***adoptive***〔ə'dɑptɪv〕*adj.* 收養的
        adoptive father 養父

    (B) biological〔‚baɪə'lɑdʒɪkl̩〕*adj.* 生物學的
        biological father 生父

    (C) legal〔'ligl̩〕*adj.* 合法的；法律的

    (D) adaptive〔ə'dæptɪv〕*adj.* 適應的

3. (**C**) Although <u>considerable</u> efforts have been made, the work still needs to be improved.

    雖然已做了<u>相當多的</u>努力，這個工作仍需改善。

    (A) selective〔sə'lɛktɪv〕*adj.* 精選的

    (B) elective〔ɪ'lɛktɪv〕*adj.* 選舉的；選修的

    (C) ***considerable***〔kən'sɪdərəbl̩〕*adj.* 相當多的

    (D) considerate〔kən'sɪdərɪt〕*adj.* 體貼的

4. (**B**) His suggestion was so <u>ridiculous</u> that no one would even consider it.

他的建議如此<u>荒謬</u>，根本沒人會考慮採用。

    (A) significant〔sɪg'nɪfəkənt〕*adj.* 重要的

    (B) ***ridiculous***〔rɪ'dɪkjələs〕*adj.* 荒謬的 (= *absurd*)

    (C) poisonous〔'pɔɪznəs〕*adj.* 有毒的 (= *toxic*)

    (D) contemporary〔kən'tɛmpə‚rɛrɪ〕*adj.* 當代的；
同時代的

5. (**A**) Your daily diet should <u>include</u> fruits and vegetables.

你的日常飲食應該要<u>包括</u>水果和蔬菜在內。

    (A) ***include***〔ɪn'klud〕*v.* 包括

    (B) exclude〔ɪk'sklud〕*v.* 排除在外

    (C) resist〔rɪ'zɪst〕*v.* 抵抗

    (D) proceed〔prə'sid〕*v.* 前進

    * daily〔'delɪ〕*adj.* 日常的   diet〔'daɪət〕*n.* 飲食

6. (**D**) Some people cannot borrow money from the bank because they do not own any real <u>estate</u>.

有些人無法向銀行借錢，因為他們沒有任何<u>不動產</u>。

    (A) capacity〔kə'pæsətɪ〕*n.* 容量

    (B) ownership〔'onə‚ʃɪp〕*n.* 所有權

    (C) possession〔pə'zɛʃən〕*n.* 財產；所有物
（常用複數形）

    (D) ***estate***〔ə'stet〕*n.* 財產；地產

    real estate 不動產；房地產 (= *real property*)

7. (**B**) In today's society, there are lots of so-called single-parent families, where children live with just one of their parents, usually after a <u>divorce</u>.

今日社會上有很多所謂的單親家庭，小孩和父母其中一方住在一起，通常是在<u>離婚</u>之後。

    (A) segregation〔ˌsɛgrɪˈgeʃən〕*n.* 隔離

    (B) ***divorce***〔dəˈvors〕*n., v.* 離婚

    (C) pursue〔pəˈsu〕*v.* 追求

    (D) lawsuit〔ˈlɔˌsut〕*n.* 訴訟

    * so-called〔ˈsoˈkɔld〕*adj.* 所謂的

8. (**C**) New discoveries enable scientists to explain why offspring should <u>resemble</u> or differ from their parents.

新發現讓科學家能夠解釋，小孩為何會和父母<u>相像</u>或不像。

    (A) mimic〔ˈmɪmɪk〕*v.* 模仿

    (B) accomplish〔əˈkamplɪʃ〕*v.* 達成

    (C) ***resemble***〔rɪˈzɛmbḷ〕*v.* 相像（= *take after*）

       （為及物動詞，直接接受詞）

    (D) terrify〔ˈtɛrəˌfaɪ〕*v.* 使驚恐

    * offspring〔ˈɔfˌsprɪŋ〕*n.* 後代子孫

re	+	semble
|		|
again +		*same*（再看也是一樣）

9. (**C**) Despite his declination, we still <u>insisted</u> on his coming to the party.

儘管他婉拒了，我們仍然<u>堅持</u>要他來參加宴會。

    (A) contract〔kənˋtrækt〕 *v.* 訂契約

    (B) contact〔kənˋtækt〕 *v.* 接觸；聯絡

    (C) *insist*〔ɪnˋsɪst〕 *v.* 堅持 < *on* >

    (D) persist〔pɚˋsɪst〕 *v.* 堅持 < *in* >

    ＊ despite〔dɪˋspaɪt〕 *prep.* 儘管 (= *in spite of*)
      declination〔͵dɛkləˋneʃən〕 *n.* 婉拒

in + sist	per + sist
| |	| |
in + stand	*through + stand*

10. (**D**) In order to <u>master</u> Chinese, Sylvia stayed in main-land China for ten years.

為了<u>精通</u>中文，西維亞在中國大陸待了十年。

    (A) multiply〔ˋmʌltə͵plaɪ〕 *v.* 繁殖

    (B) memorize〔ˋmɛmə͵raɪz〕 *v.* 背誦

    (C) maintain〔menˋten〕 *v.* 維持

    (D) *master*〔ˋmæstɚ〕 *v.* 精通

    ＊ mainland〔ˋmen͵lænd〕 *n.* 本土；大陸

TEST 26

Directions: *The following questions are incomplete sentences. You are to choose the one word that best completes the sentence.*

1. The man gave the taxi driver a small _____ for his honesty.
   (A) award
   (B) fee
   (C) reward
   (D) favor   (   )

2. Generally speaking, a college student can understand English spoken at a _____ speed.
   (A) normal
   (B) marvelous
   (C) harmonious
   (D) heavenly   (   )

3. The events of the story were told in _____ order.
   (A) phonetic
   (B) standard
   (C) chronological
   (D) telegraphic   (   )

4. Frequent demonstrations have _____ the traffic problems in the city.
   (A) altered
   (B) terminated
   (C) aggravated
   (D) soothed   (   )

5. The sound of our voices was completely _____ out by the roar of the machinery.
   (A) reduced
   (B) scattered
   (C) uncovered
   (D) drowned   (   )

6. The term paper is _____ in two days, and yet I've been unable to find all the books I need for writing it.
   (A) deadline
   (B) due
   (C) out-of-date
   (D) updated   (   )

7. The _____ of world chess grandmaster Kasparov by IBM's Deep Blue computer triggered a debate over intelligence.
   (A) failure
   (B) fight
   (C) defeat
   (D) beat   (   )

8. We can follow a baby's _____ development by observing how he learns to know objects around him.
   (A) imaginary
   (B) supernatural
   (C) conventional
   (D) intellectual   (   )

9. We couldn't carry the bags ourselves so we called for the _____, who was paid to carry luggage.
   (A) chauffeur
   (B) servant
   (C) porter
   (D) butler   (   )

10. It is time to _____ all those old and useless magazines and newspapers.
    (A) delete
    (B) discard
    (C) devise
    (D) disagree   (   )

TEST 26 詳解

1. (**C**) The man gave the taxi driver a small <u>reward</u> for his honesty.

這位男人給了計程車司機些許<u>報酬</u>，以感謝他的誠實。

(A) award〔ə'wɔrd〕*n.*（參加競賽、甄選所得的）獎；獎品；獎金

(B) fee〔fi〕*n.*（付給專業人士的）費用；入場費；入會費

(C) *reward*〔rɪ'wɔrd〕*n.*（付出勞力、服務等所得的）報酬

(D) favor〔'fevɚ〕*n.* 恩惠

2. (**A**) Generally speaking, a college student can understand English spoken at a <u>normal</u> speed.

一般說來，大學生可以聽懂以<u>正常</u>速度說出的英文。

(A) *normal*〔'nɔrml̩〕*adj.* 正常的

(B) marvelous〔'mɑrvl̩əs〕*adj.* 極好的

(C) harmonious〔hɑr'monɪəs〕*adj.* 和諧的

(D) heavenly〔'hɛvənlɪ〕*adj.* 天堂般的

3. (**C**) The events of the story were told in <u>chronological</u> order. 這個故事中的事件是<u>按照年代順序</u>來敘述。

(A) phonetic〔fo'nɛtɪk〕*adj.* 語音的

(B) standard〔'stændɚd〕*adj.* 標準的

(C) *chronological*〔ˌkrɑnə'lɑdʒɪkl̩〕*adj.* 按年代順序的

(D) telegraphic〔ˌtɛlə'græfɪk〕*adj.* 電報的

* event〔ɪ'vɛnt〕*n.* 事件　　order〔'ɔrdɚ〕*n.* 順序

4. (**C**) Frequent demonstrations have <u>aggravated</u> the traffic problems in the city.

經常舉行的示威遊行，<u>使</u>市區的交通問題<u>惡化</u>。

(A) alter〔'ɔltɚ〕*v.* 改變（= *change*）

(B) terminate〔'tɜməˌnet〕*v.* 終止（= *end*）

(C) ***aggravate***〔'ægrəˌvet〕*v.* 惡化
   （= *make worse*；*deteriorate*）

(D) soothe〔suð〕*v.* 使平靜

* frequent〔'frikwənt〕*adj.* 經常的
  demonstration〔ˌdɛmən'streʃən〕*n.* 示威遊行

```
ag + grav + ate
 |     |      |
to + heavy +  v.
```

5. (**D**) The sound of our voices was completely <u>drowned</u> out by the roar of the machinery.

我們的聲音完全被機器的轟鳴聲所<u>掩蓋</u>。

(A) reduce〔rɪ'djus〕*v.* 減少

(B) scatter〔'skætɚ〕*v.* 散播

(C) uncover〔ʌn'kʌvɚ〕*v.* 揭開

(D) ***drown***〔draun〕*v.* 淹沒；掩蓋 < *out* >

* roar〔ror〕*n.* 轟鳴聲
  machinery〔mə'ʃinərɪ〕*n.* 機器（總稱、不可數名詞）

6. (**B**) The term paper is <u>due</u> in two days, and yet I've been unable to find all the books I need for writing it.

學期報告再過二天就要交了，然而我還無法找齊所有寫報告所需的書。

 (A) deadline (ˈdɛdˌlaɪn) *n.* 最後期限

 (B) ***due*** (dju) *adj.* 到期的；該交付的

 (C) out-of-date (ˈaʊtəvˈdet) *adj.* 過時的 (= *outdated*)

 (D) updated (ʌpˈdetɪd) *adj.* 最新的 (= *up-to-date*)

  * term (tɜm) *n.* 學期

7. (**C**) The <u>defeat</u> of world chess grandmaster Kasparov by IBM's Deep Blue computer triggered a debate over intelligence.

世界棋王卡斯沛洛夫被 IBM 的電腦深藍擊敗，引發了一場關於智力的爭辯。

 (A) failure (ˈfeljɚ) *n.* 失敗 (後面不接 *by* ~)

 (B) fight (faɪt) *n., v.* 打仗；爭奪

 (C) ***defeat*** (dɪˈfit) *n., v.* 擊敗

 (D) beat (bit) *n.* 敲打；拍子

   v. 敲打；擊敗 (= *defeat*)；跳動

  * grandmaster (ˈgrændˌmæstɚ) *n.* 大師；頂尖高手

  trigger (ˈtrɪgɚ) *v.* 引發

  debate (dɪˈbet) *n.* 爭辯

  intelligence (ɪnˈtɛlədʒəns) *n.* 智力

8. (**D**) We can follow a baby's <u>intellectual</u> development by observing how he learns to know objects around him.

藉由觀察小嬰兒如何學習認識周遭物品，我們可以追蹤他的智力發展。

    (A) imaginary〔ɪˈmædʒəˌnɛrɪ〕 *adj.* 想像的

    (B) supernatural〔ˌsupɚˈnætʃərəl〕 *adj.* 超自然的

    (C) conventional〔kənˈvɛnʃən̩〕 *adj.* 傳統的

    (D) *intellectual*〔ˌɪntl̩ˈɛktʃʊəl〕 *adj.* 智力的

    * observe〔əbˈzɝv〕 *v.* 觀察

9. (**C**) We couldn't carry the bags ourselves so we called for the <u>porter</u>, who was paid to carry luggage.

我們無法自己去提袋子，所以我們付錢請<u>挑夫</u>來提行李。

    (A) chauffeur〔ʃoˈfɝ〕 *n.* 私家汽車司機

    (B) servant〔ˈsɝvənt〕 *n.* 僕人

    (C) *porter*〔ˈportɚ〕 *n.* 挑夫；行李搬運工

    (D) butler〔ˈbʌtlɚ〕 *n.* 男管家；僕役長

    * *call for* 要求；去叫～　　luggage〔ˈlʌgɪdʒ〕 *n.* 行李

10. (**B**) It is time to <u>discard</u> all those old and useless magazines and newspapers.

所有那些沒有用的舊雜誌、舊報紙都該<u>丟</u>了。

    (A) delete〔dɪˈlit〕 *v.* 刪除

    (B) *discard*〔dɪsˈkɑrd〕 *v.* 丟棄（廢物等）

    (C) devise〔dɪˈvaɪz〕 *v.* 設計

    (D) disagree〔ˌdɪsəˈgri〕 *v.* 不同意

TEST 27

Directions: *The following questions are incomplete sentences. You are to choose the one word that best completes the sentence.*

1. As college students, we should be able to tell a statesman from a _____.
   (A) politician
   (B) patriot
   (C) director
   (D) detective   (   )

2. After a long drive, he became _____ and thus pulled off the road to rest.
   (A) tricky
   (B) slender
   (C) obscure
   (D) drowsy   (   )

3. Must you _____ in other people's affairs?
   (A) disturb
   (B) interrupt
   (C) interfere
   (D) intersect   (   )

4. The injured man was taken to hospital and _____ for internal injuries.
   (A) cured
   (B) healed
   (C) operated
   (D) treated   (   )

5. There are many serious _____ to which we should devote our energy and time in life.
   (A) pursuits
   (B) precedence
   (C) precision
   (D) proportions   (   )

6. Business in that restaurant is _____, and it's nearly impossible to eat dinner there without a reservation.
   (A) flourishing
   (B) flattening
   (C) blooming
   (D) hatching   (   )

7. His works were not _____ until after his death.
   (A) appreciated
   (B) approached
   (C) applauded
   (D) appeared   (   )

8. By learning the _____ of successful learners, poor learners might increase their chances of success.
   (A) statistics
   (B) stickers
   (C) statements
   (D) strategies   (   )

9. The public _____ of the play will be held next Wednesday.
   (A) revolt
   (B) revision
   (C) revolution
   (D) rehearsal   (   )

10. Based on the findings, researchers _____ that the vaccine could have a tremendous effect on the prevention of the disease in children.
    (A) beware
    (B) narrate
    (C) recall
    (D) conclude   (   )

TEST 27 詳解

1. (**A**) As college students, we should be able to tell a
   statesman from a <u>politician</u>.

   身為大學生，我們應該要能夠分辨政治家和<u>政客</u>。

   (A) ***politician*** 〔ˌpɑləˈtɪʃən〕*n.* 政客

   (B) patriot 〔ˈpetrɪət〕*n.* 愛國者

   (C) director 〔dəˈrɛktɚ〕*n.* 董事；導演

   (D) detective 〔dɪˈtɛktɪv〕*n.* 偵探

   * statesman 〔ˈstetsmən〕*n.* 政治家

2. (**D**) After a long drive, he became <u>drowsy</u> and thus
   pulled off the road to rest.

   開了很久的車後，他有點<u>想睡</u>，所以離開公路去休息一下。

   (A) tricky 〔ˈtrɪkɪ〕*adj.* 狡猾的

   (B) slender 〔ˈslɛndɚ〕*adj.* 苗條的

   (C) obscure 〔əbˈskjʊr〕*adj.* 模糊的

   (D) ***drowsy*** 〔ˈdraʊzɪ〕*adj.* 想睡的 (= *sleepy*)

   * ***pull off*** （汽車）離開道路；停靠路邊

3. (**C**) Must you <u>interfere</u> in other people's affairs?

   你一定要去<u>干涉</u>別人的事嗎？

   (A) disturb 〔dɪˈstɝb〕*v.* 打擾（及物動詞）

   (B) interrupt 〔ˌɪntəˈrʌpt〕*v.* 打斷；打岔

   (C) ***interfere*** 〔ˌɪntəˈfɪr〕*v.* 干涉 < *in, with* >；
   妨礙 < *with* >

   (D) intersect 〔ˌɪntəˈsɛkt〕*v.* （線、道路）交叉

4. (**D**) The injured man was taken to hospital and <u>treated</u>
for internal injuries.

受傷的先生被送到醫院，<u>治療</u>他的內傷。

(A) cure〔kjur〕*v.* 治療（要用 *cure* 人 *of* 病）

(B) heal〔hil〕*v.* 治療（傷、病）

(C) operate〔'ɑpə,ret〕*v.* 動手術

（要用 *operate on* 人 *for* 病）

(D) *treat*〔trit〕*v.* 治療

treat 人 *for* 病　治療某人的某種疾病

* injured〔'ɪndʒəd〕*adj.* 受傷的

internal〔ɪn'tɝnḷ〕*adj.* 內部的

injury〔'ɪndʒərɪ〕*n.* 傷

5. (**A**) There are many serious <u>pursuits</u> to which we should
devote our energy and time in life.

在生命中，有許多我們應該投入心力和時間，認真去<u>追尋</u>
的事物。

(A) *pursuit*〔pə'sut〕*n.* 追求；追尋

(B) precedence〔prɪ'sidṇs , 'prɛsədəns〕*n.*

（時間、順序）先行；（地位、重要性）優先

(C) precision〔prɪ'sɪʒən〕*n.* 精確（= *accuracy*）

(D) proportion〔prə'porʃən〕*n.* 比例

* devote〔dɪ'vot〕*v.* 致力於；投入 < *to* >

energy〔'ɛnədʒɪ〕*n.* 精力

6. (**A**) Business in that restaurant is <u>flourishing</u>, and it's nearly impossible to eat dinner there without a reservation.

那家餐廳生意<u>興隆</u>，要去那兒吃晚餐，沒有預約幾乎不可能。

    (A) ***flourish***〔'flɜɪʃ〕*v.* 興盛

    (B) flatten〔'flætn〕*v.* 使平坦

    (C) bloom〔blum〕*v.* 開花

    (D) hatch〔hætʃ〕*v.*（蛋）孵化

    ∗ reservation〔,rɛzə'veʃən〕*n.* 預約

7. (**A**) His works were not <u>appreciated</u> until after his death.

他的作品直到他死後才受到<u>重視</u>。

    (A) ***appreciate***〔ə'priʃɪ,et〕*v.* 重視；欣賞

    (B) approach〔ə'protʃ〕*v.* 接近

    (C) applaud〔ə'plɔd〕*v.* 鼓掌

    (D) appear〔ə'pɪr〕*v.* 出現；似乎（= *seem*）

8. (**D**) By learning the <u>strategies</u> of successful learners, poor learners might increase their chances of success.

藉由學習成功學習者的<u>策略</u>，學習效率較差的人，或許可以增加成功的機會。

    (A) statistics〔stə'tɪstɪks〕*n.* 統計學；(*pl.*) 統計數字

    (B) sticker〔'stɪkə〕*n.* 貼紙

    (C) statement〔'stetmənt〕*n.* 敘述

    (D) ***strategy***〔'strætədʒɪ〕*n.* 戰略；策略

9. (**D**) The public <u>rehearsal</u> of the play will be held next Wednesday. 這齣戲正式的彩排將在下星期三舉行。

    (A) revolt〔rɪ'volt〕 *n.* 反叛

    (B) revision〔rɪ'vɪʒən〕 *n.* 修訂

    (C) revolution〔ˌrɛvə'luʃən〕 *n.* 革命

    (D) *rehearsal*〔rɪ'hɝsḷ〕 *n.* 彩排;預演

10. (**D**) Based on the findings, researchers <u>conclude</u> that the vaccine could have a tremendous effect on the prevention of the disease in children.

根據調查結果,研究人員判定,該疫苗對於預防兒童罹患此種疾病,有極大的功效。

    (A) beware〔bɪ'wɛr〕 *v.* 小心 *< of >*

       (*= be careful of*)

    (B) narrate〔næ'ret〕 *v.* 敘述

    (C) recall〔rɪ'kɔl〕 *v.* 想起

    (D) *conclude*〔kən'klud〕 *v.* 下結論;判定

    * *based on* 根據

    findings〔'faɪndɪŋz〕 *n. pl.* 調查結果

    vaccine〔'væksin〕 *n.* 疫苗

    have an effect on 對~有影響、功效

    tremendous〔trɪ'mɛndəs〕 *adj.* 極大的

    prevention〔prɪ'vɛnʃən〕 *n.* 預防

TEST 28

Directions: *The following questions are incomplete sentences. You are to choose the one word that best completes the sentence.*

1. When I saw the way he mistreated his child, it _____ my opinion that he was a bad parent.
   (A) enforced
   (B) stirred
   (C) reinforced
   (D) banned   (   )

2. As she was born with that defect, it is _____.
   (A) immature
   (B) innate
   (C) noble
   (D) naïve   (   )

3. All of my family will _____ my graduation in June.
   (A) intend
   (B) present
   (C) attend
   (D) consent   (   )

4. The weather bureau _____ an all-time record low was just around the corner.
   (A) prohibited
   (B) prospered
   (C) previewed
   (D) predicted   (   )

5. The angry father _____ his son that he would turn him out of the house if he got into trouble once more.
   (A) scolded
   (B) threatened
   (C) blamed
   (D) whispered   (   )

6. Because of road work, traffic is restricted to one
   _____ in each direction.
   (A) lane
   (B) row
   (C) alley
   (D) path   (   )

7. Medicine bottles should always be _____ labeled.
   (A) uniformly
   (B) distinctly
   (C) vaguely
   (D) conditionally   (   )

8. He sent a message to his parents abroad by _____.
   (A) microphone
   (B) phonograph
   (C) telescopes
   (D) telegram   (   )

9. The police learned from a _____ source that the
   criminal had already sneaked out of the country.
   (A) trustful
   (B) reliable
   (C) civilized
   (D) reliant   (   )

10. Having a teenager in the house is _____ at times.
    Teenagers often go their own way, refusing to listen to
    their parents.
    (A) nourishing
    (B) alarming
    (C) urging
    (D) frustrating   (   )

TEST 28 詳解

1. (**C**) When I saw the way he mistreated his child, it
<u>reinforced</u> my opinion that he was a bad parent.
當我看到他虐待孩子的方式，更<u>加深</u>我的想法，認為他
是個壞爸爸。

    (A) enforce〔ɪn'fors〕*v.* 實施

    (B) stir〔stɜ〕*v.* 激起

    (C) ***reinforce***〔,riɪn'fors〕*v.* 加強

    (D) ban〔bæn〕*v.* 禁止

    * mistreat〔mɪs'trit〕*v.* 虐待

2. (**B**) As she was born with that defect, it is <u>innate</u>.
她生來就具有那種缺陷，那是<u>天生的</u>。

    (A) immature〔,ɪmə'tjʊr〕*adj.* 不成熟的

    (B) ***innate***〔ɪn'net〕*adj.* 天生的

    (C) noble〔'nobḷ〕*adj.* 高貴的

    (D) naïve〔nɑ'iv〕*adj.* 天真的

    * ***be born with*** 天生具有

      defect〔'difɛkt〕*n.* 缺陷；缺點

3. (**C**) All of my family will <u>attend</u> my graduation in June.
我們全家人都會<u>參加</u>我六月的畢業典禮。

    (A) intend〔ɪn'tɛnd〕*v.* 打算

    (B) present〔prɪ'zɛnt〕*v.* 贈送

    (C) ***attend***〔ə'tɛnd〕*v.* 參加

    (D) consent〔kən'sɛnt〕*v.* 同意 < *to* >

4.(**D**) The weather bureau <u>predicted</u> an all-time record
low was just around the corner.
氣象局<u>預測</u>，一個空前破紀錄的最低溫即將來臨。

 (A) prohibit〔proˈhɪbɪt〕*v.* 禁止

 (B) prosper〔ˈprɑspɚ〕*v.* 繁榮

 (C) preview〔prɪˈvju〕*v.* 預習

 (D) ***predict***〔prɪˈdɪkt〕*v.* 預測

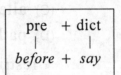

 * bureau〔ˈbjʊro〕*n.* 局
  all-time〔ˈɔlˌtaɪm〕*adj.* 空前的
  record〔ˈrɛkɚd〕*adj.* 破紀錄的
  low〔lo〕*n.* 最低點
  around the corner 即將來臨

5.(**B**) The angry father <u>threatened</u> his son that he would
turn him out of the house if he got into trouble
once more.
憤怒的父親<u>威脅</u>他的兒子說，如果他再一次惹上麻煩，
就要把他趕出家門。

 (A) scold〔skold〕*v.* 責備

 (B) ***threaten***〔ˈθrɛtn̩〕*v.* 威脅

 (C) blame〔blem〕*v.* 責備

 (D) whisper〔ˈhwɪspɚ〕*v.* 低語

 * ***get into trouble*** 惹上麻煩
  once more 再一次（= *once again*）

6. (**A**) Because of road work, traffic is restricted to one
     <u>lane</u> in each direction.
     由於道路施工，雙向各剩一個<u>車道</u>可行。

     (A) ***lane*** 〔 len 〕 *n.* 車道；巷
     (B) row 〔 ro 〕 *n.* 排；列
     (C) alley 〔'ælɪ 〕 *n.* 弄
     (D) path 〔 pæθ 〕 *n.* 小路

     * restrict 〔 rɪ'strɪkt 〕 *v.* 限制
       direction 〔 də'rɛkʃən 〕 *n.* 方向

7. (**B**) Medicine bottles should always be <u>distinctly</u> labeled.
     藥瓶理應標識<u>清楚</u>。

     (A) uniformly 〔'junə,fɔrmlɪ 〕 *adv.* 一律地
     (B) ***distinctly*** 〔 dɪ'stɪŋktlɪ 〕 *adv.* 清楚地 (= *clearly*)
     (C) vaguely 〔'veglɪ 〕 *adv.* 模糊地
     (D) conditionally 〔 kən'dɪʃənlɪ 〕 *adv.* 有條件地

     * label 〔'lebḷ 〕 *v.* 貼標籤

8. (**D**) He sent a message to his parents abroad by <u>telegram</u>.
     他以<u>電報</u>發一個訊息給他住在國外的父母。

     (A) microphone 〔'maɪkrə,fon 〕 *n.* 麥克風
     (B) phonograph 〔'fonə,græf 〕 *n.* 留聲機
     (C) telescope 〔'tɛlə,skop 〕 *n.* 望遠鏡
     (D) ***telegram*** 〔'tɛlə,græm 〕 *n.* 電報

     * abroad 〔 ə'brɔd 〕 *adv.* 在國外

9. (**B**) The police learned from a <u>reliable</u> source that the criminal had already sneaked out of the country.

警方由<u>可靠</u>消息來源得知，這個罪犯已經潛逃出境。

(A) trustful〔'trʌstfəl〕*adj.* 信任的

(B) ***reliable***〔rɪ'laɪəbḷ〕*adj.* 可靠的 (= *dependable*)

(C) civilized〔'sɪvḷ‚aɪzd〕*adj.* 有教養的

(D) reliant〔rɪ'laɪənt〕*adj.* 依賴的
　　(= *dependent*)＜ *on* ＞

　＊ source〔sors〕*n.* 來源
　　criminal〔'krɪmənḷ〕*n.* 罪犯
　　sneak〔snik〕*v.* 鬼祟行動

reli ＋ able	reli ＋ ant
｜　　｜	｜　　｜
依賴 ＋ 可以	依賴 ＋ *adj.*

10. (**D**) Having a teenager in the house is <u>frustrating</u> at times. Teenagers often go their own way, refusing to listen to their parents.

家中有青少年有時<u>令人有挫折感</u>。青少年常常我行我素，
拒絕聽父母的話。

(A) nourishing〔'nɝɪʃɪŋ〕*adj.* 滋養的

(B) alarming〔ə'lɑrmɪŋ〕*adj.* 驚人的

(C) urge〔ɝdʒ〕*v.* 催促；驅策

(D) ***frustrating***〔'frʌstretɪŋ〕*adj.* 令人有挫折感的

　＊ ***at times*** 有時　　***go one's own way*** 我行我素

TEST 29

Directions: *The following questions are incomplete sentences. You are to choose the one word that best completes the sentence.*

1. Our government has absolute _____ over the crew members in accordance with international law.
   (A) exhibition
   (B) jurisdiction
   (C) ornament
   (D) phenomenon   (   )

2. The leaders of the G-7 _____ meeting said that they would keep fighting terrorism.
   (A) seminar
   (B) summary
   (C) settlement
   (D) summit   (   )

3. The senior accounts clerk has been _____ for dishonesty.
   (A) discharged
   (B) resigned
   (C) loosened
   (D) insured   (   )

4. Democracy is believed to be the _____ of freedom.
   (A) citadel
   (B) satellite
   (C) spectacle
   (D) prison   (   )

5. The light gradually _____ and shapes and colors grew fainter.
   (A) melted
   (B) shrank
   (C) faded
   (D) subsisted   (   )

6. During an economic depression, people everywhere fear
   for their future. It's a period of tremendous upheaval
   and _____.
   (A) turbulence
   (B) marvel
   (C) stamina
   (D) stability   (   )

7. Their family has a proud and distinguished _____,
   with many family members holding important roles in
   government or industry.
   (A) heritage
   (B) heroism
   (C) ceremony
   (D) rebellion   (   )

8. Although _____ bottles are very convenient, they
   have also created a serious environmental problem.
   (A) greasy
   (B) disposable
   (C) marine
   (D) recycled   (   )

9. Many people save money to _____ for their old age.
   (A) serve
   (B) yield
   (C) provide
   (D) supply   (   )

10. Man has made many _____ that were never
    dreamed possible a century ago.
    (A) invasions
    (B) intentions
    (C) innovations
    (D) intruders   (   )

TEST 29 詳解

1. (**B**) Our government has absolute <u>jurisdiction</u> over the crew members in accordance with international law.
根據國際法，我國政府對這些機組人員有絕對的<u>管轄權</u>。

   (A) exhibition〔,ɛksə'bɪʃən〕 *n.* 展覽會

   (B) ***jurisdiction***〔,dʒʊrɪs'dɪkʃən〕 *n.* 管轄權

   (C) ornament〔'ɔrnəmənt〕 *n.* 裝飾

   (D) phenomenon〔fə'namə,nan〕 *n.* 現象

   * absolute〔'æbsə,lut〕 *adj.* 絕對的
   crew〔kru〕 *n.*（飛機、船、火車上）全體工作人員
   accordance〔ə'kɔrdn̩s〕 *n.* 一致
   in accordance with 根據；與～一致

juris	+	dict	+	ion
law	+	say	+	*n.*

2. (**D**) The leaders of the G-7 <u>summit</u> meeting said that they would keep fighting terrorism.
七國<u>高峰</u>會議的元首都說，他們會繼續對抗恐怖主義。

   (A) seminar〔'sɛmə,nar〕 *n.* 研討會

   (B) summary〔'sʌmərɪ〕 *n.* 總結

   (C) settlement〔'sɛtl̩mənt〕 *n.* 解決

   (D) ***summit***〔'sʌmɪt〕 *n.* 山頂；高峰
   summit meeting 高峰會議

   * terrorism〔'tɛrə,rɪzəm〕 *n.* 恐怖主義

3. (**A**) The senior accounts clerk has been <u>discharged</u> for dishonesty. 這位資深的會計人員因不誠實而被<u>解雇</u>。

    (A) ***discharge*** 〔 dɪs'tʃɑrdʒ 〕 *v.* 解雇 (= *dismiss*)

    (B) resign 〔 rɪ'zaɪn 〕 *v.* 辭職 (不用被動)

    (C) loosen 〔 'lusn 〕 *v.* 放鬆

    (D) insure 〔 ɪn'ʃur 〕 *v.* 保險

    * senior 〔 'sinjɚ 〕 *adj.* 資深的

4. (**A**) Democracy is believed to be the <u>citadel</u> of freedom.
民主被認為是自由的<u>堡壘</u>。

    (A) ***citadel*** 〔 'sɪtədl 〕 *n.* (保衛城市的) 堡壘；要塞

    (B) satellite 〔 'sætl͵aɪt 〕 *n.* 衛星

    (C) spectacle 〔 'spɛktəkl 〕 *n.* 景觀；(*pl.*) 眼鏡

    (D) prison 〔 'prɪzn 〕 *n.* 監獄

    * democracy 〔 də'mɑkrəsɪ 〕 *n.* 民主

5. (**C**) The light gradually <u>faded</u> and shapes and colors grew fainter. 光線逐漸<u>變暗</u>，影子和顏色越來越模糊。

    (A) melt 〔 mɛlt 〕 *v.* 溶化

    (B) shrink 〔 ʃrɪŋk 〕 *v.* 縮水；退縮

    (C) ***fade*** 〔 fed 〕 *v.* 褪色；(聲、光) 變弱；變淡

    (D) subsist 〔 səb'sɪst 〕 *v.* 生存

    * faint 〔 fent 〕 *adj.* 模糊的

6. (**A**) During an economic depression, people everywhere fear for their future. It's a period of tremendous upheaval and <u>turbulence</u>.

在經濟不景氣時，各地的人都擔心自己的未來。這是個非常<u>動亂</u>不安的時代。

(A) *turbulence* (ˋtɝbjələns) *n.* 動亂；混亂
(= *confusion* ; *disorder* ; *chaos*)

(B) marvel (ˋmɑrvḷ) *n.* 驚奇

(C) stamina (ˋstæmənə) *n.* 精力

(D) stability (stəˋbɪlətɪ) *n.* 穩定

* depression (dɪˋprɛʃən) *n.* 不景氣
tremendous (trɪˋmɛndəs) *adj.* 極大的；非常的
upheaval (ʌpˋhivḷ) *n.* 動亂

7. (**A**) Their family has a proud and distinguished <u>heritage</u>, with many family members holding important roles in government or industry.

他們的家族有非常值得誇耀的卓越<u>傳統</u>，有許多家族成員在政府及產業界擔任要職。

(A) *heritage* (ˋhɛrətɪdʒ) *n.* 遺產；傳統

(B) heroism (ˋhɛroˏɪzəm) *n.* 英雄主義

(C) ceremony (ˋsɛrəˏmonɪ) *n.* 儀式；典禮

(D) rebellion (rɪˋbɛljən) *n.* 反叛

* proud (praud) *adj.* 值得誇耀的
distinguished (dɪˋstɪŋgwɪʃt) *adj.* 著名的；卓越的

8. (**B**) Although <u>disposable</u> bottles are very convenient, they have also created a serious environmental problem.

雖然<u>用完即丟的</u>瓶子很方便，它們也製造了嚴重的環境問題。

    (A) greasy〔'grisɪ〕*adj.* 油膩的

    (B) ***disposable***〔dɪ'spozəbḷ〕*adj.* 用完即丟的

    (C) marine〔mə'rin〕*adj.* 海洋的

    (D) recycled〔ri'saɪkḷd〕*adj.* 回收再利用的

9. (**C**) Many people save money to <u>provide</u> for their old age.

許多人存錢，為老來做<u>準備</u>。

    (A) serve〔sɝv〕*v.* 服務；供應

    (B) yield〔jild〕*v.* 出產；讓步

    (C) ***provide***〔prə'vaɪd〕*v.* 提供；準備

        provide for 為～做準備

    (D) supply〔sə'plaɪ〕*v.* 提供；滿足（及物動詞）

10. (**C**) Man has made many <u>innovations</u> that were never dreamed possible a century ago.

人類已經發展出許多<u>新事物</u>，這些東西在一個世紀前都是不可能想得到的。

    (A) invasion〔ɪn'veʒən〕*n.* 侵略

    (B) intention〔ɪn'tɛnʃən〕*n.* 意圖

    (C) ***innovation***〔͵ɪnə'veʃən〕*n.* 革新；新事物

    (D) intruder〔ɪn'trudɚ〕*n.* 侵入者

TEST 30

Directions: *The following questions are incomplete sentences. You are to choose the one word that best completes the sentence.*

1. If you can't remember, let me try to _____ your memory.
   (A) remind
   (B) wake
   (C) refresh
   (D) portray   (   )

2. The watch my father wears is a _____ Swiss make.
   (A) genial
   (B) genuine
   (C) gentle
   (D) glorious   (   )

3. He is thinking of whether to buy a well-known _____ of car or not.
   (A) trademark
   (B) make
   (C) mark
   (D) label   (   )

4. The purpose of the conference is to _____ a petition to the legislature.
   (A) argue
   (B) confiscate
   (C) address
   (D) omit   (   )

5. The principle of natural selection is often _____ as 'the survival of the fittest.'
   (A) summarized
   (B) comprised
   (C) compared
   (D) summoned   (   )

6. At least 1000 depositors were _____ to have rushed
   to the bank to get their deposits back.
   (A) executed
   (B) expressed
   (C) established
   (D) estimated   (   )

7. You can feel certain that her decision is _____.
   She won't change it.
   (A) illogical
   (B) impregnable
   (C) informal
   (D) irrevocable   (   )

8. Don't be so _____ about your work; I think it's
   excellent.
   (A) humble
   (B) breathtaking
   (C) monotonous
   (D) sympathetic   (   )

9. Since she was accustomed to having her own room, it
   was difficult for her to _____ a roommate.
   (A) forecast
   (B) prevent
   (C) tolerate
   (D) insert   (   )

10. I was _____ that he was innocent. I gave him my
    one hundred percent trust.
    (A) convinced
    (B) struggled
    (C) condensed
    (D) challenged   (   )

TEST 30 詳解

1. (**C**) If you can't remember, let me try to <u>refresh</u> your memory. 如果你不記得了，讓我來試試喚起你的記憶。

    (A) remind〔rɪ'maɪnd〕v. 提醒

    (B) wake〔wek〕v. 叫醒 < *up* >

    (C) ***refresh***〔rɪ'frɛʃ〕v. 提神

        refresh *one's* ***memory*** 重新喚起某人的記憶

    (D) portray〔por'tre〕v. 描繪

2. (**B**) The watch my father wears is a <u>genuine</u> Swiss make. 我爸爸配戴的手錶是<u>真正</u>瑞士製的錶。

    (A) genial〔'dʒinjəl〕adj. 親切的

    (B) ***genuine***〔'dʒɛnjuɪn〕adj. 真正的

    (C) gentle〔'dʒɛntḷ〕adj. 溫和的

    (D) glorious〔'glorɪəs〕adj. 光榮的

    * Swiss〔swɪs〕adj. 瑞士的

      make〔mek〕n. ～製；樣式

3. (**B**) He is thinking of whether to buy a well-known <u>make</u> of car or not. 他正在考慮是否要買一部著名<u>廠牌</u>的車。

    (A) trademark〔'tred,mɑrk〕n. 商標

    (B) ***make***〔mek〕n. 廠牌；品牌

    (C) mark〔mɑrk〕n. 記號

    (D) label〔'lebḷ〕n. 標籤

    * ***think of*** 考慮 (= *consider*)

4. (**C**) The purpose of the conference is to <u>address</u> a petition to the legislature.

這次會議的目的，是要向立法機關<u>提出</u>請願。

    (A) argue〔ˈɑrgju〕*v.* 爭辯

    (B) confiscate〔ˈkɑnfɪsˌket〕*v.* 沒收；充公

    (C) ***address***〔əˈdrɛs〕*v.* 提出（抱怨、訴願等）< *to* >

    (D) omit〔oˈmɪt〕*v.* 遺漏；省略

    * purpose〔ˈpɝpəs〕*n.* 目的

      conference〔ˈkɑnfərəns〕*n.* 會議

      petition〔pəˈtɪʃən〕*n.* 請願

      legislature〔ˈlɛdʒɪsˌletʃə〕*n.* 立法機關

5. (**A**) The principle of natural selection is often <u>summarized</u> as 'the survival of the fittest.'

自然淘汰的原則常被<u>總結</u>爲「最適者生存」。

    (A) ***summarize***〔ˈsʌməˌraɪz〕*v.* 總結

      比較：summary〔ˈsʌmərɪ〕*n.* 摘要

    (B) comprise〔kəmˈpraɪz〕*v.* 組成

    (C) compare〔kəmˈpɛr〕*v.* 比較 < *with* >

    (D) summon〔ˈsʌmən〕*v.* 召喚

    * principle〔ˈprɪnsəpḷ〕*n.* 原則

      natural selection 自然淘汰

      survival〔səˈvaɪvḷ〕*n.* 生存

      fit〔fɪt〕*adj.* 適合的

6. (**D**) At least 1000 depositors were <u>estimated</u> to have rushed to the bank to get their deposits back.

據<u>估計</u>，至少有一千名存戶趕到該銀行，把存款領回。

(A) execute (ˈɛksɪˌkjut) v. 執行

(B) express (ɪkˈsprɛs) v. 表達

(C) establish (əˈstæblɪʃ) v. 建立

(D) *estimate* (ˈɛstəˌmet) v. 估計

* depositor (dɪˈpazɪtɚ) n. 存款者

rush (rʌʃ) v. 匆忙   deposit (dɪˈpazɪt) n. 存款

7. (**D**) You can feel certain that her decision is <u>irrevocable</u>. She won't change it.

你可以確定，她的決定是<u>不會變更的</u>。她不會改變的。

(A) illogical (ɪˈladʒɪkl̩) adj. 不合邏輯的

(B) impregnable (ɪmˈprɛgnəbl̩) adj. 攻不破的

(C) informal (ɪnˈfɔrml̩) adj. 不正式的

(D) *irrevocable* (ɪˈrɛvəkəbl̩) adj. 不會變更的；
不能取消的

8. (**A**) Don't be so <u>humble</u> about your work; I think it's excellent. 別對你的作品如此<u>謙虛</u>；我覺得很棒。

(A) *humble* (ˈhʌmbl̩) adj. 謙虛的

(B) breathtaking (ˈbrɛθˌtekɪŋ) adj. 驚人的

(C) monotonous (məˈnatn̩əs) adj. 單調的

(D) sympathetic (ˌsɪmpəˈθɛtɪk) adj. 有同情心的；
贊成的 < to >

9. (**C**) Since she was accustomed to having her own room,
it was difficult for her to <u>tolerate</u> a roommate.

因為她擁有自己的房間習慣了，要忍受室友同住，對她而言
相當困難。

(A) forecast〔for'kæst〕*v.* 預測

(B) prevent〔prɪ'vɛnt〕*v.* 預防；避免

(C) ***tolerate***〔'tɑlə,ret〕*v.* 忍受
(= *bear* ; *endure* ; *stand* ; *put up with*)

(D) insert〔ɪn'sɝt〕*v.* 插入

* ***be accustomed to*** + ***N/V-ing*** 習慣於

10. (**A**) I was <u>convinced</u> that he was innocent. I gave him
my one hundred percent trust.

我相信他是無辜的。我百分之百信任他。

(A) ***convince***〔kən'vɪns〕*v.* 說服；使相信
be convinced 相信 (= *believe*)

(B) struggle〔'strʌgl̩〕*v.* 掙扎；奮鬥

(C) condense〔kən'dɛns〕*v.* 濃縮

(D) challenge〔'tʃælɪndʒ〕*v.* 挑戰

* innocent〔'ɪnəsn̩t〕*adj.* 無辜的

TEST 31

Directions: *The following questions are incomplete sentences. You are to choose the one word that best completes the sentence.*

1. These statistics show 75% of motorcyclists die in traffic accidents because they do not wear _____.
   (A) hermits
   (B) helmets
   (C) hangers
   (D) hamlets   (   )

2. We should not _____ behind other nations in space exploration.
   (A) solve
   (B) flee
   (C) lag
   (D) plot   (   )

3. More than 500 _____ viewers rushed out of the theater as the alarm rang.
   (A) panicked
   (B) fearless
   (C) rural
   (D) afraid   (   )

4. Although some have better verbal skills than others, almost everyone can _____ his first language well.
   (A) acquaint
   (B) articulate
   (C) abandon
   (D) assure   (   )

5. In Taipei, it is difficult to find areas of _____ beauty.
   (A) unhurt
   (B) unharmed
   (C) untouched
   (D) unspoiled   (   )

6. The old factory was _____ and replaced by a new commercial building.
   - (A) disabled
   - (B) dispensed
   - (C) disrupted
   - (D) dismantled   (   )

7. Chinese culture values the _____ of the group over the desires of the individual.
   - (A) harmony
   - (B) dependence
   - (C) competence
   - (D) reunion   (   )

8. We hope to _____ the steps of our company's internal reforms.
   - (A) explode
   - (B) accelerate
   - (C) isolate
   - (D) undergo   (   )

9. He declared in the newspaper that he was not _____ for the debts of his runaway wife.
   - (A) liable
   - (B) payable
   - (C) subject
   - (D) countless   (   )

10. He felt an irresistible _____ to cry out at that scene.
   - (A) input
   - (B) impulse
   - (C) index
   - (D) immersion   (   )

TEST 31 詳解

1. (**B**) These statistics show 75% of motorcyclists die in
traffic accidents because they do not wear <u>helmets</u>.
這些統計數字顯示，百分之七十五的機車騎士在車禍中喪
生，是因為沒有戴<u>安全帽</u>。

 (A) hermit ﹝ˈhɝmɪt﹞ *n.* 隱士

 (B) ***helmet*** ﹝ˈhɛlmɪt﹞ *n.* 安全帽；頭盔

 (C) hanger ﹝ˈhæŋɚ﹞ *n.* 掛鉤

 (D) hamlet ﹝ˈhæmlɪt﹞ *n.* 小村莊

 * statistics ﹝stəˈtɪstɪks﹞ *n. pl.* 統計數字

  motorcyclist ﹝ˈmotɚˌsaɪklɪst﹞ *n.* 機車騎士

2. (**C**) We should not <u>lag</u> behind other nations in space
exploration. 我們不應在太空探險中<u>落後</u>於其他國家。

 (A) solve ﹝sɑlv﹞ *v.* 解決

 (B) flee ﹝fli﹞ *v.* 逃走

 (C) ***lag*** ﹝læg﹞ *v.* 落後

  lag behind 落後 (= *fall behind*)

 (D) plot ﹝plɑt﹞ *v.* 陰謀

 * exploration ﹝ˌɛkspləˈreʃən﹞ *n.* 探險

3. (**A**) More than 500 <u>panicked</u> viewers rushed out of the theater as the alarm rang.

當警鈴響時，五百多名<u>驚慌的</u>觀眾衝出戲院。

(A) ***panicked***〔'pænɪkt 〕 *adj.* 驚慌的（ = *panicky*）

(B) fearless〔'fɪrlɪs 〕 *adj.* 不害怕的；勇敢的

(C) rural〔'rʊrəl 〕 *adj.* 鄉下的

(D) afraid〔 ə'fred 〕 *adj.* 害怕的（ 不置於名詞前 ）

* alarm〔 ə'lɑrm 〕 *n.* 警鈴；警報

4. (**B**) Although some have better verbal skills than others, almost everyone can <u>articulate</u> his first language well.

雖然有些人的語言技巧比別人好，但幾乎每個人都能<u>清楚表達</u>自己的母語。

(A) acquaint〔 ə'kwent 〕 *v.* 使認識

(B) ***articulate***〔 ɑr'tɪkjə͵let 〕 *v.* 清楚表達

(C) abandon〔 ə'bændən 〕 *v.* 放棄

(D) assure〔 ə'ʃʊr 〕 *v.* 確定

* verbal〔'vɝbḷ 〕 *adj.* 語言的

5. (**D**) In Taipei, it is difficult to find areas of <u>unspoiled</u> beauty. 在台北，很難找到<u>未喪失自然美的</u>地區。

(A) unhurt〔 ʌn'hɝt 〕 *adj.* 未受傷的

(B) unharmed〔 ʌn'hɑrmd 〕 *adj.* 未受損傷的

(C) untouched〔 ʌn'tʌtʃt 〕 *adj.* 沒有碰過的

(D) ***unspoiled***〔 ʌn'spɔɪld 〕 *adj.* 未受損壞的；未喪失原有自然美的

6. (**D**) The old factory was <u>dismantled</u> and replaced by a new commercial building.

這間舊廠房被<u>拆除</u>，取而代之的是一棟新的商業大樓。

(A) disable ﹝ dɪsˈebl̩ ﹞ v. 使殘廢

(B) dispense ﹝ dɪˈspɛns ﹞ v. 分配

(C) disrupt ﹝ dɪsˈrʌpt ﹞ v. 使混亂

(D) ***dismantle*** ﹝ dɪsˈmæntl̩ ﹞ v. 拆除 (= *tear down*)

＊ replace ﹝ rɪˈples ﹞ v. 取代

commercial ﹝ kəˈmɝʃəl ﹞ adj. 商業的

7. (**A**) Chinese culture values the <u>harmony</u> of the group over the desires of the individual.

中國文化重視團體的<u>協調</u>，更甚於個人的慾望。

(A) ***harmony*** ﹝ ˈhɑrmənɪ ﹞ n. 協調；和諧

(B) dependence ﹝ dɪˈpɛndəns ﹞ n. 依賴 < *on* >

(C) competence ﹝ ˈkɑmpətəns ﹞ n. 能力；勝任

(D) reunion ﹝ riˈjunjən ﹞ n. 重聚

＊ value ﹝ ˈvælju ﹞ v. 重視   desire ﹝ dɪˈzaɪr ﹞ n. 慾望

8. (**B**) We hope to <u>accelerate</u> the steps of our company's internal reforms. 我們希望<u>加速</u>公司內部改革的腳步。

(A) explode ﹝ ɪkˈsplod ﹞ v. 使爆炸

(B) ***accelerate*** ﹝ ækˈsɛləˌret ﹞ v. 加速

(C) isolate ﹝ ˈaɪsl̩ˌet ﹞ v. 使孤立

(D) undergo ﹝ ˌʌndəˈgo ﹞ v. 經歷

＊ internal ﹝ ɪnˈtɝnl̩ ﹞ adj. 內部的

reform ﹝ rɪˈfɔrm ﹞ n. 改革

9. (**A**) He declared in the newspaper that he was not <u>liable</u>
for the debts of his runaway wife.
他在報紙上宣布，他沒<u>有義務</u>清償逃妻的債務。

    (A) ***liable*** (ˈlaɪəbḷ) *adj.* (法律上) 有義務的；
        有責任的 < *for* >

    (B) payable (ˈpeəbḷ) *adj.* 應付的 < *to sb.* >

    (C) subject (ˈsʌbdʒɪkt) *adj.* 服從的；易遭受的 < *to* >

    (D) countless (ˈkauntlɪs) *adj.* 無數的

    ＊ declare (dɪˈklɛr) *v.* 宣布   debt (dɛt) *n.* 債務
       runaway (ˈrʌnəˌwe) *adj.* 逃走的

10. (**B**) He felt an irresistible <u>impulse</u> to cry out at that
scene. 他看到那個景象，禁不住<u>衝動</u>想要大聲喊叫。

    (A) input (ˈɪnˌput) *n.* 輸入

    (B) ***impulse*** (ˈɪmpʌls) *n.* 衝動

        比較：pulse (pʌls) *n.* 脈搏

    (C) index (ˈɪndɛks) *n.* 索引

    (D) immersion (ɪˈmɝʃən) *n.* 沈入

    ＊ irresistible (ˌɪrɪˈzɪstəbḷ) *adj.* 難以抗拒的
       scene (sin) *n.* 景象

```
im + pulse
 |     |
in  + drive (驅策)
```

TEST 32

Directions: *The following questions are incomplete sentences. You are to choose the one word that best completes the sentence.*

1. He spent ten years in the army and for most of the time he was _____ abroad.
   (A) camped
   (B) situated
   (C) placed
   (D) stationed   (   )

2. An argument is _____ because they dislike each other so much.
   (A) invariable
   (B) invaluable
   (C) inevitable
   (D) insolvable   (   )

3. The directions were so _____ that half of them did so, and the other half did something else.
   (A) ambiguous
   (B) apprehensive
   (C) sedentary
   (D) secretive   (   )

4. She went in person to the office which _____ the forms and got what she wanted.
   (A) dissuaded
   (B) sprinkled
   (C) patrolled
   (D) issued   (   )

5. If you need advice on tax affairs, consult a(n) _____.
   (A) accountant
   (B) auctioneer
   (C) pharmacist
   (D) prosecutor   (   )

6. If you read English half an hour every day, the amount of reading you do will be _____.
   (A) mediocre
   (B) cautious
   (C) gorgeous
   (D) enormous   (   )

7. With his charisma, he is the best one to _____ the role of the leader of the project.
   (A) overlook
   (B) achieve
   (C) worship
   (D) assume   (   )

8. It's best not to tell her off because she's very _____ and she may start crying immediately.
   (A) sensible
   (B) sensitive
   (C) parallel
   (D) paranoid   (   )

9. After peace _____ started, Iraq announced that its soldiers had left Iran.
   (A) negotiations
   (B) confrontations
   (C) organizations
   (D) measurements   (   )

10. The machine is operated by hand; that is, it is operated _____.
    (A) notably
    (B) manually
    (C) annually
    (D) technically   (   )

TEST 32 詳解

1. (**D**) He spent ten years in the army and for most of the time he was <u>stationed</u> abroad.

他從軍十年，且大部分時間都<u>駐守</u>在國外。

   (A) camp〔kæmp〕v. 露營

   (B) situated〔'sɪtʃu,etɪd〕adj. 位於

   (C) place〔ples〕v. 安置

   (D) **station**〔'steʃən〕v. 部署；駐紮

   * army〔'ɑrmɪ〕n. 軍隊
     abroad〔ə'brɔd〕adv. 在國外

2. (**C**) An argument is <u>inevitable</u> because they dislike each other so much.

爭論是<u>無法避免的</u>，因爲他們都非常討厭對方。

   (A) invariable〔ɪn'vɛrɪəbl̩〕adj. 不變的

   (B) invaluable〔ɪn'væljuəbl̩〕adj. 非常珍貴的

   (C) **inevitable**〔ɪn'ɛvətəbl̩〕adj. 無法避免的
        (= *unavoidable*)

   (D) insolvable〔ɪn'sɑlvəbl̩〕adj. 無法解決的

   * argument〔'ɑrgjəmənt〕n. 爭論
     dislike〔dɪs'laɪk〕v. 不喜歡；討厭

in + evit + able	un + avoid + able
| | |	| | |
not + *avoid* + 可以	*not* + *avoid* + 可以

3. (**A**) The directions were so <u>ambiguous</u> that half of them did so, and the other half did something else.

說明太<u>模稜兩可</u>，以至於他們有一半的人照做，而另一半的人卻沒這樣做。

(A) ***ambiguous*** 〔æm'bɪgjʊəs 〕 *adj*. 模稜兩可的

(B) apprehensive 〔,æprɪ'hɛnsɪv 〕 *adj*. 憂慮的

(C) sedentary 〔'sɛdn̩,tɛrɪ 〕 *adj*. 久坐的

(D) secretive 〔 sɪ'kritɪv 〕 *adj*. 守口如瓶的

* directions 〔 də'rɛkʃənz 〕 *n. pl*. 說明

4. (**D**) She went in person to the office which <u>issued</u> the forms and got what she wanted.

她親自到<u>發給</u>表格的辦事處，得到她所要的。

(A) dissuade 〔 dɪ'swed 〕 *v*. 勸阻 < *from* >

(B) sprinkle 〔'sprɪŋkl̩ 〕 *v*. 灑（水、液體）

(C) patrol 〔 pə'trol 〕 *v*. 巡邏

(D) ***issue*** 〔'ɪʃju 〕 *v*. 發給；發行

* ***in person*** 親自 (= *personally*)

5. (**A**) If you need advice on tax affairs, consult an <u>accountant</u>. 如果你需要稅務方面的建議，可請教<u>會計師</u>。

(A) ***accountant*** 〔 ə'kaʊntənt 〕 *n*. 會計師

(B) auctioneer 〔,ɔkʃən'ɪr 〕 *n*. 拍賣人

(C) pharmacist 〔'farməsɪst 〕 *n*. 藥劑師

(D) prosecutor 〔'prasɪ,kjutɚ 〕 *n*. 檢察官

* consult 〔 kən'sʌlt 〕 *v*. 請教

6. (**D**) If you read English half an hour every day, the amount of reading you do will be <u>enormous</u>.

如果你每天讀半小時英文，你所閱讀的量就會很<u>龐大</u>。

(A) mediocre〔‚midɪ'okɚ〕 *adj.* 平凡的

(B) cautious〔'kɔʃəs〕 *adj.* 小心的（ = *careful* ）

(C) gorgeous〔'gɔrdʒəs〕 *adj.* 美麗的

(D) *enormous*〔ɪ'nɔrməs〕 *adj.* 龐大的
    (= *huge* ; *great* ; *tremendous* ; *massive*)

7. (**D**) With his charisma, he is the best one to <u>assume</u> the role of the leader of the project.

由於他具有領袖氣質，他是<u>擔任</u>這個計劃領導者的最佳人選。

(A) overlook〔‚ovɚ'luk〕 *v.* 俯瞰；忽視

(B) achieve〔ə'tʃiv〕 *v.* 達成

(C) worship〔'wɝʃəp〕 *v.* 崇拜

(D) *assume*〔ə'sjum〕 *v.* 擔任（角色、職位）

* charisma〔kə'rɪzmə〕 *n.* 領袖氣質；個人魅力

8. (**B**) It's best not to tell her off because she's very <u>sensitive</u> and she may start crying immediately.

最好別責罵她，因為她很<u>敏感</u>，可能會馬上開始哭。

(A) sensible〔'sɛnsəbḷ〕 *adj.* 明智的

(B) *sensitive*〔'sɛnsətɪv〕 *adj.* 敏感的 < *to* >

(C) parallel〔'pærə‚lɛl〕 *adj.* 平行的 < *to* >

(D) paranoid〔'pærə‚nɔɪd〕 *adj.* 偏執狂的；妄想症的

* *tell off* 責罵（ = *scold* ）

9. (**A**) After peace <u>negotiations</u> started, Iraq announced
that its soldiers had left Iran.

和<u>談</u>開始後，伊拉克宣布已從伊朗撤軍。

(A) ***negotiation*** 〔 nɪˌgoʃɪˈeʃən 〕 *n.* 談判

(B) confrontation 〔ˌkɑnfrʌnˈteʃən 〕 *n.* 對抗

(C) organization 〔ˌɔrgənəˈzeʃən 〕 *n.* 組織

(D) measurement 〔ˈmɛʒəmənt 〕 *n.* 測量；(*pl.*) 尺寸

* Iraq 〔 ɪˈrɑk 〕 *n.* 伊拉克

announce 〔 əˈnauns 〕 *v.* 宣布

soldier 〔ˈsoldʒɚ 〕 *n.* 士兵　　Iran 〔 iˈrɑn 〕 *n.* 伊朗

10. (**B**) The machine is operated by hand; that is, it is
operated <u>manually</u>.

這部機器要用手動；也就是，要<u>用手工</u>操作。

(A) notably 〔ˈnotəblɪ 〕 *adv.* 顯著地

(B) ***manually*** 〔ˈmænjʊəlɪ 〕 *adv.* 用手工 (= *by hand*)

(C) annually 〔ˈænjʊəlɪ 〕 *adv.* 每年地 (= *yearly*)

(D) technically 〔ˈtɛknɪkl̩ɪ 〕 *adv.* 技術上地

* operate 〔ˈɑpəˌret 〕 *v.* 操作

that is 也就是；換句話說 (= *in other words*)

manu	+	al	+	ly
hand	+	*adj.*	+	*adv.*

TEST 33

Directions: *The following questions are incomplete sentences. You are to choose the one word that best completes the sentence.*

1. According to the _____ of the contract, tenants must give six months notice if they intend to leave.
   - (A) flaws
   - (B) reins
   - (C) terms
   - (D) strings   (　)

2. A man was arrested on _____ of drug trafficking.
   - (A) behalf
   - (B) suspicion
   - (C) confession
   - (D) verdict   (　)

3. A _____ respect for traditional culture is fundamental to Chinese values.
   - (A) promising
   - (B) protective
   - (C) profound
   - (D) provocative   (　)

4. The teacher tried her best to _____ the need for good manners into the children.
   - (A) inspire
   - (B) instill
   - (C) instruct
   - (D) infect   (　)

5. When his wife started seeing more of the tennis coach, he became very _____.
   - (A) arrogant
   - (B) heartfelt
   - (C) jealous
   - (D) persistent   (　)

6. No matter how _____ our society becomes, work will still remain the center of our existence.

   (A) affluent
   (B) absolute
   (C) ambitious
   (D) apparent   (   )

7. I want to know what the medicine _____ of because I am allergic to some drugs.

   (A) constitutes
   (B) constructs
   (C) composes
   (D) consists   (   )

8. Many stores use _____ to attract customers to buy their products at a lower price.

   (A) coupons
   (B) cones
   (C) cowards
   (D) cottages   (   )

9. Miss Smith uses _____ approaches in teaching because she finds that students enjoy new ways of learning.

   (A) mysterious
   (B) optional
   (C) supplementary
   (D) novel   (   )

10. We walked in a deserted village and didn't meet a _____.

    (A) personality
    (B) character
    (C) soul
    (D) spirit   (   )

TEST 33 詳解

1. (**C**) According to the <u>terms</u> of the contract, tenants must give six months notice if they intend to leave.

根據契約中的<u>條件</u>，房客如果打算要離開，必須六個月前先行通知。

    (A) flaw〔flɔ〕 *n.* 缺點

    (B) rein〔ren〕 *n.* 韁繩

    (C) ***terms***〔tɜmz〕 *n. pl.* 條件

    (D) string〔strɪŋ〕 *n.* 細繩；線

    * contract〔'kɑntrækt〕 *n.* 契約
      tenant〔'tɛnənt〕 *n.* 房客　　notice〔'notɪs〕 *n.* 通知
      intend〔ɪn'tɛnd〕 *v.* 打算

2. (**B**) A man was arrested on <u>suspicion</u> of drug trafficking.

一名男子因涉嫌販毒被逮捕。

    (A) behalf〔bɪ'hæf〕 *n.* 方面
      on behalf of sb. 代表某人；爲了某人

    (B) ***suspicion***〔sə'spɪʃən〕 *n.* 懷疑；嫌疑
      on (the) suspicion of 因涉嫌~

    (C) confession〔kən'fɛʃən〕 *n.* 承認

    (D) verdict〔'vɜdɪkt〕 *n.* 判決

    * arrest〔ə'rɛst〕 *v.* 逮捕
      trafficking〔'træfɪkɪŋ〕 *n.* (非法) 交易

3. (**C**) A <u>profound</u> respect for traditional culture is fundamental to Chinese values.

對傳統文化<u>非常</u>尊崇，是中國人價值觀的根本。

    (A) promising〔'prɑmɪsɪŋ〕*adj.* 有希望的

    (B) protective〔prə'tɛktɪv〕*adj.* 保護的

    (C) *profound*〔prə'faʊnd〕*adj.* 深遠的；極度的

    (D) provocative〔prə'vɑkətɪv〕*adj.* 挑釁的

    * fundamental〔͵fʌndə'mɛntl̩〕*adj.* 根本的
       values〔'væljʊz〕*n., pl.* 價值觀

4. (**B**) The teacher tried her best to <u>instill</u> the need for good manners into the children.

老師盡全力，把良好禮儀的必要性，<u>逐漸灌輸</u>給孩子們。

    (A) inspire〔ɪn'spaɪr〕*v.* 鼓舞；激勵

    (B) *instill*〔ɪn'stɪl〕*v.* 逐漸灌輸＜ *in , into* ＞

    (C) instruct〔ɪn'strʌkt〕*v.* 教導（＝ *teach*）

    (D) infect〔ɪn'fɛkt〕*v.* 感染

    * manners〔'mænəz〕*n. pl.* 禮儀

5. (**C**) When his wife started seeing more of the tennis coach, he became very <u>jealous</u>.

當他太太越來越常去找那位網球教練時，他變得很<u>嫉妒</u>。

    (A) arrogant〔'ærəgənt〕*adj.* 傲慢的

    (B) heartfelt〔'hɑrt͵fɛlt〕*adj.* 衷心的

    (C) *jealous*〔'dʒɛləs〕*adj.* 嫉妒的

    (D) persistent〔pə'sɪstənt〕*adj.* 持久的

    * coach〔kotʃ〕*n.* 教練

6. (**A**) No matter how <u>affluent</u> our society becomes, work will still remain the center of our existence.

無論我們的社會變得多富裕，工作將仍然是我們生活的重心。

    (A) ***affluent*** (ˈæfluənt) *adj.* 富裕的 (= *wealthy*)

    (B) absolute (ˈæbsəˌlut) *adj.* 絕對的

    (C) ambitious (æmˈbɪʃəs) *adj.* 有抱負的

    (D) apparent (əˈpærənt) *adj.* 明顯的 (= *obvious*)

    * existence (ɪgˈzɪstəns) *n.* 存在；生活

7. (**D**) I want to know what the medicine <u>consists</u> of because I am allergic to some drugs.

我要知道這種藥的組成成分為何，因為我對某些藥物過敏。

    (A) constitute (ˈkɑnstəˌtjut) *v.* 組成

        (此處應用 *be constituted of*)

    (B) construct (kənˈstrʌkt) *v.* 建築 (= *build*)

    (C) compose (kəmˈpoz) *v.* 組成

        (此處應用 *be composed of*)

    (D) ***consist*** (kənˈsɪst) *v.* 組成　　***consist of*** 由～組成

    * allergic (əˈlɝdʒɪk) *adj.* 過敏的 < *to* >

8. (**A**) Many stores use <u>coupons</u> to attract customers to buy their products at a lower price. 許多商店利用折價券，來吸引顧客以較低的價格購買他們的商品。

    (A) ***coupon*** (ˈkupɑn) *n.* 折價券

    (B) cone (kon) *n.* 圓錐形物體

    (C) coward (ˈkaʊəd) *n.* 懦夫

    (D) cottage (ˈkɑtɪdʒ) *n.* 農舍

9. (**D**) Miss Smith uses <u>novel</u> approaches in teaching because she finds that students enjoy new ways of learning.

史密斯老師使用<u>新奇的</u>教學方法，因為她發現學生很喜歡新的學習方法。

   (A) mysterious〔mɪˈstɪrɪəs〕*adj.* 神秘的

   (B) optional〔ˈɑpʃənl̩〕*adj.* 選擇的（= *elective*）

   (C) supplementary〔͵sʌpləˈmɛntərɪ〕*adj.* 補充的

   (D) ***novel***〔ˈnɑvl̩〕*adj.* 新奇的（= *new* ; *innovative*）

   * approach〔əˈprotʃ〕*n.* 方法（= *method*）

10. (**C**) We walked in a deserted village and didn't meet a <u>soul</u>. 我們走在一個荒廢的村莊裡，一個<u>人</u>也沒看到。

   (A) personality〔͵pɝsn̩ˈælətɪ〕*n.* 人格

   (B) character〔ˈkærɪktɚ〕*n.* 角色；人物

   (C) ***soul***〔sol〕*n.* 靈魂；人

   not ~ a soul 一個人也沒有（用於否定句）

   (D) spirit〔ˈspɪrɪt〕*n.* 精神；靈魂；帶有～特質的人

   （與形容詞連用）

   * deserted〔dɪˈzɝtɪd〕*adj.* 荒廢的

   village〔ˈvɪlɪdʒ〕*n.* 村莊

TEST 34

Directions: *The following questions are incomplete sentences. You are to choose the one word that best completes the sentence.*

1. The so-called greenhouse effect is excessive levels of carbon dioxide in the _____.
   (A) temperature
   (B) atmosphere
   (C) comets
   (D) meteors   (   )

2. Something about him _____ our instant attention and deference.
   (A) confines
   (B) conserves
   (C) commands
   (D) commends   (   )

3. He has an excellent _____ as a criminal lawyer.
   (A) popularity
   (B) fame
   (C) regard
   (D) reputation   (   )

4. The different ideas have been _____ into one uniform plan.
   (A) interpreted
   (B) interviewed
   (C) integrated
   (D) inspected   (   )

5. The committee took just thirty minutes to _____ the conclusion that action was necessary.
   (A) pitch
   (B) stitch
   (C) preach
   (D) reach   (   )

6. The prime minister will lead a(n) _____ to attend the inauguration ceremony of that country's new president.

   (A) representative
   (B) delegation
   (C) diplomacy
   (D) envoy   (   )

7. The family was made homeless through no _____ of their own.

   (A) merits
   (B) baits
   (C) responsibility
   (D) fault   (   )

8. The study of human beings is called _____.

   (A) geology
   (B) anthropology
   (C) psychology
   (D) astrology   (   )

9. The minister _____ his resignation to the premier yesterday, but the premier asked him to reconsider his decision.

   (A) organized
   (B) retreated
   (C) tendered
   (D) proposed   (   )

10. The mayor declared that the city was on the _____ of financial collapse and had to lay off 10 percent of the city's work force.

    (A) circumstance
    (B) verge
    (C) outline
    (D) outlook   (   )

TEST 34 詳解

1. (**B**) The so-called greenhouse effect is excessive levels
   of carbon dioxide in the <u>atmosphere</u>.
   所謂的溫室效應,就是<u>大氣</u>之中二氧化碳的含量過高。

   (A) temperature (ˈtɛmprətʃɚ) *n.* 溫度

   (B) ***atmosphere*** (ˈætməsˌfɪr) *n.* 大氣

   (C) comet (ˈkɑmɪt) *n.* 彗星

   (D) meteor (ˈmitɪɚ) *n.* 流星;隕石

   * ***greenhouse effect*** 溫室效應
     excessive (ɪkˈsɛsɪv) *adj.* 過度的
     level (ˈlɛvḷ) *n.* 程度
     carbon dioxide 二氧化碳

2. (**C**) Something about him <u>commands</u> our instant
   attention and deference.
   他的某項特質<u>博得</u>我們立即的注意及尊敬。

   (A) confine (kənˈfaɪn) *v.* 限制

   (B) conserve (kənˈsɝv) *v.* 保存

   (C) ***command*** (kəˈmænd) *v.* 博得;贏得 (尊敬等)

   (D) commend (kəˈmɛnd) *v.* 稱讚 (= *compliment*)

   * instant (ˈɪnstənt) *adj.* 立即的
     attention (əˈtɛnʃən) *n.* 注意
     deference (ˈdɛfərəns) *n.* 尊敬 (= *respect*)

3. (**D**) He has an excellent <u>reputation</u> as a criminal lawyer.

他是一位極負盛名的刑事訴訟律師。

(A) popularity〔ˌpɑpjəˈlærətɪ〕*n.* 受歡迎

(B) fame〔fem〕*n.* 名聲（不可數名詞，不加 *a*）

(C) regard〔rɪˈgɑrd〕*n.* 評價；尊敬

(D) *reputation*〔ˌrɛpjəˈteʃən〕*n.* 名聲

（習慣用 *a reputation*）

＊ criminal〔ˈkrɪmənl̩〕*adj.* 刑事的；刑法的

4. (**C**) The different ideas have been <u>integrated</u> into one uniform plan.

這些不同的意見已被整合成一個統一的計劃。

(A) interpret〔ɪnˈtɝprɪt〕*v.* 口譯

(B) interview〔ˈɪntəˌvju〕*v.* 面談

(C) *integrate*〔ˈɪntəˌgret〕*v.* 整合

(D) inspect〔ɪnˈspɛkt〕*v.* 檢查

＊ uniform〔ˈjunəˌfɔrm〕*adj.* 一致的

5. (**D**) The committee took just thirty minutes to <u>reach</u> the conclusion that action was necessary.

委員會只用了三十分鐘，達成必須採取行動的結論。

(A) pitch〔pɪtʃ〕*v.* 投擲

(B) stitch〔stɪtʃ〕*v.* 縫（一針）

(C) preach〔pritʃ〕*v.* 說敎

(D) *reach*〔ritʃ〕*v.* 達成

＊ committee〔kəˈmɪtɪ〕*n.* 委員會

6. (**B**) The prime minister will lead a <u>delegation</u> to attend the inauguration ceremony of that country's new president.

行政院長將帶領一個<u>代表團</u>，參加該國新總統的就職典禮。

   (A) representative〔͵rɛprɪˊzɛntətɪv〕*n.* 代表人
   (B) *delegation*〔͵dɛləˊgeʃən〕*n.* 代表團
   (C) diplomacy〔dɪˊploməsɪ〕*n.* 外交
   (D) envoy〔ˊɛnvɔɪ〕*n.* 外交使節；公使

   ＊ *prime minister* 行政院長
   attend〔əˊtɛnd〕*v.* 參加
   inauguration〔ɪn͵ɔgjəˊreʃən〕*n.* 就職
   ceremony〔ˊsɛrə͵monɪ〕*n.* 典禮

7. (**D**) The family was made homeless through no <u>fault</u> of their own.

這一家人被弄得無家可歸，卻不是他們自己的<u>錯</u>。

   (A) merit〔ˊmɛrɪt〕*n.* 優點；功勞
   (B) bait〔bet〕*n.* 誘餌
   (C) responsibility〔rɪ͵spansəˊbɪlətɪ〕*n.* 責任
   (D) *fault*〔fɔlt〕*n.* 過錯

8. (**B**) The study of human beings is called <u>anthropology</u>.

研究人類的學問被稱為<u>人類學</u>。

   (A) geology〔dʒiˊalədʒɪ〕*n.* 地質學
   (B) *anthropology*〔͵ænθrəˊpalədʒɪ〕*n.* 人類學
   (C) psychology〔saɪˊkalədʒɪ〕*n.* 心理學
   (D) astrology〔əˊstralədʒɪ〕*n.* 占星術

9. (**C**) The minister <u>tendered</u> his resignation to the premier yesterday, but the premier asked him to reconsider his decision.

部長昨天向總理提出辭呈，但總理請他再考慮一下他的決定。

(A) organize（'ɔrgən,aɪz) *v.* 組織

(B) retreat（rɪ'trit) *v.* 撤退

(C) *tender*（'tɛndə) *v.* 提出

(D) propose（prə'poz) *v.* 提議；求婚

* minister（'mɪnɪstə) *n.* 部長
  resignation（,rɛzɪg'neʃən) *n.* 辭職；辭呈
  premier（'primɪə , prɪ'mɪr) *n.* 總理；首相

10. (**B**) The mayor declared that the city was on the <u>verge</u> of financial collapse and had to lay off 10 percent of the city's work force.

市長宣布，該市已瀕臨財務崩潰，不得不裁撤百分之十的市政府員工。

(A) circumstance（'sɜkəm,stæns) *n.* 情況
   (通常用 *under/in the circumstances*)

(B) *verge*（vɜdʒ) *n.* 邊緣
   on the verge of 瀕臨（ 常指不好的情況 ）

(C) outline（'aut,laɪn) *n.* 輪廓；綱要

(D) outlook（'aut,luk) *n.* 看法 < *on* >

* mayor（'meə) *n.* 市長　　declare（dɪ'klɛr) *v.* 宣布
  financial（fə'nænʃəl) *adj.* 財務的
  collapse（kə'læps) *n.* 崩潰　　*lay off* 解雇
  work force 人力；員工人數

TEST 35

Directions*: The following questions are incomplete sentences. You are to choose the one word that best completes the sentence.*

1. If this _____ does not end, the government may announce the measure of water rationing.
   (A) drought
   (B) flood
   (C) epidemic
   (D) famine   (   )

2. Many casualties were caused because people had not been warned of the danger until disaster was _____.
   (A) intimate
   (B) interior
   (C) imminent
   (D) impractical   (   )

3. I was filled with _____ when I heard my favorite old songs.
   (A) nonsense
   (B) notion
   (C) nostalgia
   (D) novelty   (   )

4. All visitors are requested to _____ with the regulations.
   (A) compile
   (B) comply
   (C) conduct
   (D) converse   (   )

5. Babies _____ before they learn to walk.
   (A) crawl
   (B) slip
   (C) linger
   (D) limp   (   )

6. People arriving late will not be _____ to enter the concert hall.
   - (A) violated
   - (B) permitted
   - (C) rejected
   - (D) imported   ( )

7. Most of the skyscrapers are centered in the commercial _____ of the city.
   - (A) distribution
   - (B) dominance
   - (C) district
   - (D) domain   ( )

8. As soon as the exams were over, the students all went their _____ ways.
   - (A) distinctive
   - (B) restricted
   - (C) perspective
   - (D) respective   ( )

9. Advertisers _____ credibility when they make exaggerated claims for the products they promote.
   - (A) sacrifice
   - (B) advocate
   - (C) capture
   - (D) offend   ( )

10. People in the Caucasus Mountains in the former Soviet Union are famous for their _____.
   - (A) delivery
   - (B) antiquity
   - (C) longevity
   - (D) nationality   ( )

TEST 35 詳解

1. (**A**) If this <u>drought</u> does not end, the government may announce the measure of water rationing.

如果<u>旱象</u>不止，政府可能會宣布限水措施。

(A) ***drought*** 〔 draʊt 〕 *n.* 乾旱

(B) flood 〔 flʌd 〕 *n.* 水災

(C) epidemic 〔 ͵ɛpə'dɛmɪk 〕 *n.* 傳染病

(D) famine 〔 'fæmɪn 〕 *n.* 飢荒

＊ announce 〔 ə'naʊns 〕 *v.* 宣布

measure 〔 'mɛʒɚ 〕 *n.* 措施

ration 〔 'ræʃən 〕 *v.* 限量供應；配給

2. (**C**) Many casualties were caused because people had not been warned of the danger until disaster was <u>imminent</u>.

直到災難<u>逼近</u>，人們才收到危險警告，因而造成許多人死傷。

(A) intimate 〔 'ɪntəmɪt 〕 *adj.* 親密的 (= *close*)

(B) interior 〔 ɪn'tɪrɪɚ 〕 *adj.* 內部的

(C) ***imminent*** 〔 'ɪmənənt 〕 *adj.* 逼近的；迫切的

(D) impractical 〔 ɪm'præktɪkḷ 〕 *adj.* 不切實際的

＊ casualty 〔 'kæʒʊəltɪ 〕 *n.* 死傷者

disaster 〔 dɪz'æstɚ 〕 *n.* 災難

3. (**C**) I was filled with <u>nostalgia</u> when I heard my favorite
old songs.

聽到我最喜歡的老歌，我心中充滿懷舊之情。

　　(A) nonsense〔'nɑnsɛns〕*n.* 無意義；胡說八道

　　(B) notion〔'noʃən〕*n.* 概念 (= *idea* ; *concept*)

　　(C) ***nostalgia***〔nɑ'stældʒɪə〕*n.* 懷舊

　　(D) novelty〔'nɑvl̩tɪ〕*n.* 新奇

4. (**B**) All visitors are requested to <u>comply</u> with the
regulations.　所有訪客都被要求遵守規定。

　　(A) compile〔kəm'paɪl〕*v.* 編輯

　　(B) ***comply***〔kəm'plaɪ〕*v.* 遵守 < *with* >

　　(C) conduct〔kən'dʌkt〕*v.* 進行

　　(D) converse〔kən'vɝs〕*v.* 談話 < *with sb.* >

　　* request〔rɪ'kwɛst〕*v.* 要求
　　　 regulation〔ˌrɛgjə'leʃən〕*n.* 規定 (= *rule*)

```
com    + ˋply
 |         |
together + fold
```

5. (**A**) Babies <u>crawl</u> before they learn to walk.

小寶寶在學會走路前先會爬。

　　(A) ***crawl***〔krɔl〕*v.* 爬

　　(B) slip〔slɪp〕*v.* 滑倒

　　(C) linger〔'lɪŋgɚ〕*v.* 徘徊

　　(D) limp〔lɪmp〕*v.* 跛行

6. (**B**) People arriving late will not be <u>permitted</u> to enter the concert hall.

晚到的人都不被<u>允許</u>進入音樂廳。

(A) violate 〔'vaɪə,let 〕 v. 違反

(B) ***permit*** 〔 pə'mɪt 〕 v. 允許

(C) reject 〔 rɪ'dʒɛkt 〕 v. 拒絕

(D) import 〔 ɪm'port 〕 v. 進口

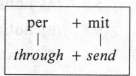

 * ***concert hall*** 音樂廳

7. (**C**) Most of the skyscrapers are centered in the commercial <u>district</u> of the city.

大部分的摩天大樓都集中在該市的商業<u>區</u>。

(A) distribution 〔,dɪstrə'bjuʃən 〕 n. 分配

(B) dominance 〔'dɑmənəns 〕 n. 支配

(C) ***district*** 〔'dɪstrɪkt 〕 n. 地區

(D) domain 〔 do'men 〕 n. 領土

 * skyscraper 〔'skaɪ,skrepə 〕 n. 摩天大樓
   center 〔'sɛntə 〕 v. 集中
   commercial 〔 kə'mɝʃəl 〕 adj. 商業的

8. (**D**) As soon as the exams were over, the students all went their <u>respective</u> ways.

考試一結束，學生們全部<u>各自</u>離開。

(A) distinctive 〔 dɪ'stɪŋktɪv 〕 adj. 獨特的

(B) restricted 〔 rɪ'strɪktɪd 〕 adj. 受限制的

(C) perspective 〔 pə'spɛktɪv 〕 adj. 透視法的

(D) ***respective*** 〔 rɪ'spɛktɪv 〕 adj. 各自的

9. (**A**) Advertisers <u>sacrifice</u> credibility when they make exaggerated claims for the products they promote.

當廣告商對於他們所促銷的商品做出誇大的宣傳時，他們就<u>犧牲</u>了可信度。

(A) ***sacrifice***〔'sækrə͵faɪs〕 *v.* 犧牲

(B) advocate〔'ædvə͵ket〕 *v.* 主張；提倡

(C) capture〔'kæptʃɚ〕 *v.* 捕捉

(D) offend〔ə'fɛnd〕 *v.* 冒犯

＊ credibility〔͵krɛdə'bɪlətɪ〕 *n.* 可信度

exaggerated〔ɪg'zædʒə͵retɪd〕 *adj.* 誇大的

claim〔klem〕 *n.* 宣稱

promote〔prə'mot〕 *v.* 促銷

10. (**C**) People in the Caucasus Mountains in the former Soviet Union are famous for their <u>longevity</u>.

前蘇聯高加索山區的居民以<u>長壽</u>著稱。

(A) delivery〔dɪ'lɪvərɪ〕 *n.* 遞送

(B) antiquity〔æn'tɪkwətɪ〕 *n.* 古代；古舊

比較：antique〔æn'tik〕 *adj.* 古代的   *n.* 古董

(C) ***longevity***〔lɑn'dʒɛvətɪ〕 *n.* 長壽

(D) nationality〔͵næʃən'ælətɪ〕 *n.* 國籍

＊ Caucasus〔'kɔkəsəs〕 *n.* 高加索

former〔'fɔrmɚ〕 *adj.* 以前的   ***Soviet Union*** 蘇聯

long + evity	antiqu + ity
| |	| |
long + *n.*	*before* + *n.*

TEST 36

Directions: *The following questions are incomplete sentences. You are to choose the one word that best completes the sentence.*

1. Since we cannot reach any agreement now, let's _____ the meeting for a month.
   (A) adjust
   (B) adjourn
   (C) relay
   (D) recess   (   )

2. On behalf of my family, I would like to express our _____ to all of you.
   (A) gratitude
   (B) gesture
   (C) gossip
   (D) gallery   (   )

3. We _____ when we are bored and tired.
   (A) pant
   (B) sign
   (C) cough
   (D) yawn   (   )

4. The unknown often fills our minds with _____, making us feel uncertain and nervous.
   (A) anxiety
   (B) enmity
   (C) modesty
   (D) poverty   (   )

5. The artist was so _____ that he created beautiful statues out of junk metal.
   (A) resourceful
   (B) reputable
   (C) resentful
   (D) reproducible   (   )

6. After a lot of difficulty, he _____ to open the door.
    (A) managed
    (B) succeeded
    (C) strengthened
    (D) strolled   (   )

7. His firm _____ of the value of education made him study hard and earn top honors in his class.
    (A) convention
    (B) contention
    (C) contraction
    (D) conviction   (   )

8. Archaeologists estimated the age of the buried city after examining the _____ found in the ruins.
    (A) melodies
    (B) postures
    (C) artifacts
    (D) borders   (   )

9. Tales of overnight riches have fueled a general _____ for lotteries and gambling.
    (A) torch
    (B) capability
    (C) fondness
    (D) glue   (   )

10. His new appointment takes _____ from the beginning of next month.
    (A) shape
    (B) shelter
    (C) effect
    (D) offense   (   )

TEST 36 詳解

1. (**B**) Since we cannot reach any agreement now, let's
   <u>adjourn</u> the meeting for a month.
   既然我們現在無法達成協議，那就將會議<u>延後</u>一個月。

    (A) adjust〔əˈdʒʌst〕*v.* 調整

    (B) ***adjourn***〔əˈdʒɝn〕*v.* 休會；延期

    (C) relay〔rɪˈle〕*v.* 轉播；傳達

    (D) recess〔rɪˈsɛs，ˈrisɛs〕*v.* 休息

    * agreement〔əˈgrimənt〕*n.* 一致；協議

2. (**A**) On behalf of my family, I would like to express our
   <u>gratitude</u> to all of you.
   我謹代表我們全家，向你們大家致上我們的<u>感激</u>之意。

    (A) ***gratitude***〔ˈgrætəˌtjud〕*n.* 感激

    (B) gesture〔ˈdʒɛstʃɚ〕*n.* 姿勢

    (C) gossip〔ˈgasəp〕*n.* 閒話

    (D) gallery〔ˈgælərɪ〕*n.* 美術館

    * ***on behalf of*** 代表

3. (**D**) We <u>yawn</u> when we are bored and tired.
   當我們無聊、疲倦時，會<u>打呵欠</u>。

    (A) pant〔pænt〕*v.* 喘氣

    (B) sign〔saɪn〕*v.* 簽名

    (C) cough〔kɔf〕*v.* 咳嗽

    (D) ***yawn***〔jɔn〕*v.* 打呵欠

4. (**A**) The unknown often fills our minds with <u>anxiety</u>, making us feel uncertain and nervous.

未知的事物常使我們心中充滿<u>焦慮</u>，讓我們覺得不確定、緊張。

    (A) ***anxiety*** 〔 æŋˈzaɪətɪ 〕 *n.* 焦慮

    (B) enmity 〔ˈɛnmətɪ 〕 *n.* 敵意

    (C) modesty 〔ˈmɑdəstɪ 〕 *n.* 謙虛

    (D) poverty 〔ˈpɑvətɪ 〕 *n.* 貧窮

    * uncertain 〔 ʌnˈsɝtṇ 〕 *adj.* 不確定的

5. (**A**) The artist was so <u>resourceful</u> that he created beautiful statues out of junk metal.

這位藝術家十分<u>善於運用變化</u>，他利用廢鐵做出美麗的雕塑品。

    (A) ***resourceful*** 〔 rɪˈsorsfəl 〕 *adj.* 善於應變的

    (B) reputable 〔ˈrɛpjətəbḷ 〕 *adj.* 名聲好的

    (C) resentful 〔 rɪˈzɛntfəl 〕 *adj.* 憤怒的

    (D) reproducible 〔ˌriprəˈdjusəbḷ 〕 *adj.* 可複製的

    * statue 〔ˈstætʃu 〕 *n.* 雕像

    junk 〔 dʒʌŋk 〕 *n.* 垃圾；廢物

6. (**A**) After a lot of difficulty, he <u>managed</u> to open the door.

幾經困難後，他<u>設法</u>將門打開了。

    (A) ***manage*** 〔ˈmænɪdʒ 〕 *v.* 設法做到 < *to* + *V* >

    (B) succeed 〔 səkˈsid 〕 *v.* 成功 < *in* >

    (C) strengthen 〔ˈstrɛŋθən 〕 *v.* 加強

    (D) stroll 〔 strol 〕 *v.* 閒逛

7. (**D**) His firm <u>conviction</u> of the value of education made him study hard and earn top honors in his class.

他對教育的價值<u>信念</u>堅定，使他努力用功，並得到全班最優異的成績。

    (A) convention〔kən'vɛnʃən〕*n.* 會議；習俗

    (B) contention〔kən'tɛnʃən〕*n.* 爭論

    (C) contraction〔kən'trækʃən〕*n.* 收縮；感染

    (D) *conviction*〔kən'vɪkʃən〕*n.* 判罪；信念

    * firm〔fɜm〕*adj.* 堅定的

      honors〔'ɑnɚz〕*n. pl.* 優異的成績

8. (**C**) Archaeologists estimated the age of the buried city after examining the <u>artifacts</u> found in the ruins.

考古學家在研究遺跡中發現的<u>人工製品</u>後，估計出這個被掩埋的都市的年代。

    (A) melody〔'mɛlədɪ〕*n.* 旋律

    (B) posture〔'pɑstʃɚ〕*n.* 姿勢

    (C) *artifact*〔'ɑrtɪ,fækt〕*n.* 人工製品

    (D) border〔'bɔrdɚ〕*n.* 邊緣；邊界

    * archaeologist〔,ɑrkɪ'ɑlədʒɪst〕*n.* 考古學家

      estimate〔'ɛstə,met〕*v.* 估計

      bury〔'bɛrɪ〕*v.* 掩埋

      examine〔ɪg'zæmɪn〕*v.* 檢查

      ruins〔'ruɪnz〕*n. pl.* 廢墟；遺跡

arti +	fact
|	|
art +	*make , do*

9. (**C**) Tales of overnight riches have fueled a general
<u>fondness</u> for lotteries and gambling.

一夜致富的故事，引發了大眾對樂透彩和賭博的<u>愛好</u>。

(A) torch〔tɔrtʃ〕*n.* 火炬

(B) capability〔͵kepə'bɪlətɪ〕*n.* 能力

(C) *fondness*〔'fɑndnɪs〕*n.* 愛好 < *for* >

(D) glue〔glu〕*n.* 黏膠

* overnight〔'ovɚ'naɪt〕*adj.* 一夜之間的
  fuel〔'fjuəl〕*v.* 供給燃料；激發
  lottery〔'lɑtərɪ〕*n.* (樂透) 彩卷
  gambling〔'gæmblɪŋ〕*n.* 賭博

10. (**C**) His new appointment takes <u>effect</u> from the beginning
of next month.　他的新職位從下個月起<u>生效</u>。

(A) shape〔ʃep〕*n.* 形狀　　take shape　成形；實現

(B) shelter〔'ʃɛltɚ〕*n.* 避難　　take shelter　躲避

(C) *effect*〔ɪ'fɛkt〕*n.* 影響；效果
take effect　生效 (= *become effective*)

(D) offense〔ə'fɛns〕*n.* 冒犯　　take offense　生氣

* appointment〔ə'pɔɪntmənt〕*n.* 任命；職位

```
ef  +   fect
|        |
out + make , do
```

TEST 37

Directions: *The following questions are incomplete sentences. You are to choose the one word that best completes the sentence.*

1. Sometimes Prof. Hardin talks very fast, and his lecture is _____ to us.
   (A) incomplete
   (B) incomprehensible
   (C) indirect
   (D) inaccurate   (   )

2. A dog's sense of smell is far _____ than man's.
   (A) nosier
   (B) moodier
   (C) duller
   (D) keener   (   )

3. The quarterback called the _____ and the team won the game.
   (A) shots
   (B) rolls
   (C) quits
   (D) bluff   (   )

4. The government _____ his service by giving him a medal.
   (A) recognized
   (B) recited
   (C) reassured
   (D) reclined   (   )

5. It is not always easy for students to make the _____ from elementary school to junior high school.
   (A) transmission
   (B) transition
   (C) transference
   (D) transaction   (   )

6. Louise has a great sense of humor, but she also knows when to be _____.

    (A) contagious
    (B) religious
    (C) sarcastic
    (D) solemn   (   )

7. Crossing streets in the wrong place is against the law; therefore, a pedestrian can be fined for _____.

    (A) double-parking
    (B) overtaking
    (C) trespassing
    (D) jaywalking   (   )

8. The restaurant around the corner serves a wide _____ of foods.

    (A) elite
    (B) prominence
    (C) variety
    (D) amateur   (   )

9. Drug addicts often _____ crimes such as robbery in order to get money to buy drugs.

    (A) commit
    (B) commute
    (C) excel
    (D) excite   (   )

10. During the discussion, not every student in the class agreed to practice _____ marriage before getting married.

    (A) magical
    (B) trial
    (C) tryout
    (D) crystal   (   )

TEST 37 詳解

1. (**B**) Sometimes Prof. Hardin talks very fast, and his lecture is <u>incomprehensible</u> to us.
有時，哈定教授講課非常快，所以他的課我們<u>無法理解</u>。

    (A) incomplete〔͵ɪnkəm'plit〕 *adj.* 不完整的

    (B) ***incomprehensible***〔͵ɪnkɑmprɪ'hɛnsəbḷ〕 *adj.*
        無法理解的

    (C) indirect〔͵ɪndə'rɛkt〕 *adj.* 間接的

    (D) inaccurate〔ɪn'ækjərɪt〕 *adj.* 不正確的

    ＊ lecture〔'lɛktʃɚ〕 *n.* 講課

2. (**D**) A dog's sense of smell is far <u>keener</u> than man's.
狗的嗅覺遠比人類<u>敏銳</u>。

    (A) nosy〔'nozɪ〕 *adj.* 愛打聽的

    (B) moody〔'mudɪ〕 *adj.* 不高興的

    (C) dull〔dʌl〕 *adj.* 遲鈍的

    (D) ***keen***〔kin〕 *adj.* 敏銳的

3. (**A**) The quarterback called the <u>shots</u> and the team won the game. 該隊由四分衛<u>發號施令</u>，贏得比賽。

    (A) ***shot***〔ʃɑt〕 *n.* 射擊   ***call the shots*** 發號施令

    (B) roll〔rol〕 *n.* 名冊   call the roll 點名

    (C) quit〔kwɪt〕 *v.* 停止   call it quits 到此為止

    (D) bluff〔blʌf〕 *n.* 嚇唬   call the bluff 虛張聲勢

    ＊ quarterback〔'kwɔrtɚ͵bæk〕 *n.* (美式足球的) 四分衛

4. (**A**) The government <u>recognized</u> his service by giving
him a medal. 政府頒贈勳章給他，<u>表揚他的貢獻</u>。

    (A) ***recognize*** 〔'rɛkəɡ‚naɪz 〕 *v.* 承認；表揚（功績等）

    (B) recite 〔 rɪ'saɪt 〕 *v.* 背誦

    (C) reassure 〔‚riə'ʃur 〕 *v.* 使安心

    (D) recline 〔 rɪ'klaɪn 〕 *v.* 斜倚

    ＊ service 〔'sɝvɪs 〕 *n.* 服務；貢獻
        medal 〔'mɛdḷ 〕 *n.* 獎牌；勳章

5. (**B**) It is not always easy for students to make the
<u>transition</u> from elementary school to junior high
school. 學生從小學到國中的<u>轉變</u>過程不太容易適應。

    (A) transmission 〔 træns'mɪʃən 〕 *n.* 傳送

    (B) ***transition*** 〔 træn'zɪʃən 〕 *n.* 轉變；過渡期

    (C) transference 〔 træns'fɝəns 〕 *n.* 轉移

    (D) transaction 〔 træns'ækʃən 〕 *n.* 交易

    ＊ ***elementary school*** 小學

6. (**D**) Louise has a great sense of humor, but she also
knows when to be <u>solemn</u>.
路易絲非常幽默，但她知道何時該<u>嚴肅</u>一點。

    (A) contagious 〔 kən'tedʒəs 〕 *adj.* 傳染性的

    (B) religious 〔 rɪ'lɪdʒəs 〕 *adj.* 宗教的

    (C) sarcastic 〔 sɑr'kæstɪk 〕 *adj.* 諷刺的

    (D) ***solemn*** 〔'sɑləm 〕 *adj.* 嚴肅的（ = *serious* ）

7. (**D**) Crossing streets in the wrong place is against the law; therefore, a pedestrian can be fined for <u>jaywalking</u>.

在錯誤的地方過馬路是違法的;因此,行人可能因<u>任意穿越馬路</u>而受罰。

(A) double-park〔ˋdʌblˋpɑrk〕*v.* 並排停車

(B) overtake〔͵ovɚˋtek〕*v.* 超 (車)

(C) trespass〔ˋtrɛspəs〕*v.* 侵入 < *on* >

(D) *jaywalk*〔ˋdʒe͵wɔk〕*v.* 任意穿越馬路

* *against the law* 違法的 (= *illegal*)
  pedestrian〔pəˋdɛstrɪən〕*n.* 行人
  fine〔faɪn〕*v.* 罰款

8. (**C**) The restaurant around the corner serves a wide <u>variety</u> of foods.

轉角那家餐廳供應的食物<u>種類</u>繁多。

(A) elite〔ɪˋlit〕*n.* 菁英

(B) prominence〔ˋprɑmənəns〕*n.* 卓越

(C) *variety*〔vəˋraɪətɪ〕*n.* 種類;變化

    a (*wide*) *variety of* 種類繁多的;各式各樣的

(D) amateur〔ˋæmə͵tʃur〕*n.* 業餘愛好者

    (↔ *professional n.* 職業選手)

* *around the corner* 在轉角
  serve〔sɝv〕*v.* 供應 (食物、餐點)

var	+	iety
change	+	*n.*

9. (**A**) Drug addicts often <u>commit</u> crimes such as robbery in order to get money to buy drugs.

吸毒者常犯下搶劫等罪行，為了要得到買毒品的錢。

(A) *commit*〔kə'mɪt〕*v.* 犯（罪）

commit a crime 犯罪

(B) commute〔kə'mjut〕*v.* 通勤

(C) excel〔ɪk'sɛl〕*v.* 勝過

(D) excite〔ɪk'saɪt〕*v.* 使興奮

* addict〔'ædɪkt〕*n.* 上癮者

```
com   +  mit
 |        |
together + send
```

10. (**B**) During the discussion, not every student in the class agreed to practice <u>trial</u> marriage before getting married.

在討論會上，並非班上每位同學，都贊成結婚前先試婚。

(A) magical〔'mædʒɪkḷ〕*adj.* 魔術的

(B) *trial*〔'traɪəl〕*n.* 試驗　　*trial marriage* 試婚

(C) tryout〔'traɪ,aut〕*n.* 甄選

(D) crystal〔'krɪstḷ〕*n.* 水晶

crystal (wedding) anniversary 水晶婚紀念

（結婚十五週年）

* practice〔'præktɪs〕*v.* 實行

TEST 38

Directions: *The following questions are incomplete sentences. You are to choose the one word that best completes the sentence.*

1. The manic-depressive usually _____ between great excitement and deep depression.
   (A) speculates
   (B) contaminates
   (C) fluctuates
   (D) punctuates   (   )

2. She _____ a large sum of money to that orphanage.
   (A) donated
   (B) deceived
   (C) detected
   (D) dodged   (   )

3. He spends little time with his family because his job _____ him to travel a lot.
   (A) inquires
   (B) requires
   (C) quests
   (D) requests   (   )

4. A child's development is influenced more strongly by his or her environment than by _____ factors.
   (A) heroic
   (B) hazardous
   (C) hereditary
   (D) heritable   (   )

5. He is a man of great _____, and I'm confident that he will achieve his goal eventually.
   (A) ritual
   (B) radiation
   (C) recipe
   (D) resolution   (   )

6. There is always excitement at the Olympics when a previous record of performance is _____.
   - (A) survived
   - (B) surveyed
   - (C) surpassed
   - (D) surrendered   ( )

7. Fish are cold-blooded and can _____ their body temperature with their surroundings.
   - (A) regulate
   - (B) suspend
   - (C) darken
   - (D) ridicule   ( )

8. He worries about his health, and the worry makes him ill. It's a _____ circle.
   - (A) vibrant
   - (B) vigorous
   - (C) virtuous
   - (D) vicious   ( )

9. Aspirin can _____ the suffering of a headache or certain cold symptoms.
   - (A) paralyze
   - (B) duplicate
   - (C) alleviate
   - (D) elevate   ( )

10. One stormy night the old bridge _____ into the river without warning.
    - (A) submerged
    - (B) collapsed
    - (C) degenerated
    - (D) immersed   ( )

TEST 38 詳解

1. (**C**) The manic-depressive usually <u>fluctuates</u> between great excitement and deep depression.

躁鬱症患者通常心情<u>起伏</u>不定，時而興奮，時而沮喪。

(A) speculate〔'spɛkjə,let〕v. 思考；推測

(B) contaminate〔kən'tæmə,net〕v. 污染

(= *pollute*)

(C) ***fluctuate***〔'flʌktʃu,et〕v. 上下移動；波動

(D) punctuate〔'pʌŋktʃu,et〕v. 加標點符號

* manic-depressive〔'mænɪkdɪ,prɛsɪv〕*adj.* 躁鬱症的

depression〔dɪ'prɛʃən〕*n.* 沮喪；憂鬱症

```
fluctu + ate
  |       |
wave  +   v.
```

2. (**A**) She <u>donated</u> a large sum of money to that orphanage.

她<u>捐贈</u>了一大筆錢給那家孤兒院。

(A) ***donate***〔'donet〕v. 捐贈

(B) deceive〔dɪ'siv〕v. 欺騙

(C) detect〔dɪ'tɛkt〕v. 偵測

(D) dodge〔dadʒ〕v. 閃避

```
don + ate
 |     |
give + v.
```

* sum〔sʌm〕*n.* 金額

orphanage〔'ɔrfənɪdʒ〕*n.* 孤兒院

3. (**B**) He spends little time with his family because his job <u>requires</u> him to travel a lot.

他和家人相處時間很少，因爲他的工作<u>需要</u>到處旅行。

    (A) inquire〔ɪnˋkwaɪr〕v. 詢問

    (B) *require*〔rɪˋkwaɪr〕v. 需要

    (C) quest〔kwɛst〕v. 尋求

    (D) request〔rɪˋkwɛst〕v. 要求

4. (**C**) A child's development is influenced more strongly by his or her environment than by <u>hereditary</u> factors.

小孩的發展受到環境的影響，比受到<u>遺傳</u>因素的影響更大。

    (A) heroic〔hɪˋro·ɪk〕*adj.* 英勇的

    (B) hazardous〔ˋhæzɚˌdəs〕*adj.* 危險的（= *dangerous*）

    (C) *hereditary*〔həˋrɛdəˌtɛrɪ〕*adj.* 遺傳的

    (D) heritable〔ˋhɛrətəbḷ〕*adj.* 可繼承的

    * factor〔ˋfæktɚ〕*n.* 因素

5. (**D**) He is a man of great <u>resolution</u>, and I'm confident that he will achieve his goal eventually.

他是個非常有<u>決心</u>的人，我有信心他終將達成他的目標。

    (A) ritual〔ˋrɪtʃʊəl〕*n.* 儀式

    (B) radiation〔ˌredɪˋeʃən〕*n.* 輻射

    (C) recipe〔ˋrɛsəpɪ〕*n.* 食譜

    (D) *resolution*〔ˌrɛzəˋluʃən〕*n.* 決心

    * confident〔ˋkɑnfədənt〕*adj.* 有信心的

      eventually〔ɪˋvɛntʃʊəlɪ〕*adv.* 終於

6. (**C**) There is always excitement at the Olympics when a previous record of performance is <u>surpassed</u>.

奧運會中，當某個項目先前的記錄被<u>超越</u>時，大家總是非常興奮。

    (A) survive〔səˋvaɪv〕*v.* 生存

    (B) survey〔səˋve〕*v.* 調查

    (C) ***surpass***〔səˋpæs〕*v.* 超越 (= *exceed* ; *beat*)

    (D) surrender〔səˋrɛndɚ〕*v.* 投降

      * ***the Olympics*** 奧運會 (= *the Olympic Games*)

7. (**A**) Fish are cold-blooded and can <u>regulate</u> their body temperature with their surroundings.

魚是變溫動物，可以根據環境<u>調節</u>自己的體溫。

    (A) ***regulate***〔ˋrɛgjəˏlet〕*v.* 調節

    (B) suspend〔səˋspɛnd〕*v.* 暫停

    (C) darken〔ˋdɑrkən〕*v.* 變暗

    (D) ridicule〔ˋrɪdɪˏkjul〕*v.* 嘲笑

8. (**D**) He worries about his health, and the worry makes him ill. It's a <u>vicious</u> circle.

他擔心自己的健康，而這種憂慮又使他生病。這是<u>惡性</u>循環。

    (A) vibrant〔ˋvaɪbrənt〕*adj.* 振動的；活潑的

    (B) vigorous〔ˋvɪgərəs〕*adj.* 精力充沛的 (= *energetic*)

    (C) virtuous〔ˋvɝtʃuəs〕*adj.* 有品德的

    (D) ***vicious***〔ˋvɪʃəs〕*adj.* 邪惡的

      vicious circle 惡性循環

9. (**C**) Aspirin can <u>alleviate</u> the suffering of a headache or certain cold symptoms.

阿斯匹靈可以<u>減輕</u>頭痛或某些感冒的症狀。

    (A) paralyze〔'pærə‚laɪz〕v. 麻痺

    (B) duplicate〔'djuplə‚ket〕v. 複製

    (C) *alleviate*〔ə'livɪ‚et〕v. 減輕 (= *relieve* ; *ease*)

    (D) elevate〔'ɛlə‚vet〕v. 提高

    ＊ aspirin〔'æspərɪn〕n. 阿斯匹靈

       symptom〔'sɪmptəm〕n. 症狀

```
al  +  levi  +  ate
 |       |       |
to  +  light  +  v.
```

10. (**B**) One stormy night the old bridge <u>collapsed</u> into the river without warning.

一個狂風暴雨的夜晚，這座老舊的橋毫無預警地突然<u>塌陷</u>到河裏。

    (A) submerge〔səb'mɝdʒ〕v. 沉入

    (B) *collapse*〔kə'læps〕v. 崩潰；崩塌

    (C) degenerate〔dɪ'dʒɛnə‚ret〕v. 墮落

    (D) immerse〔ɪ'mɝs〕v. 浸入

    ＊ *without warning* 毫無預警地；突然地

```
col  +   lapse
 |        |
all  +  slip , glide ( 全部滑落 )
```

TEST 39

Directions: *The following questions are incomplete sentences. You are to choose the one word that best completes the sentence.*

1. We found it of _____ importance to rebuild the old bridge.
   - (A) proficient
   - (B) critical
   - (C) attractive
   - (D) puzzling   (   )

2. He is used to exaggerating, so you had better _____ much of what he says.
   - (A) disappoint
   - (B) disclose
   - (C) discount
   - (D) disguise   (   )

3. The oil _____ out of the well in large quantities.
   - (A) gushed
   - (B) pressed
   - (C) flung
   - (D) tossed   (   )

4. The Chinese Children Foundation offers _____ to abusive parents.
   - (A) counseling
   - (B) counter
   - (C) maxim
   - (D) maximum   (   )

5. Cooks, waiters, and other restaurant help must be _____; without them, the restaurant cannot function.
   - (A) offensive
   - (B) trustworthy
   - (C) tolerable
   - (D) edible   (   )

6. The stronger the _____, the faster a person will learn a foreign language.

   (A) motion
   (B) commotion
   (C) motivation
   (D) promotion   (   )

7. Though Sam had seen the accident, he was _____ to act as a witness.

   (A) capable
   (B) agreeable
   (C) reluctant
   (D) willing   (   )

8. He is not a close friend of mine; he is just a nodding _____.

   (A) executive
   (B) athlete
   (C) preacher
   (D) acquaintance   (   )

9. Two hundred years ago, it was _____ that humans would be able to walk on the moon.

   (A) unilateral
   (B) unshakable
   (C) intelligible
   (D) inconceivable   (   )

10. Salaried workers are being left behind by _____, and it is getting harder for them to buy houses.

    (A) inhabitants
    (B) statesmen
    (C) speculators
    (D) legislators   (   )

TEST 39 詳解

1. (**B**) We found it of <u>critical</u> importance to rebuild the old
bridge. 我們覺得重建那座舊橋<u>非常</u>重要。

    (A) proficient〔prə'fɪʃənt〕*adj.* 熟練的 < *in* >

    (B) *critical*〔'krɪtɪkḷ〕*adj.* 非常重要的

    (C) attractive〔ə'træktɪv〕*adj.* 有吸引力的

    (D) puzzling〔'pʌzḷɪŋ〕*adj.* 令人困惑的

    * *be of importance* 重要的 (= *be important*)
      rebuild〔rɪ'bɪld〕*v.* 重建

2. (**C**) He is used to exaggerating, so you had better
<u>discount</u> much of what he says.
他習慣誇大其辭，所以，對於他所說的大部分的話，你最
好<u>打點折扣</u>。

    (A) disappoint〔ˌdɪsə'pɔɪnt〕*v.* 使失望

    (B) disclose〔dɪs'kloz〕*v.* 揭露

    (C) *discount*〔dɪs'kaʊnt〕*v.* 打折

    (D) disguise〔dɪs'gaɪz〕*v.* 偽裝

    * *be used to* + *N/V-ing* 習慣於
      exaggerate〔ɪg'zædʒəˌret〕*v.* 誇張

dis + count	dis + close
| |	| |
not + *count* (不算)	*not* + *close* (沒有關閉)

3. (**A**) The oil <u>gushed</u> out of the well in large quantities.

　　　石油從油井中大量<u>噴出</u>。

　　　(A) ***gush*** 〔 gʌʃ 〕 *v.* 噴出；湧出

　　　(B) press 〔 prɛs 〕 *v.* 壓

　　　(C) fling 〔 flɪŋ 〕 *v.* 拋；擲

　　　(D) toss 〔 tɔs 〕 *v.* 投擲

　　　＊ well 〔 wɛl 〕 *n.* 井　　***in large quantities*** 大量

4. (**A**) The Chinese Children Foundation offers <u>counseling</u> to abusive parents.

　　　中華兒童基金會提供<u>輔導</u>，給虐待小孩的父母親。

　　　(A) ***counseling*** 〔 'kaʊnsḷɪŋ 〕 *n.* 輔導

　　　(B) counter 〔 'kaʊntɚ 〕 *n.* 櫃台

　　　(C) maxim 〔 'mæksɪm 〕 *n.* 格言；座右銘

　　　(D) maximum 〔 'mæksəməm 〕 *n.* 最大值

　　　＊ foundation 〔 faʊn'deʃən 〕 *n.* 基金會
　　　　 abusive 〔 ə'bjusɪv 〕 *adj.* 虐待的

5. (**B**) Cooks, waiters and other restaurant help must be <u>trustworthy</u>; without them, the restaurant cannot function. 廚師、服務生和餐廳其他的幫手都必須很<u>可靠</u>；沒有他們，餐廳就無法運作。

　　　(A) offensive 〔 ə'fɛnsɪv 〕 *adj.* 無禮的

　　　(B) ***trustworthy*** 〔 'trʌst,wɝðɪ 〕 *adj.* 可靠的；值得信任的

　　　(C) tolerable 〔 'tɑlərəbḷ 〕 *adj.* 可容忍的

　　　(D) edible 〔 'ɛdəbḷ 〕 *adj.* 可食用的

　　　＊ function 〔 'fʌŋkʃən 〕 *v.* 運作

6. (**C**) The stronger the <u>motivation</u>, the faster a person will learn a foreign language.

一個人<u>動機</u>越強烈，學習外語的速度就越快。

(A) motion〔'moʃən〕*n.* 動作

(B) commotion〔kə'moʃən〕*n.* 暴動

(C) *motivation*〔,motə've ʃən〕*n.* 動機；刺激

(= *incentive*)

(D) promotion〔prə'moʃən〕*n.* 升遷

7. (**C**) Though Sam had seen the accident, he was <u>reluctant</u> to act as a witness.

雖然山姆看見了那場意外，但他<u>不願意當證人</u>。

(A) capable〔'kepəbḷ〕*adj.* 能夠的 < *of* >

(B) agreeable〔ə'griəbḷ〕*adj.* 愉快的

(C) *reluctant*〔rɪ'lʌktənt〕*adj.* 不願意的 (= *unwilling*)

(D) willing〔'wɪlɪŋ〕*adj.* 願意的

* *act as* 擔任　　witness〔'wɪtnɪs〕*n.* 證人

8. (**D**) He is not a close friend of mine; he is just a nodding <u>acquaintance</u>.

他不算是我的密友；他只是<u>點頭之交</u>。

(A) executive〔ɪg'zɛkjʊtɪv〕*n.* 主管

(B) athlete〔'æθlit〕*n.* 運動員

(C) preacher〔'pritʃɚ〕*n.* 提倡者

(D) *acquaintance*〔ə'kwentəns〕*n.* 相識之人

nodding acquaintance 點頭之交

9. (**D**) Two hundred years ago, it was <u>inconceivable</u> that humans would be able to walk on the moon.

二百年前，人類能夠走在月球上，是<u>無法想像的</u>。

(A) unilateral 〔ˌjunɪˈlætərəl 〕 *adj.* 單方面的
(= *one-sided*)

(B) unshakable 〔 ʌnˈʃekəbl̩ 〕 *adj.* 不能動搖的；堅定的
(= *firm*)

(C) intelligible 〔 ɪnˈtɛlɪdʒəbl̩ 〕 *adj.* 可了解的；清晰的
(= *understandable*)

(D) *inconceivable* 〔ˌɪnkənˈsivəbl̩ 〕 *adj.* 無法想像的
(= *unimaginable*)

in + conceiv + able
| | |
not + 想像 + 可以

un + imagin + able
| | |
not + 想像 + 可以

10. (**C**) Salaried workers are being left behind by <u>speculators</u>, and it is getting harder for them to buy houses.

薪水階級被<u>投機炒作者</u>遠拋在後，對他們而言，買房子越來越困難了。

(A) inhabitant 〔 ɪnˈhæbətənt 〕 *n.* 居民

(B) statesman 〔ˈstetsmən 〕 *n.* 政治家

(C) *speculator* 〔ˈspɛkjəˌletɚ 〕 *n.* 投機者

(D) legislator 〔ˈlɛdʒɪsˌletɚ 〕 *n.* 立法委員

* salaried 〔ˈsælərɪd 〕 *adj.* 領薪水的
   leave behind 超過

TEST 40

Directions: *The following questions are incomplete sentences. You are to choose the one word that best completes the sentence.*

1. Heart disease is the _____ cause of death because it has far-reaching effects on the entire body.
   (A) minor
   (B) leading
   (C) supporting
   (D) rare   (   )

2. Once a big source of _____ goods, Taiwan is now a growing market for real items.
   (A) counterfeit
   (B) paradise
   (C) brand
   (D) orientation

3. As long as he can do the job well, his age is _____.
   (A) immense
   (B) immobile
   (C) irrelevant
   (D) inadequate   (   )

4. All you see is the _____ of the iceberg; six-sevenths of it is underwater.
   (A) tag
   (B) tip
   (C) tent
   (D) tone   (   )

5. Tonight there are no clouds and stars _____ in the night sky.
   (A) stagger
   (B) stutter
   (C) twinkle
   (D) sparkle   (   )

6. The total _____ from last month's charity dance were far more than expected.
   - (A) earnings
   - (B) acquisitions
   - (C) winnings
   - (D) requisitions   (   )

7. The exhibition brought together the works of several _____ artists.
   - (A) radical
   - (B) renowned
   - (C) trivial
   - (D) transient   (   )

8. Kevin is more _____ than George and always tells us jokes and funny stories.
   - (A) stern
   - (B) miserable
   - (C) gloomy
   - (D) cheerful   (   )

9. If you read between the _____, this letter is really a request for money.
   - (A) passages
   - (B) paragraphs
   - (C) lines
   - (D) articles   (   )

10. He chose his eldest son as his _____ and let him take over the company.
    - (A) critic
    - (B) tenant
    - (C) tyrant
    - (D) successor   (   )

TEST 40 詳解

1. (**B**) Heart disease is the <u>leading</u> cause of death because it has far-reaching effects on the entire body.

心臟病是死亡的<u>主</u>因，因爲它對全身會產生深遠的影響。

(A) minor ('maɪnə) *adj.* 次要的

(B) *leading* ('lidɪŋ) *adj.* 主要的 (= *major*)

(C) supporting (sə'portɪŋ) *adj.* 陪襯的

(D) rare (rɛr) *adj.* 罕見的

* far-reaching ('far'ritʃɪŋ) *adj.* 深遠的
entire (ɪn'taɪr) *adj.* 整個的

2. (**A**) Once a big source of <u>counterfeit</u> goods, Taiwan is now a growing market for real items.

台灣曾經是<u>仿冒品</u>的大宗之一，但現在已是越來越大的眞品市場。

(A) *counterfeit* ('kauntə,fɪt) *n.* 仿冒品；贗品
adj. 仿冒的 (= *fake*)

(B) paradise ('pærə,daɪs) *n.* 天堂

(C) brand (brænd) *n.* 品牌

(D) orientation (,orɪɛn'teʃən) *n.* 適應

* source (sors) *n.* 來源
item ('aɪtəm) *n.* 物品

```
counter + feit
   |        |
against  +  make  (違反去做)
```

3. (**C**) As long as he can do the job well, his age is <u>irrelevant</u>.
只要他能把這個工作做好，他的年齡<u>沒有關係</u>。

    (A) immense〔ɪˋmɛns〕*adj.* 巨大的

    (B) immobile〔ɪˋmobḷ〕*adj.* 不動的

    (C) *irrelevant*〔ɪˋrɛləvənt〕*adj.* 無關的；不重要的

    (D) inadequate〔ɪnˋædəkwɪt〕*adj.* 不足的

    ＊ *as long as* 只要

4. (**B**) All you see is the <u>tip</u> of the iceberg; six-sevenths of it is underwater.
你所看到的只是冰山的<u>一角</u>；冰山的七分之六都在水底下。

    (A) tag〔tæg〕*n.* 標籤

    (B) *tip*〔tɪp〕*n.* 尖端

        tip of the iceberg 冰山的一角

    (C) tent〔tɛnt〕*n.* 帳篷

    (D) tone〔ton〕*n.* 語調

    ＊ iceberg〔ˋaɪs͵bɝg〕*n.* 冰山

5. (**C**) Tonight there are no clouds and stars <u>twinkle</u> in the night sky. 今晚沒有雲，繁星在夜空中<u>閃爍</u>。

    (A) stagger〔ˋstægɚ〕*v.* 搖晃

    (B) stutter〔ˋstʌtɚ〕*v.* 口吃（= *stammer*）

    (C) *twinkle*〔ˋtwɪŋkḷ〕*v.* (星星、眼睛) 閃爍

    (D) sparkle〔ˋsparkḷ〕*v.* (目光、寶石) 閃耀

6. (**B**) The total <u>acquisitions</u> from last month's charity dance were far more than expected.

上個月慈善舞會的總<u>所得</u>比預料中高出很多。

(A) earnings (ˈɜnɪŋz) *n. pl.* 賺得的收入;所得

(B) ***acquisition*** (ˌækwəˈzɪʃən) *n.* 所得;獲得物

(C) winnings (ˈwɪnɪŋz) *n. pl.* 獎金;贏得的利益

(D) requisition (ˌrɛkwəˈzɪʃən) *n.* 要求

＊ total (ˈtotl̩) *adj.* 全部的

charity (ˈtʃærətɪ) *n.* 慈善

7. (**B**) The exhibition brought together the works of several <u>renowned</u> artists.

此次展覽會將數位<u>知名</u>藝術家的作品集合在一起。

(A) radical (ˈrædɪkl̩) *adj.* 徹底的

(B) ***renowned*** (rɪˈnaʊnd) *adj.* 著名的

  (= *famous* ; *well-known*)

(C) trivial (ˈtrɪvɪəl) *adj.* 瑣碎的

(D) transient (ˈtrænʃənt) *adj.* 短暫的

 ＊ exhibition (ˌɛksəˈbɪʃən) *n.* 展覽會

8. (**D**) Kevin is more <u>cheerful</u> than George and always tells us jokes and funny stories.

凱文比喬治更<u>開朗</u>,他總是會說笑話和有趣的故事給我們聽。

(A) stern (stɜn) *adj.* 嚴厲的 (= *severe*)

(B) miserable (ˈmɪzərəbl̩) *adj.* 悲慘的

(C) gloomy (ˈglumɪ) *adj.* 憂鬱的

(D) ***cheerful*** (ˈtʃɪrfəl) *adj.* 愉快的;開朗的

9. (**C**) If you read between the <u>lines</u>, this letter is really a request for money.

如果你能領會言外之意，這封信事實上是來要錢的。

(A) passage〔'pæsɪdʒ〕*n.* 通過；段落

(B) paragraph〔'pærə,græf〕*n.* 段落

(C) *line*〔laɪn〕*n.*（文章的）行

    read between the lines 探究字裏行間的意義；

    領會言外之意

(D) article〔'ɑrtɪkl̩〕*n.* 文章

  * request〔rɪ'kwɛst〕*n.* 要求

10. (**D**) He chose his eldest son as his <u>successor</u> and let him take over the company.

他選擇他的長子當繼任者，讓他接管公司。

(A) critic〔'krɪtɪk〕*n.* 評論者

(B) tenant〔'tɛnənt〕*n.* 房客

(C) tyrant〔'taɪrənt〕*n.* 暴君

(D) *successor*〔sək'sɛsə〕*n.* 繼任者

  * *take over* 接管

suc	+ cess	+ or
under	+ go	+ 人

TEST 41

Directions: *The following questions are incomplete sentences. You are to choose the one word that best completes the sentence.*

1. Cultural elements shouldn't be viewed in _____ but be viewed in the totality of the culture.
   (A) association
   (B) consolation
   (C) adaptation
   (D) isolation   (   )

2. The proposal to increase taxation met with a lot of _____ comments.
   (A) disorderly
   (B) adverse
   (C) distasteful
   (D) averse   (   )

3. The thunder _____ in the distance.
   (A) rustled
   (B) rumbled
   (C) tinkled
   (D) crashed   (   )

4. A _____ is a doctor who treats people suffering from mental illness rather than physical diseases.
   (A) psychiatrist
   (B) surgeon
   (C) nutritionist
   (D) dentist   (   )

5. My mother is very _____ with purchases and saves us a lot of money.
   (A) extravagant
   (B) righteous
   (C) thrifty
   (D) economic   (   )

6. She _____ dressing formally to wearing sports clothes.
   - (A) refers
   - (B) prefers
   - (C) recedes
   - (D) precedes   (   )

7. Studies indicate that adults need a(n) _____ of six hours sleep a day.
   - (A) element
   - (B) minimum
   - (C) title
   - (D) extent   (   )

8. Since Mary does not answer the telephone, I _____ that she is not home.
   - (A) exceed
   - (B) exclaim
   - (C) suppose
   - (D) concede   (   )

9. It is _____ recognized that taking a walk after dinner is desirable.
   - (A) subjectively
   - (B) subtly
   - (C) universally
   - (D) regretfully   (   )

10. My father had to tutor students in private in order to _____ his salary as a teacher.
    - (A) augment
    - (B) expand
    - (C) impose
    - (D) inflate   (   )

TEST 41 詳解

1. (**D**) Cultural elements shouldn't be viewed in <u>isolation</u> but be viewed in the totality of the culture.

文化的要素不應該以<u>分離</u>的角度，而應以整體的文化來觀察。

   (A) association〔ə,soʃɪ'eʃən〕*n.* 關聯；協會
   (B) consolation〔,kɑnsə'leʃən〕*n.* 安慰
   (C) adaptation〔,ædəp'teʃən〕*n.* 適應
   (D) ***isolation***〔,aɪsḷ'eʃən〕*n.* 孤立；分離
   　　 in isolation 孤立地；分離地

   * element〔'ɛləmənt〕*n.* 要素
   　 totality〔to'tælətɪ〕*n.* 整體

2. (**B**) The proposal to increase taxation met with a lot of <u>adverse</u> comments.

加稅的提議遭受許多<u>反對的聲浪</u>。

   (A) disorderly〔dɪs'ɔrdəlɪ〕*adj.* 無秩序的
   (B) ***adverse***〔əd'vɜs , 'ædvɜs〕*adj.* 反對的；逆向的
   　　 < *to* >
   (C) distasteful〔dɪs'testfəl〕*adj.* 討厭的 < *to* >
   (D) averse〔ə'vɜs〕*adj.* 討厭的；反對的 < *to* >
   　　（不置於名詞前）

   * proposal〔prə'pozḷ〕*n.* 提議
   　 taxation〔tæks'eʃən〕*n.* 稅金；課稅
   　 meet with 遭遇
   　 comment〔'kɑmɛnt〕*n.* 評論；意見

3. (**B**) The thunder <u>rumbled</u> in the distance.

遠方雷聲隆隆。

(A) rustle〔'rʌsḷ〕*v.* (樹葉、紙) 沙沙作響

(B) ***rumble***〔'rʌmbḷ〕*v.* (雷、炮、肚子) 發出隆隆聲

(C) tinkle〔'tɪŋkḷ〕*v.* 發出叮噹聲

(D) crash〔kræʃ〕*v.* 相撞；墜毀

* thunder〔'θʌndɚ〕*n.* 雷   ***in the distance*** 在遠方

4. (**A**) A <u>psychiatrist</u> is a doctor who treats people suffering from mental illness rather than physical diseases.

精神科醫師治療心理有病，而非身體有病的病人。

(A) ***psychiatrist***〔saɪ'kaɪətrɪst〕*n.* 精神科醫師

(B) surgeon〔'sɝdʒən〕*n.* 外科醫生

(C) nutritionist〔nju'trɪʃənɪst〕*n.* 營養學家

(D) dentist〔'dɛntɪst〕*n.* 牙科醫師

* ***suffer from*** 罹患   mental〔'mɛntḷ〕*adj.* 心理的
　rather than 而非   physical〔'fɪzɪkḷ〕*adj.* 身體的

5. (**C**) My mother is very <u>thrifty</u> with purchases and saves us a lot of money.

我媽媽買東西非常節省，因此為我們省了不少錢。

(A) extravagant〔ɪk'strævəgənt〕*adj.* 浪費的

(B) righteous〔'raɪtʃəs〕*adj.* 正直的

(C) ***thrifty***〔'θrɪftɪ〕*adj.* 節省的

(D) economic〔͵ikə'nɑmɪk〕*adj.* 經濟 (學) 的
　　(此處應用 *economical adj.* 節省的)

* purchase〔'pɝtʃəs〕*n.* 購物

6. (**B**) She <u>prefers</u> dressing formally to wearing sports clothes.

她較喜歡正式的穿著，勝過穿運動服。

    (A) refer〔rɪ'fɝ〕*v.* 提及；參考 < *to* >

    (B) ***prefer***〔prɪ'fɝ〕*v.* 比較喜歡；偏愛

       prefer A to B 比較喜歡 A 勝過 B

    (C) recede〔rɪ'sid〕*v.* 後退

    (D) precede〔prɪ'sid〕*v.* 領先

    ＊ formally〔'fɔrməlɪ〕*adv.* 正式地

7. (**B**) Studies indicate that adults need a <u>minimum</u> of six hours sleep a day.

研究顯示，成年人一天<u>最少</u>需要六小時睡眠。

    (A) element〔'ɛləmənt〕*n.* 要素

    (B) ***minimum***〔'mɪnəməm〕*n.* 最小值

       (↔ *maximum*)

    (C) title〔'taɪt!〕*n.* 標題

    (D) extent〔ɪk'stɛnt〕*n.* 程度

    ＊ indicate〔'ɪndə,ket〕*v.* 顯示 (= *show*)

8. (**C**) Since Mary does not answer the telephone, I <u>suppose</u> that she is not home.

由於瑪麗沒有接電話，我<u>認為</u>她不在家。

    (A) exceed〔ɪk'sid〕*v.* 超過

    (B) exclaim〔ɪk'sklem〕*v.* 呼喊

    (C) ***suppose***〔sə'poz〕*v.* 認為；猜想

    (D) concede〔kən'sid〕*v.* 讓步

9. (**C**) It is <u>universally</u> recognized that taking a walk after dinner is desirable.

一般人普遍承認，晚餐後去散個步很不錯。

    (A) subjectively〔səbˋdʒɛktɪvlɪ〕*adv.* 主觀地

    (B) subtly〔ˋsʌtḷɪ〕*adv.* 細微地

    (C) ***universally***〔ˏjunəˋvɝsḷɪ〕*adv.* 普遍地

    (D) regretfully〔rɪˋgrɛtfəlɪ〕*adv.* 後悔地

    * recognize〔ˋrɛkəgˏnaɪz〕*v.* 承認

      desirable〔dɪˋzaɪrəbḷ〕*adj.* 值得要的

10. (**A**) My father had to tutor students in private in order to <u>augment</u> his salary as a teacher.

爲了要增加擔任教師的薪水，父親必須私底下收家教學生。

    (A) ***augment***〔ɔgˋmɛnt〕*v.* 增加（= *increase*）

    (B) expand〔ɪkˋspænd〕*v.* 擴張

    (C) impose〔ɪmˋpoz〕*v.* 強加 < *on* >

    (D) inflate〔ɪnˋflet〕*v.*（輪胎、通貨）膨脹

    * tutor〔ˋtjutɚ〕*v.* 擔任家教

      in private 私下地（= *privately*）

      salary〔ˋsælərɪ〕*n.* 薪水

aug	+	ment
|		|
increase	+	*v.*

TEST 42

Directions: *The following questions are incomplete sentences. You are to choose the one word that best completes the sentence.*

1. The square was so crowded that I had to _____ my way out of there.
   (A) block
   (B) elbow
   (C) combat
   (D) pioneer   (   )

2. _____ activity should be avoided after an operation.
   (A) Proper
   (B) Routine
   (C) Academic
   (D) Strenuous   (   )

3. In order to save time, I took a _____ flight to San Francisco.
   (A) nonstop
   (B) nonstick
   (C) nonverbal
   (D) nonprofit   (   )

4. The auditorium was very big, so I had to use a microphone to _____ my voice.
   (A) exaggerate
   (B) lengthen
   (C) boast
   (D) amplify   (   )

5. The speaker's main _____ was how to eliminate hunger in this world.
   (A) topic
   (B) package
   (C) occasion
   (D) obstacle   (   )

6. Corruption in the city's largest bank was _____ in the local newspaper.

    (A) defected

    (B) exposed

    (C) reposed

    (D) perfected   (   )

7. By not objecting to the proposal, Mrs. Jones gave it her _____ support.

    (A) illusory

    (B) implicit

    (C) impotent

    (D) illicit   (   )

8. Tom didn't tell Alice his secret because he thought she was _____.

    (A) unequivocal

    (B) unbelievable

    (C) untrustworthy

    (D) unutterable   (   )

9. After sealing all the envelopes, the secretary _____ stamps to them.

    (A) obtained

    (B) detained

    (C) attached

    (D) detached   (   )

10. Please be _____ with me about the outcome of the medical check-up.

    (A) logical

    (B) honesty

    (C) straighten

    (D) frank   (   )

TEST 42 詳解

1. (**B**) The square was so crowded that I had to <u>elbow</u>
   my way out of there.
   廣場上太擁擠了，我得<u>用手肘擠開</u>人群才能離開。

    (A) block〔blɑk〕v. 堵塞

    (B) *elbow*〔'ɛl͵bo〕n. 手肘　v. 用肘推擠
       elbow one's way 用手肘擠開人群前進

    (C) combat〔'kɑmbæt〕v. 戰鬥

    (D) pioneer〔͵paɪə'nɪr〕v. 開拓

    * square〔skwɛr〕n. 廣場

2. (**D**) <u>Strenuous</u> activity should be avoided after an
   operation. 手術後要避免從事<u>費力的</u>活動。

    (A) proper〔'prɑpɚ〕adj. 適合的

    (B) routine〔ru'tin〕adj. 例行的

    (C) academic〔͵ækə'dɛmɪk〕adj. 學術的

    (D) *strenuous*〔'strɛnjuəs〕adj. 費力的

    * operation〔͵ɑpə'reʃən〕n. 手術

3. (**A**) In order to save time, I took a <u>nonstop</u> flight to San
   Francisco. 為了節省時間，我搭<u>直飛</u>班機前往舊金山。

    (A) *nonstop*〔'nɑn'stɑp〕adj. 直達的

    (B) nonstick〔nɑn'stɪk〕adj. 不沾鍋的

    (C) nonverbal〔nɑn'vɝbḷ〕adj. 非語言的

    (D) nonprofit〔nɑn'prɑfɪt〕adj. 非營利的

4. (**D**) The auditorium was very big, so I had to use a
microphone to <u>amplify</u> my voice.

演講廳非常大，所以我必須用麥克風來<u>擴大</u>我的音量。

(A) exaggerate〔ɪgˋzædʒəˏret〕v. 誇大

(B) lengthen〔ˋlɛŋθən〕v. 延長

(C) boast〔bost〕v. 自誇

(D) ***amplify***〔ˋæmpləˏfaɪ〕v. 擴大

＊ auditorium〔ˏɔdəˋtorɪəm〕n. 演講廳
microphone〔ˋmaɪkrəˏfon〕n. 麥克風；擴音器

5. (**A**) The speaker's main <u>topic</u> was how to eliminate
hunger in this world.

這位演講者的演講<u>主題</u>是，如何消除全世界的飢餓問題。

(A) ***topic***〔ˋtɑpɪk〕n. 主題

(B) package〔ˋpækɪdʒ〕n. 包裝

(C) occasion〔əˋkeʒən〕n. 場合

(D) obstacle〔ˋɑbstəkl̩〕n. 障礙

＊ eliminate〔ɪˋlɪməˏnet〕v. 消除（= *get rid of*）

6. (**B**) Corruption in the city's largest bank was <u>exposed</u>
in the local newspaper.

當地報社<u>揭發</u>了該市最大銀行所發生的貪污事件。

(A) defect〔dɪˋfɛkt〕v. 脫離；背叛

(B) ***expose***〔ɪkˋspoz〕v. 暴露；揭發

(C) repose〔rɪˋpoz〕v. 休息

(D) perfect〔pɚˋfɛkt〕v. 使完美

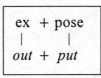

＊ corruption〔kəˋrʌpʃən〕n. 貪污；舞弊

7. (**B**) By not objecting to the proposal, Mrs. Jones gave it her <u>implicit</u> support.

既然不反對這項提議，瓊斯太太就暗示了她的支持。

(A) illusory〔ɪˈlusərɪ〕*adj.* 幻想的

(B) *implicit*〔ɪmˈplɪsɪt〕*adj.* 暗示的

(C) impotent〔ˈɪmpətənt〕*adj.* 無能的

(D) illicit〔ɪˈlɪsɪt〕*adj.* 非法的

* *object to* 反對 (= *oppose* ; *be opposed to*)
proposal〔prəˈpozl̩〕*n.* 提議

```
im  + pli  + cit
 |      |      |
in  + fold + adj. (摺在裏面的)
```

8. (**C**) Tom didn't tell Alice his secret because he thought she was <u>untrustworthy</u>.

湯姆沒有把他的秘密告訴愛麗絲，因爲他認爲她靠不住。

(A) unequivocal〔͵ʌnɪˈkwɪvəkl̩〕*adj.* 不含糊的；
清楚的 (= *clear*)

(B) unbelievable〔͵ʌnbɪˈlivəbl̩〕*adj.* 不可思議的
(= *incredible*)

(C) *untrustworthy*〔ʌnˈtrʌst͵wɝðɪ〕*adj.* 靠不住的

(D) unutterable〔ʌnˈʌtərəbl̩〕*adj.* 說不出的

```
un + trust + worthy
 |     |       |
not + 信任  +  值得
```

9. (**C**) After sealing all the envelopes, the secretary
<u>attached</u> stamps to them.

封上所有信封後，秘書把郵票<u>貼上</u>。

(A) obtain〔əb'ten〕*v.* 獲得

(B) detain〔dɪ'ten〕*v.* 拘留

(C) ***attach***〔ə'tætʃ〕*v.* 貼上；附著 < *to* >

(D) detach〔dɪ'tætʃ〕*v.* 拆開；分離 < *from* >

* seal〔sil〕*v.* 封住

envelope〔'ɛnvə,lop〕*n.* 信封

at + tach	de + tach
| 　　 |	| 　　 |
to + 栓住	*away* + 栓住

10. (**D**) Please be <u>frank</u> with me about the outcome of the
medical check-up.

請<u>坦白</u>告訴我體檢的結果。

(A) logical〔'lɑdʒɪkl̩〕*adj.* 合邏輯的

(B) honesty〔'ɑnɪstɪ〕*n.* 誠實（在此應用形容詞 *honest* ）

(C) straighten〔'stretn̩〕*v.* 變直；整理

（在此應用形容詞 *straight* 或 *straightforward* ）

(D) ***frank***〔fræŋk〕*adj.* 坦白的

* outcome〔'aut,kʌm〕*n.* 結果（ = *result* ）

medical check-up 體檢

INDEX

心得筆記欄

心得筆記欄

心得筆記欄

中高級英語字彙 420 題

主　　　　編／劉　毅

發　行　所／學習出版有限公司　　　　☎ (02) 2704-5525

郵　撥　帳　號／0512727-2 學習出版社帳戶

登　記　證／局版台業 2179 號

印　刷　所／裕強彩色印刷有限公司

台　北　門　市／台北市許昌街 10 號 2 F　　　☎ (02) 2331-4060

台灣總經銷／紅螞蟻圖書有限公司　　　☎ (02) 2795-3656

美國總經銷／ Evergreen Book Store　　☎ (818) 2813622

本公司網址　www.learnbook.com.tw

電 子 郵 件　learnbook@learnbook.com.tw

> 售價：新台幣二百二十元正

2012 年 7 月 1 日新修訂

ISBN 957-519-652-X